THE NATURAL HISTORY OF THE VAMPIRE

by the same author

A Pocketful of Rye
(*Short Stories*)
The Seahorse
A Literary Lion
Conquering Heroes
The Syndicate
The Summer that Bled
(*the biography of Hannah Senesh*)

THE NATURAL HISTORY OF THE VAMPIRE

BY

Anthony Masters

FOUNDED 1838

GPPS

G. P. Putnam's Sons, New York

First American Edition 1972

SBN: 399-10931-5
Library of Congress Catalog
Card Number: 70-175268

Printed in the United States of America

To my brother Paul, whose occult interests stimulated the writing of this work, and to the memory of the late Reverend Montague Summers who was the original 'vampire analyst'.

Contents

List of Illustrations

Between pages 116 and 117

Introduction

This book is an entertainment built round a contemporarily much abused mass-media figure—the vampire. It is also an analysis of the way vampire belief ravaged its way around the world from the eleventh century to present times.

There are two kinds of vampire: mythical and real. Both were killers. The mythical vampire killed thousands out of self-generating fear that created a death-wish—similar to the power of a witch-doctor. The real-life vampire killed in more modest quantities but usually in a more horrific way—and was judged in court to be a psychotic killer. Both kinds of vampire are documented here.

I have begun this book by debating the causes of the fear that created mythical vampirism and the climate for real-life vampirism, and have continued by analysing vampire practice and vampire protection throughout the world, the vampire in pagan times and later the vampire as the all too convenient enemy of institutionalised religion. I have then attempted to rationalise the sexual, religious and psychiatric motivation behind the creation of the vampire cult. In the second half of the book I have discussed the vampire in literature as well as his rôle as a latter-day entertainer and have concluded by portraying some present-day aspects of vampirism.

In writing *The Natural History of the Vampire* I have tried not only to improve the status of the vampire, whose appearances on the screen have not always helped the actuality of his true reign of terror, but I have also tried to demonstrate how mass hysteria is created and appallingly fulfilled.

In compiling this work I was given enthusiastic assistance by a large number of people and organisations. Principal amongst these were: ABC Television of America, Campbell Black, Professor Cottie A. Burland, Bill Butler, Professor T. Cartwright of the Nuffield Institute of Comparative Medicines at the Zoological Society of London, Brian Collins, Lovett Edwards, The Folklore Society, Deric R. James, Christopher Lee, Brighton and Hove Public Library, Wandsworth Library, Kensington & Chelsea Public Library, the Catholic Central Library, The Wellcome Foundation and the Guildhall Library, Muz Murray, P. Ross Nichols, Dr Dennis E. Rhodes, Gabriel Ronay, The Society of Authors, the Staatsbibliothek of Vienna, Dr O. W. Samson, the University of Chicago Press, Ruth Wynn Owen, Dennis Wheatley, Colin Wilson, Michael Carreras, Brian Laurance and Howard Brandy of Hammer Films and my wife, Robina Masters, for checking and editing the manuscript of this book.

Finally I would like to thank posthumously the late Reverend Montague Summers whose works *The Vampire: His Kith and Kin* and *The Vampire in Europe* were a constant source of help and stimulation to me.

London, 1971 — Anthony Masters

Part One

The Human Vampire or Psychic Sponge: Origins

Do you imagine that we see the hundred thousandth part of what exists? Consider, for example, the wind, which is the greatest of the forces of nature. It knocks men down, it demolishes houses, it uproots trees, stirs up the sea into mountainous waves, it breaks away the cliffs and drives great ships on to the rocks. The wind whistles, groans, bellows, sometimes it even kills. Have you seen it? It exists nevertheless.

The words of St Michel as imagined by Guy de Maupassant in his short story 'The Horla'.

From Webster's International Dictionary:
A blood-sucking ghost or re-animated body of a dead person; a soul or re-animated body of a dead person, believed to come from the grave and wander about by night sucking the blood of persons asleep causing their death.

From Witney's Century Dictionary:
A kind of spectral body which, according to a superstition existing among the slavic and other races on the lower Danube, leaves the grave during the night and maintains a semblance of life by sucking the warm blood of living men and women while they are asleep. Dead wizards, werewolves, heretics and other outcasts become vampires, as do also the illegitimate offspring of parents themselves illegitimate, and anyone killed by a vampire.

From Encyclopaedia Britannica:
The persons who turn vampires are in general wizards, suicides, or those who come to a violent end, or have been cursed by their parents or by the Church. But anyone may become a vampire, if an animal leaps over the corpse or a bird flies over it.

Vampirism was one of the most demonic outbreaks of mass hysteria ever to sweep the world. Its origins are rooted at the beginning of time and almost all of them are founded on superstition, later swelling to massive proportions with the advent of Christianity. If the Church had ignored superstition instead of officially condemning it as the work of the devil, then the waves of vampire belief would not have been so widespread and so intense.

In the twentieth century, living in a synthetic and oversophisticated society, it is difficult to feel the cold and foetid breath of superstition. Yet in primitive societies and later in societies that were shrugging off paganism and accepting Christianity, superstition was a dominant force. The Church of England asks its communicants to drink the symbolic blood of Jesus Christ. 'The Blood of our Lord Jesus Christ, which was shed for thee, preserve thy body and soul unto everlasting life. Drink this in remembrance that Christ's Blood was shed for thee, and be thankful.' The Jewish law of sacrifice clearly denotes the difference between spreading the blood as life and offering it as food. The Israelites were not allowed to drink the blood of the flesh (which is life) but must pour it on the earth. The blood should be sprinkled before the sanctuary, put upon the horns of the altar and then sprinkled or poured out. It must never be drunk. ('Their drink offerings of blood will I not offer.' See Leviticus I, Deuteronomy XII, 23; Psalms XVI, 4.)

Blood is the key factor in the origins of the vampire myth. Some believed that the soul lived within the blood; others, more simply, that it was the source of life. At all costs it must be protected as the fount of virility: warriors drank the blood of their slain enemies to gain their strength. Blood was essentially sacred and played a prominent part in ritual worship and sacrifice—throughout the ages the gods have demanded it and in order to propitiate them Man has obediently complied. Some races have a blood taboo, considering blood to be unclean, but although feelings on the subject may differ, they are always strong.

If it is natural to die through loss of blood it is logical to think one could live again through drinking blood. All societies have had their beliefs about the whereabouts and activities of the dead, and a constant factor in these beliefs was the feeling that many categories of people were reluctant to depart this life and that constant draughts of blood were all they required to carry on as before. It was felt that the dead were uneasy in their graves, that many of them were hostile or openly malignant and would be only too pleased to drain others of their life-blood. The dead who were unable to achieve divine status were particularly uneasy and therefore apt to roam; blood would give them a second birth. The undead, those who emerge from the grave and suck the blood of humans to give them life, are known as vampires. Their history is universal; they span the ages and have appeared in the legends of all races and all religions.

John Heinrich Zopfius, in his *Dissertatio de Vampiris*

Seruiensibus (published in Germany in 1733), describes vampires as follows:

> Vampires issue forth from their graves in the night, attack people sleeping quietly in their beds, suck out all the blood from their bodies and destroy them. They beset men, women and children alike sparing neither age nor sex. Those who are under the fatal malignity of their influence complain of suffocation and a total deficiency of spirits, after which they soon expire. Some who, when at the point of death, have been asked if they can tell what is causing their decease, reply that such and such persons, lately dead, have arisen from the tomb to torment and torture them.

Obviously there are many factors in men's habits, religious beliefs and customs that have led to or fostered the vampire. The most significant of these are described below.

Cannibalism

People have been eating each other for centuries. Man is a carnivorous animal and hungers for meat. This hunger needs repression and if indulged can become a definite addiction. The succulent fleshy crispness of blood-red steak, the bland texture of chicken breast, the delicate and savoury tang of a slim slice of beef... simply cooked, how tempting they can be. How ravishing they are when garnished. But what would they be like in their raw state? Many people have found them quite palatable. Man is an intelligent animal. He also considers himself sacred. With this in mind he is loath to masticate his neighbour. But, if blindfolded, would he really detect the difference between steak Diane and thigh flambé? Would his tastebuds differentiate between roast leg of lamb and roast leg of man?

There is no doubt that since the earliest times Man has eaten the flesh of his fellow human beings.

According to Montague Summers in *The Vampire: Its Kith and Kin*:

> Primitive people so frequently aligned men and animals in their thinking that it is possible that human flesh was not considered significantly different from other foodstuffs. There is *probably no*

instinctive aversion to eating it; the horror shown by civilized, and by many primitive, peoples was developed by convention, parallel to their aversion to eating other foods considered unorthodox, unclean, or unfit for human consumption, much as the pig and the dog are unclean for all Semitic peoples. The abhorrence of such foods is an extraordinarily deep emotion, not dictated by biological necessity.

In 1927, in the Chinese village of Choukoutien, some forty miles south-west of Pekin, a single tooth was discovered which enabled the anatomist Davidson Black to identify a creature closely related to *Pithecanthropus erectus*, the Javan ape-man already discovered by a Dutch anatomist. Later excavations brought to light the bones and skulls of some forty contemporaries of Black's *Pithecanthropus Pekinensis*, together with a number of their weapons and implements. Charred remains of bones lying on their hearths gave an insight into this primitive man's cooking habits, and there was clear evidence in some curiously broken-up skulls that the brains had been extracted, and cooked. If Pekin Man was, as this evidence strongly suggests, an eater of human flesh, he was also something of an epicure in this respect. And Pekin Man, like Java Man, lived some 500,000 years ago!

Neanderthal Man, living some 220,000 years ago in Central Europe, was almost certainly a cannibal; there is evidence for this in the caves and rock shelters of the Dordogne, particularly at Le Moustier, from which comes the term 'Mousterian' culture, and from skeletal remains in a Mousterian settlement at Krapina, in Croatia. Cro-Magnon Man, living some 75,000 years ago and called for the first time *Homo sapiens*, was an eater at times of the flesh of his fellows, if one is to judge by evidence found in the caves of Aurignac, near Toulouse, from which the term 'Aurignacian' derives.

Mesolithic and Neolithic Man, between 10,000 and 2,000 years BC, maintained the traditions of their ancestors in this respect: there is evidence of this in Switzerland and elsewhere and in the later Bronze Age, when Man first began working metal, he was still on occasion an eater of human flesh.

Instances of cannibalism continued throughout history. In the sixteenth century it was the custom and, indeed, the prerogative for many European executioners to retain the blood and parts of the body of the executed—to 'make what use of them they would'. In the eighteenth century, the Zingaris of Bohemia ate human flesh, Rajahs drank the blood from the severed heads of their executed prisoners and in the nineteenth century a Chinese executioner ate the heart and brains of his victims.

However, the eating of the actual flesh itself is comparatively irrelevant to vampirism. What *was* important was the transfer of virility, of soul-stuff or of life-giving blood from the dead to the living. Occasionally the blood was licked off the spear, occasionally hands went unwashed of blood for a certain period and occasionally the blood would be drunk, like milk still warm from the cow.

As Man became more sophisticated cannibalism became taboo. Those who indulged in cannibalistic practices were the abnormal, the mentally sick whose 'case histories' were faithfully recorded by their contemporaries and are now studied by psychologists.

Necrophilia, which basically means sexual attraction to corpses, also plays a part in cannibalistic rites. This particular mental disease has been divided into three parts by the psychiatrist Wulffen:

a. Lust Murder. The sexual act is completed with a body *after* murder.
b. Necrophagy. Parts of a mutilated corpse are eaten.
c. Necrostuprum. Body-stealing.

There are many examples of these more 'civilised' cannibal practices, all of which are rooted in fact but inevitably have become legendary—grossly exaggerated and distorted. Here are two pieces of grisly folklore involving not only cannibalism but the ever-vital transmutation of blood.

The Monster of Montluel (Justine Lafayette and Martin Dummolard) France 1888.
This was one of the most appalling examples of cannibalism yet recorded and at the same time poses psychiatric questions, the depths of which have never really been plumbed. Both Lafayette and Dummolard were necrophilists, the former being a flesh-eater and the latter a blood-drinker.

Martin first met the enormous Justine when she was running a workman's boarding-house in Lyon. She was a hideous, moustachioed slab of a woman, whilst Martin was considerably younger, extremely good-looking and totally impressionable. Somehow Justine was able to get the young man into her power and it was likely she used drugs, probably a combination of hypnotics and depressants, to do so. Whilst he was in a permanently dazed condition she married him, introducing him 'at the same time to her favourite study of the black arts—a heritage which ran several generations back in her family'. Trading on Martin's psychosis, Justine put him through a complexity of rites associated with black magic—out of which he emerged broken and obedient. Ordered to make his first kill, Martin attacked a fifteen-year-old girl behind a derelict warehouse on the riverbank. He ripped at her throat and drained the body of most of its blood—a fact substantiated by the horrified pathologists who later examined the body. But what was considerably more nauseating was the fact that the flesh of her upper arms and thighs had been sliced neatly away.

There then broke out in Montluel a complete terror campaign that reduced the town to a silent, echoing desolation at nightfall. But despite the fact that everybody locked themselves in, Martin was still able to use his seductive powers on at least eighty young girls in five years. They were all found in the same way: with their throats cut, their bodies drained of blood and the fleshiest, meatiest parts of their bodies neatly sliced away. Meanwhile, Martin became more obsessed with his blood fetish and Justine waxed even fatter on her appalling diet. Eventually Martin was captured, whilst attacking some children, and Justine, never far away from him, was also caught. A wildly sensational trial followed, which terminated in Justine being guillotined and Martin being sent to an institution. There he lived for some forty years, mostly in a placid and vegetable-like condition. But occasionally his lycanthropic self would emerge and he would be reduced to a snarling, slathering animal. Psychiatrists were unable to properly define Justine's influence over Martin, but whatever it was, it was strong—strong enough for its domination to remain some forty years after her execution.

Sawney Beane (East Lothian, Fifteenth Century)
Beane was the son of a peasant in East Lothian near Edinburgh. For no reason he and his girl friend left home and set up house in a cave on the coast of Galloway. Survival would have been impossible for the pair and the romance would have soon foundered had they not begun robbing travellers and dragging them back to the cave, which was part of a complex of subterranean caverns that ran under the sea for about a mile. There the victims were eaten—a diet that kept Beane and his girl in excellent health. They were in such fine fettle that they were able to raise eight sons and six daughters, all of whom inherited their parents' lust for human meat. Grandchildren also emerged and the cannibalistic family lived safely for several generations until their hideaway was eventually penetrated and the whole group was captured. In 1435 they were executed in Edinburgh amid great excitement and relief, although their executioners were almost as barbaric as the Beanes in the tortures they imposed.

In his book, *The Vampire: His Kith and Kin,** Montague Summers, the famous theatre critic and occult investigator, relates two instances of cannibalism. The first is from the Bible, recalling the horrors perpetrated when Jerusalem was besieged by Benadad of Syria during the reign of King Joram.

> Benadad King of Syria gathered together all his army and went up, and besieged Samaria. And there was a great famine in Samaria; and so long did the siege continue, till the head of an ass was sold for fourscore pieces of silver, and the fourth part of a cabe of pigeon's dung, for five pieces of silver. And as the King of Israel was passing by the wall, a certain woman cried out to him, saying: Save me, my Lord, O King. And he said: If the Lord doth not save thee how can I save thee? Out of the barn floor, or out of the winepress? And the King said to her: What aileth thee? And she answered: This woman said to me: give thy son, that we may eat him today, and we will eat my son tomorrow. So we boiled my son, and ate him. And I said to her on the next day: Give thy son that we may eat him. And she hath hid her son. When the King heard

* Published in 1928 by Kegan, Paul, Trench, Trubner & Co.

> this, he rent his garments, and passed by upon the wall. And all the people saw the hair-cloth which he wore within next to his flesh.

Montague Summers also quotes from a paper entitled *Necrophilism*, which was read in 1874 at a meeting of the Medico-Psychological Association in Glasgow by W. A. F. Browne, at one time Commissioner for Lunacy in Scotland. The quote relates to the savage reprisals evoked by Queen Elizabeth in Ireland when fertile pasture was burnt, soon becoming a total wilderness.

> The miserable poor ... out of every corner of the woods and glens came creeping forth upon thin hands, for their legs could not bear them, they looked like anatomes of death; they spoke like ghosts crying out of their graves; they did eat the dead carrions; happy when they could find them: yea, they did eat one another soon after; insomuch as the very carcasses they spared not to scrape out of their very graves.

When starving people eat each other, the strong survive through the weak. Superstition dictated and religion implied that the transmutation of blood from one to another would give strength and life. In times of plague, persecution and famine many people preferred not to know what was going on (in just the same way as German villages near wartime extermination camps preferred not to know what was going on) and therefore it was necessary to invent a reason for the attacks on the living and the dismembering of the dead. What better scapegoat could they have than the vampire? What better legend could be supported than the vampire myth? The vampire was traditionally both hungry and anxious for greater virility. Although his diet was largely blood he has been known, in certain areas, to devour gobbets of flesh. It is obvious that blood-sucking man built up the ominous legend of the gore-covered grave-lurker in order to cover up his own activities.

It is strange that although all forms of cannibalism were closely linked to vampire belief, vampirism, as a mystical force, had its main power-structure in central Europe rather than central Africa or Asia. But this area of Europe was noted for its poverty and for its pestilence and famine and Man was therefore continually forced to turn to his neighbour for nourishment—as well as for a transference of the vital life-blood.

Sacrifice

Sacrifice has a number of meanings but those responsible for igniting the vampire cult are basically the sacrificing of a victim, either to appease an angry god or to bribe him to promote one side against another in war, or the mutilation of the body itself to achieve the same ends.

In some cases the gift need not be a human being or part of a human being at all. Certain economies could be achieved, as in the case of the burnt offering of the Greeks, who sacrificed only the bones and fat of the ox, keeping the meat for themselves. Apparently their gods were content with this paltry diet and showed no signs of indigestional hell-fire. However, it was more usual for the worshipper to offer part of his own body—a finger-joint was a popular choice with many primitive peoples. In Tonga a portion of the little finger is severed as a sacrifice in order to speed the recovery of a sick relative (of higher rank). New Zealanders hung hair on trees in the graveyards as a substitute for their souls, thus hoping to cheat death. In India, mothers severed their own fingers and offered them as sacrifices so that they would not lose the children they bore.

Strangely, blood replaced carnage in many continents as a method of sacrifice and was thought to be just as effective as more dramatic offerings. A typical example of ritual bloodshed is the worshipper who draws drops of blood from his forefinger, praying at the same time.

The sacrifice of others, however, was a more popular pastime. The Greeks, practising economy again, offered criminals or prisoners of war to the gods. In Peru, when a lord was dangerously ill he would offer the gods one of his own sons so that he would be taken in his stead. Tribes in Northern Europe sacrificed slaves, the Aztecs poured the blood of their victims into their idols' mouths, and so on. The gods, however, were not the only blood-suckers and there were numerous spirits, usually evil, who also had to have sacrifices made to them for appeasement.

Ancestor worship

George Laurence Gomme, the British folklorist, says:

> On the one hand there is a definite representation of a cult of the dead based on the fear of dead kindred and found in isolated patches of the country; on the other hand there is a definite representation of a cult of the dead based on the love of the dead kindred and found generally prevalent over the country.*

These two different aspects of ancestor worship are as sharply divided in emotion yet as drawn together in practice as the two different aspects of sacrifice. Ancestors, like the gods, had to be appeased. General respect in life and in death was not enough. They were inclined to behave more neurotically and nastily in death than they ever did in life. Two facets of ancestor worship are examined below.

A. *Fear of the Dead Kindred*
It was always absolutely essential to speed the spirit on its way once death had taken place. At all costs the late departed must join the family's ancestors without delay. Should there be a delay the spirit would take offence, would hover malignantly around and when it did reach its eventual destination would have singled out defaulting members of the family for retribution. Precautions for the spirit's escape include the opening of windows and doors, the putting out of the fire in the hearth (in case the spirit doggedly refused conventional exits and insisted on the chimney), and keeping a careful watch on the corpse.

Fear of the malevolent ghost is described by the Reverend Atkinson, in his book *Forty Years in a Moorland Parish*:

> There is no doubt that the self-murderer or the doer of some atrocious deed of violence, murder, or lust was buried by some lonely road-side, in a road crossing or by the wild shadow-substance of other bodies, for that purpose; the body was made secure by pinning it to the bottom of the grave by aid of the driven

* *The British Folklorist*, published by Routledge & Kegan Paul (1962).

> stake. And there were other means adopted with the same end in view. The head was severed from the body and laid between the legs or placed under the arm—between the side and the arm, that is—or the feet and legs were bound together with a strong rope; or the corpse might be cut up into some hollow vessel capable of containing the pieces, and carried away quite beyond the precincts of the village and deposited in some bog or morass.

There is a direct link here between the old English attitude to the suicide or the murderer and the ritual savagery of the old pagan tribes.

B. Fear of the Ancestor Gods

If one carefully examines what is often called the totem complex it soon becomes apparent that at the bottom of the totem is dead Father, then Grandfather, then Great-Grandfather, and so on until at the very top of the totem is the first creator, and therefore God—or a god. Rather like the arduous 'begatting' sequences in the Old Testament, one ends up with somebody who was the issue of nobody—and therefore begat himself. If he or she could do that—alone and unaided—they must hold divine conception. The higher up the totem pole that primitive people worshipped the greater the sacrifice that was made. If recently-dead Father and not so recently-dead Grandfather were liverish and apt to return as irritable *revenants* then ancestors further back could turn into veritable demons if unappeased. The gods at the top of the totem were the most easily annoyed and each had his or her personal hang-up or neurosis. If annoyed they would send thunderbolts, pestilence or plague upon the offending community, not deigning to step down from their eyries themselves, unless under special mystical circumstances. Vintage ancestors were the most active as smiters and terror-mongers whilst the recently dead fussed and niggled around the family hearthside. The family would worship their ancestors at home whilst the tribe would worship their gods publicly. Both practices involved sacrifice and both practices amply illustrate the totem complex.

Plague

Outbreaks of plague are extremely rare today, but from the twelfth century until the seventeenth plague was rife. Thousands of people had to be buried quickly under primitive conditions in inadequate crypts. Some of the people were still alive when they were buried, some died in the funeral cart. A very real terror besieged those who witnessed the deaths of others: fear of contamination, fear of sacrilege and ultimately fear of death itself. In areas afflicted by the plague the dead walked (because they were not quite dead) and moved in their coffins (because they had been buried alive). Rats and starving domestic animals gnawed at children and the resultant carnage was blamed on the vampire. To show how quickly terror can spread and how deadly it can be, Montague Summers relates a macabre fable.

> A pilgrim making his way to Baghdad was overtaken on his journey by a grisly figure. 'Who are you?' asked the pilgrim. 'I am the Plague,' was the response, 'and I am going to Baghdad to kill a thousand people.' On his return journey the pilgrim overtook the spectre and stopping him said, 'Why did you tell me you were only going to kill a thousand people in Baghdad, whereas I found ten thousand of your victims in the city?' 'I spoke truly,' said the Plague, 'I killed but one thousand, the remainder died from fright.'

Consecrated ground became overfull, and the dead were buried in trenches and pits. The passing bell tolled continuously and the dead and the near-dead piled up in their thousands. During the Black Death in England a troupe called the Flagellantes arrived from Hungary and walked through the streets lashing at themselves 'till the blood ran down their shoulders that the plague might be stayed'. As death claimed family after family in the plague-afflicted lands of central Europe hysteria set in and desperate sacrifices were made in order to achieve salvation through divine appeasement. In the mind's eye vengeful dead ancestors walked by night seeking life, corpses lunged and tore at each other and the whole psychosis of these countries was one of dark and venomous fear—a climate in which to create vampires.

In England in 1665 the death-roll was 144,991 after four mammoth plagues had swept the country. However this was closely followed by the purging by fire when a large portion of foul and pestilent London was burnt to the ground.

The following account of the London plague appears in Bertram Puckle's book, *Funeral Customs, Their Origin and Development*, published in 1926:

> Some sort of organization seems to have existed with a view to stamping out the epidemic, for the city was divided into districts each with nurses, watchers and grave-diggers.
>
> The women who tended the sick carried a red staff in their hands that those whom they met might avoid them. The infected houses were marked with a cross and a prayer—a cry to Heaven when nothing more could be expected of material assistance. The warning cry 'Bring out your dead' and the rumble of the 'dead-carts' disturbed the stillness of the night, all too short for the collection of the bodies from the streets and houses.
>
> The following regulations were drawn up by the City Fathers in their desperate attempts to arrest the spread of the plague:
>
> 'That burial of the dead by this visitation be at most convenient hours always, either before sunrise or before sunsetting, with the privity of the churchwardens or constable, and not otherwise, and that no neighbours or friends be suffered to accompany the corpse to church, or to enter the house visited, upon pain of having his house shut up or be imprisoned, and that no corpse dying of infection shall be buried, or remain in any church in time of common prayer, sermon, or lecture; and that no children be suffered at time of burial of any corpse in any church, churchyard, or burying place, to come near the corpse, coffin or grave, and that all the graves be at least six feet deep; and further, all public assemblies at other burials are to be forborne during the continuance of the visitation.'
>
> The regulations further enjoined that the houses which the plague had visited were to be marked with a red cross on the middle of the door one foot in length, and the words 'Lord have mercy on us' to be also inscribed.
>
> In view of the regulation that none might follow to the grave, the corpse was hurried out of the house at night, wrapped in any sort of an improvised shroud, to be committed to the pits, with, or more likely without, a muttered prayer from the labourer already accustomed to the sickening sight of wholesale slaughter.

Liberal libations of beer and tobacco and good pay were the only consolations of a sorely tried official, who, from force of circumstances, or some sense of duty, was pressed into this service.

Whatever the efforts made it was certainly not science that finally overcame a national calamity which, nurtured in a hotbed of filth, would, once it had started, have sorely taxed our most earnest efforts today.

All that we have to remind us of this last of a series of plagues is the old burial grounds, over the entrance to which may be seen the sculptured representation of skull and cross-bones distinguishing the sites of the plague cemeteries.

In the Brompton Road, once far removed from habitation, a row of empty houses stood for many years, which none would occupy. They were built on the spot where many thousands of victims of the plague lay buried.

There is an account by another historian, James Anthony Froude, of the symptoms and progress of the disease.

If it broke out in a foreign town it picked out the English residents with undeviating accuracy. The sufferers were generally men between thirty and forty years of age, and the stouter and healthier they were the more readily they caught the infection.

The symptoms were a sudden perspiration accompanied by faintness and drowsiness. Those who were taken with full stomachs died immediately, and those who caught cold 'shivered into dissolution in a few hours'.

The disease produced in the victim an intense desire to sleep, which, if yielded to, quickly proved fatal. So rapid was the disorder that of seven householders who supped together in the City of London, six before morning were corpses.

Catalepsy

The incidence of suspended animation was a particularly important and logical basis of vampire belief. In many cases it resulted in premature burial and the dreadful crypt incidents that this involved. The supposed corpse would wake in the coffin and have little idea of what nightmarish circumstances he or she was in. It is impossible to imagine the slow torture of dawning realisation, and the agony of mind and body that would overtake one. To lie in the coffin in a vault or crypt that would only be opened again to admit the next corpse, perhaps in half a century's time; the futile wrenching at the coffin lid from an extraordinarily cramped position; the screams of despair evoked by the claustrophobia of the situation; then hunger and death in limited contortion. A situation born only of dreams—yet it was a reality to some hundreds of cataleptics in the past.

If sounds were heard in the crypt most people were too frightened to investigate. If they did have the courage then the evidence of the undead, the vampire, was all too plain to discern—twisted positions, torn shrouds and blood. But were these evidence of vampirism? Or merely the desperate struggle of the cataleptic to free himself from his premature grave? The blood itself is easily explained, for the panic-stricken victim had either bloodied his limbs in fruitless beating at the coffin lid or, worse still, had bitten in hunger at his own flesh.

Montague Summers comments on catalepsy in *The Vampire: His Kith and Kin*:

> Some authorities consider catalepsy as almost entirely, if not wholly, psychic, and certainly not a disease in any correct sense of the word, although it may be a symptom of obscure diseases arising from nervous disorders. A medical authority has pronounced that 'in itself catalepsy is never fatal'. It belongs to the domain of hypnotism, and is said to be refreshing to the subject, specially when he is exhausted by long mental exertion or physical toil. Very often it arises from conscious or sub-conscious autosuggestion, and it has been described as 'the supreme effort of nature to give the tired nerves their needed repose'. No doubt the fatal mistake so often made in the past was that of endeavouring by drastic measures to hasten restoration to consciousness, instead of allowing nature to recuperate at will. If the attempt is successful it comes as a fearful shock to the nerves which are craving for rest; if the effort is seemingly without result the patient is in imminent danger of an autopsy or of being buried alive, a tragedy which, it is to be feared, has happened to very many.

It did indeed happen to very many. American statistics in the early 1900s show that not less than one case a week of premature burial was discovered. In France, also, a physician named Brutier published a pamphlet in the eighteenth century entitled

Dissertations On The Uncertainty of the Signs of Death and Premature Burials. In it he claims that 'out of 181 cases fifty-five were buried alive, four dissected alive, fifty-three woke in their coffins before being buried, and seventy-two others were pronounced dead whilst still alive'. To the layman any victim of catalepsy would appear to be very dead. But nevertheless the nervous and circulating systems all continue whilst the heart-beat and respiration do the same—albeit weakly.

Finally, here is an extract from a dissertation on catalepsy and vampirism by Dr Herbert Mayo, who was Professor of Anatomy at King's College, London. His book was called *On the Truths Contained in Popular Superstitions*, and is dated 1851.

> ...let us content ourselves with a notion not so monstrous, but still startling enough: that the bodies, which were found in the so-called Vampyr state, instead of being in a new or mystical condition, were simply alive in the common way, or had been so for some time subsequent to their interment; that, in short, they were the bodies of persons who had been buried alive, and whose life, where it yet lingered, was finally extinguished through the ignorance and barbarity of those who disinterred them. In the following sketch ... the correctness of this inference comes out with terrific force.
>
> Erasmus Francisci, in his remarks upon the description of the Dukedom of Krain by Valvasor, speaks of a man of the name of Grando, in the district of Kring, who died, was buried, and became a Vampyr, and as such was exhumed for the purpose of having a stake thrust through him.
>
> 'When they opened his grave, after he had been long buried, his face was found with a colour, and his features made natural sorts of movements, as if the dead man smiled. He even opened his mouth as if he would inhale fresh air. They held the crucifix before him, and called in a loud voice, "See, this is Jesus Christ who redeemed your soul from hell, and died for you." After the sound had acted on his organs of hearing, and he had connected perhaps some ideas with it, tears began to flow from the dead man's eyes. Finally, when after a short prayer for his poor soul they proceeded to hack off his head, the corpse uttered a screech, and turned and rolled just as if it had been alive—and the grave was full of blood.'
>
> We have thus succeeded in interpreting one of the unknown terms in the Vampyr-theorem. The suspicious character, who had

some dark way of nourishing himself in the grave, turns out to be an unfortunate gentleman (or lady) whom his friends had buried under a mistake while he was still alive, and who, if they afterwards mercifully let him alone, died sooner or later either naturally or of the premature interment—in either case, it is to be hoped, with no interval of restored consciousness. The state which thus passed for death and led to such fatal consequences, apart from superstition, deserves our serious consideration; for, although of very rare, it is of continual occurrence, and society is not sufficiently on its guard against a contingency so dreadful when overlooked. When the nurse or the doctor has announced that all is over—that the valued friend or relative has breathed his last—no doubt crosses any one's mind of the reality of the sad event. Disease is now so well understood—every step in its march laid down and foreseen—the approach of danger accurately estimated—the liability of the patient, according to his powers of resisting it, to succumb earlier or to hold out longer—all is theoretically so clear, that a wholesome suspicion of error in the verdict of the attendants seldom suggests itself. The evil I am considering ought not, however, to be attributed to redundance of knowledge: it arises from its partial lack—from a too general neglect of one very important section in pathological science. The laity, if not the doctors too, constantly lose sight of the fact, that there exists an alternative to the fatal event of ordinary disease; that a patient is liable at any period of illness to deviate, or, as it were, to slide off, from the customary line of disease into another and a deceptive route—*instead of death, to encounter apparent death.*

The Germans express this condition of the living body by the term *scheintod*, which signifies exactly *apparent death*; and it is perhaps a better term than our English equivalent, 'suspended animation'. But both these expressions are generic terms, and a specific term is still wanted to denote the present class of instances. To meet this exigency, I propose, for reasons which will afterwards appear, to employ the term 'death-trance' to designate the cases we are investigating.

Death-trance is, then, one of the forms of suspended animation: there are several others. After incomplete poisoning, after suffocation in either of its various ways, after exposure to cold in infants newly born, a state is occasionally met with, of which (however each may still differ from the rest) the common feature is an apparent suspension of the vital actions. But all of these so-cited instances agree in another important respect, which second inter-agreement separates them as a class from death-trance. They represent, each and all, a period of conflict between the effects of certain deleterious impressions and the vital principle, the latter struggling against the weight and force of the former. Such is not the case in death-trance.

Death-trance is a positive status—a period of repose—the duration of which is sometimes definite and predetermined, though unknown. Thus the patient, the term of the death-trance having expired, occasionally suddenly wakes, entirely and at once restored. Oftener, however, the machinery which has been stopped seems to require to be jogged—then it goes on again.

The basis of death-trance is suspension of the action of the heart, and of the breathing, and of voluntary motion; generally likewise feeling and intelligence, and the vegetative changes in the body, are suspended. With these phenomena is joined loss of external warmth; so that the usual evidence of life is gone. But there have occurred varieties of this condition, in which occasional slight manifestations of one or other of the vital actions have been observed.

Death-trance may occur as a primary affection, suddenly or gradually. The diseases the course of which it is liable, as it were, to bifurcate, or to graft itself upon, are first and principally all disorders of the nervous system. But in any form of disease, when the body is brought to a certain degree of debility, death-trance may supervene. Age and sex have to do with its occurrence; which is more frequent in the young than in the old, in women than in men—differences evidently connected with greater irritability of the nervous system. Accordingly, women in labour are among the most liable to death-trance....

I might exemplify death-trance by many a well-authenticated romantic story. —A noise heard in a vault; the people instead of breaking open the door, go for the keys, and for authority to act, and return too late; the unfortunate person is found dead, having previously gnawn her hand and arm in agony. —A lady is buried with a jewel of value on her finger; thieves open the vault to possess themselves of the treasure; the ring cannot be drawn from the finger, and the thieves proceed to cut the finger off; the lady, wakening from her trance, scares the thieves away, and recovers. —A young married lady dies and is buried; a former admirer to whom her parents had refused her hand, bribes the sexton to let him see once more the form he loved. The body opportunely comes to life at this moment, and flies from Paris with its first lover to England, where they are married. Venturing to return to France, the lady is recognised, and is reclaimed by her previous husband through a suit at law; her counsel demurs, on the ground of the desertion and burial; but the law not admitting this plea, she flies again to England with her preserver, to avoid the judgment of the parliament of Paris, in the acts of which the case stands recorded. There are one or two other cases that I dare not cite, the particulars of which transcend the wildest flights of imagination...

To return to the former subject of the Vampyr superstition. The second element which we have yet to explain is the Vampyr visit and its consequence—the lapse of the party visited into death-trance. There are two ways of dealing with this knot; one is to cut it, the other to untie it.

It may be cut, by denying the supposed connection between the Vampyr visit and the supervention of death-trance in the second party. Nor is the explanation thus obtained devoid of plausibility. There is no reason why death-trance should not, in certain seasons and places, be *epidemic*. Then the persons most liable to it would be those of weak and irritable nervous systems. Again a first effect of the epidemic might be further to shake the nerves of weaker subjects. These are exactly the persons who are likely to be infected with imaginary terrors, and to dream, or even to fancy, they have seen Mr and Mrs such a one, the last victims of the epidemic. The dream or impression upon the senses might again recur, and the sickening patient have already talked of it to his neighbours, before he himself was seized with death-trance. On this supposition, the Vampyr visit would sink into the subordinate rank of a mere premonitory symptom.

To myself, I must confess, this explanation, the best I am yet in a position to offer, appears barren and jejune; and not at all to do justice to the force and frequency, or, as tradition represents the matter, the universality of the Vampyr visit as a precursor of the victim's fate. Imagine how strong must have been the conviction of the reality of the apparition, how common a feature it must have been, to have led to the laying down of the unnatural and repulsive process customarily followed at the Vampyr's grave, as the regular and proper preventive of ulterior consequences.

I am disposed, therefore, rather to try and untie this knot, and with that object to wait, hoping that something may turn up in the progress of these inquiries to assist me in its solution. In the mean time, I would beg leave to consider this second half of the problem a compound phenomenon, the solutions of the two parts of which may not emerge simultaneously. The Vampyr visit is one thing; its presumed contagious effect another. The Vampyr visit! Well, it is clear the Vampyr could not have left his grave bodily—or, at all events, if he could, he never could have buried himself again. Yet in his grave they always found him. So the body could not have been the visitant. Then, in popular language, it was the ghost of the Vampyr that haunted its future victim.

A more contemporary medical explanation of states of cataplexy, sleep paralysis and catalepsy is as follows:

Cataplexy. An attack to which sufferers from narcolepsy are liable but which differs from sleep in that although the patient loses all power of movement and of maintaining posture, consciousness is preserved. Sometimes tremor of the head and muscular twitching occur at the onset, but these may be absent. The patient sinks limply to the ground with the eyes closed. The muscles are hypotonic and the pupils may fail to react to light, the tendon reflexes may be diminished or lost. Though completely unable to move or to utter a sound, the patient is fully aware of all that is happening. Cataplectic attacks usually last for less than a minute and recovery is rapid. They are commonly precipitated by strong emotion, pleasurable or otherwise, and the patient may be unable to move until he has controlled his emotion.

Sleep Paralysis. This resembles cataplexy except that instead of being precipitated during the day by emotion it usually occurs during the period of falling asleep or of awakening—often accompanied by intense anxiety. However, a touch will usually rapidly disperse the paralysis.

Catalepsy. A morbid condition in which there is a sudden suspension of sensibility and voluntary movement with waxy rigidity of the limbs and body, these maintaining any posture in which they are placed. The pulse and respiration are slow and the body is cold. The condition is of nervous origin and may be found in association with hypnosis, hysteria and epilepsy. The attack may last for any period between a few minutes and several days. *Local catalepsy*—catalepsy in which a single group of muscles or a single organ is effected. *Organic catalepsy* can be induced by destructive lesions in certain parts of the brain and is met with in its most severe form in association with schizophrenia. Extreme catalepsy may continue for weeks, months or even years.

Hysterical Trance, as in deep sleep, may last for hours, weeks or days and cases have been reported of patients being buried alive (some deliberately—as Fakirs). In more severe cases the heart and respiration may become so feeble that death is simulated. An hysterical trance may be caused by auto-suggestion, hypnotic state or may follow an hysterical fit.

Here, then, were very plausible foundations for vampire belief. Some of the more grotesque incidents are described in the next section.

Premature burial

It was not unknown for East European peasants to exhume the dead in order to define whether or not the corpse had ascended or descended. Owing to the rudimentary methods of defining death, many people were buried alive and on being exhumed would be in an entirely different position from that in which they were buried. The victim would be face down in the coffin, so as to inhale the maximum amount of air, and during the process of suffocating the occupant would bite at his lips and fingers, draining blood and often filling the coffin with gore. This unfortunate person would then be represented as a blood-sucking vampire.

One rather amusing example of premature burial is drawn from a Norse legend. Two chieftains known as Asmund and Assueit made an alliance known as a Brotherhood of Arms. This not only meant the strongest possible friendship in life but eternal friendship in death. If one died then the other was to be interred, alive, in his tomb. Some years later Assueit was killed in battle and it was Asmund's rôle to join his dead friend, despite the fact that he was still very much alive. The tomb was built large enough to contain not just the two friends but their war-horses and trophies. The mausoleum was sealed, leaving the living to watch over the dead. A century later a group of Swedish travellers arrived in the district and, hearing of the legend, were determined to exhume both Asmund and Assueit, partly to gauge the truth of the legend and partly because they wanted to plunder the tomb. With fervent interest the Swedes uncovered the entrance to the gigantic tomb and gained entry. But directly penetration had been made, the sound of a great battle was heard echoing in the vaults below. A soldier was sent down on a rope—and disappeared. A few minutes later, violent tugging was felt and the rest of the party began to haul what they assumed was the soldier to the surface. But instead a wild and bloody figure emerged—Asmund. Quickly taking stock of his situation, Asmund lectured the assembled Swedes on his century of entombed adventure. Life had been far from dull; apparently, directly the vault had been sealed Assueit rose ill-temperedly from his death-bed. He was also hungry—and briskly ate his way through both war-horses. His appetite unappeased, Assueit leapt upon Asmund and they were locked in mortal combat (so the story goes) for a century. By coincidence Asmund won just as the Swedes arrived. Having recounted this dramatic story Asmund collapsed and died. The Swedes then took Assueit's body, removed it from the tomb and cremated it. Then they replaced Asmund, now alone in the vault, and once again sealed the entrance.

One of the strongest advocates of taking precautions against the tragic possibility of premature burial was an Austrian physician named Franz Hartmann. In 1896 he published a book entitled *Premature Burial* that proved to be a veritable chronicle of horrors. He vehemently believed that the medical profession of the day knew little or nothing when it came to determining whether or not a patient was dead. Over and over again he repeated the theory that decomposition was the only reliable proof of actual death. He believed that when a person appeared dead, the only way to be absolutely certain was to keep the body around for a few days until there was no doubt about its condition. Furthermore he enthusiastically subscribed to a plan proposed by Colonel Edward P. Vollum of the U.S. Army Medical Corps. Under the plan, provision was made that anyone buried without an autopsy, or without having been embalmed, be interred with a bottle of chloroform within reach so that if they revived they could easily commit suicide with a minimum of suffering.

Although Hartmann makes fascinating reading, it is impossible to accept everything he reports as fact. For instance, he cites many cases of victims who were buried for days or weeks and then returned to life, but obviously if a person in a state of catalepsy were to be buried for any appreciable length of time he would soon suffocate. Some of the cases recorded by Hartmann are worth examining, however, in an effort to understand the origins of vampire beliefs. Two of these are as follows:

> In the village of Merva, near Gorizia, a woman by the name of Scalettari died a victim of indigestion. In due time she was buried. On the following day someone passing through the cemetery near the grave heard cries as if issuing from within the tomb. He reported the case to the police, who caused the grave to be opened, and it was then discovered that the woman had just died after a horrible struggle. Her body was still warm, and her arms and face were scratched and bleeding, owing to the attempts she had made to free herself from her terrible position.
>
> In the year 1856 there died a man in a Hungarian village; it is customary there to dig the graves in rows. As the grave-digger was making a new grave he heard sounds as of knocking proceeding from a grave where a man had been buried a few days previously. Terrified, he went to the priest, and with the priest to the police. At last permission was granted to open the grave; but by this time its occupant had died in reality. The fact that he had been buried alive was made evident by the condition of the body and by the wounds which the man had inflicted upon himself by biting his shoulders and arms.

Hartmann, although little more than a crank, certainly mirrored the fears of a good many people—particularly during this period.

Montague Summers relates cases which, although they have slightly hilarious connotations, were nevertheless serious symptoms of the fear of being buried alive—a fear that not only contributed heavily to vampire belief but also spread like wildfire throughout Europe.

> A lady who is now the head matron of one of the largest orphan asylums in the United States has been given over as dead no less than twice by the physicians in attendance; her body has

twice been shrouded in the decent cerements of the grave; and twice she has been resuscitated by her friends. On the second occasion, in view of the former experience, extraordinary precautions were taken. All known tests were applied by the physicians, and humanly speaking all possible doubt was set at rest. The doctors had actually left the house, and the undertaker was at his sad business. It chanced that the body was pierced by a pin, and to the joy of her friends it was noted that a small drop of blood shortly afterwards oozed from the puncture. The family insisted upon the preparations being stayed; vigorous treatment was unremittingly applied, and the patient returned to life. Today she is an exceptionally active and energetic administratrix. It should be remarked that the lady declared that she had never for a moment lost consciousness, that she was fully cognizant of all that went on around her, that she perfectly understood the meaning of all the tests which were so assiduously employed, but that all the while she felt the utmost indifference with regard to the result. The verdict of the physicians that she was dead did not cause her either the slightest surprise or the smallest alarm.

A very similar accident occurred to a gentleman of good estate, one of the most prominent citizens of Harrisburg, in Pennsylvania. After a long illness he apparently died from inflammatory rheumatism, which was complicated with heart trouble. All preparations were made for the funeral, but his wife determined that this should not take place for at least a week, so great was her fear of premature burial. In the course of two or three days it was noticed that the body had moved; the eyes were wide open, and one of the arms had altered the position in which it had been carefully placed. His wife shrieked out his name, upon which he slowly arose, and with assistance was supported to a chair. Even before the arrival of the physicians, who were instantly summoned, he had regained a marked degree of strength, together with an ability of movement which had not been possible throughout the whole course of his illness. He was soon in excellent health, and what is very remarkable, he stated that during the time of suspended animation he was perfectly aware of everything that was going on all around, that the grief of his family filled him with terrible agony, and he dreaded the preparations of interment, but that he was unable to move a muscle or utter a word.

There are dozens of different stories, some proven and others not, that illustrate the rising of the dead from their graves. There are few public memorials to substantiate their rising—although there is one in London at St Giles, Cripplegate, where there is a monument dedicated to a woman named Constance Whitney. Above the scroll there is a picture of a lady rising from her coffin—and this picture represents an actual occasion. She had not died, but had merely been buried in a state of catalepsy. The sexton saved her from a lingering death when he opened her coffin to steal a ring from her finger. Luckily the lady happened to wake as the cool air flooded her narrow prison.

Body-snatching

Here was another reason for the dead leaving their tombs—but this time the circumstances were completely outside their control. The bodies were snatched—by the Resurrection Men. These professional grave-diggers sold corpses to anatomical students. The first wave of body-snatching began in France in the seventeenth century when the Paris Faculty of Medicine was only allowed one corpse a year. This intolerable situation was alleviated by a Doctor Mauriccau who was later accused of 'illegally obtaining corpses' from the Saint Sulpice cemetery.

But the real scandal broke during the nineteenth century in Britain, a period when scientific and medical research was in the ascendant. A number of 'resurrection men' began to operate, opening a considerable traffic with medical schools and teaching hospitals. The Barber Surgeon's Company received a grant of four corpses each year which was supplemented by the bodies of all criminals whose offences brought them to the gallows. Top prices, however, were paid for 'additional subjects' and no embarrassing questions were asked. As a result guards were put upon the newly interred to ensure that they stayed interred. The tightening security led to murder in the streets—and the bodies continued to flow into the clutches of the anatomical students.

Another aspect of body-snatching was holding a corpse to ransom—providing he was a wealthy one. A victim of this practice was the unfortunate twenty-fifth Earl of Crawford whose body was stolen from the family vault at Dunecht (near Aberdeen). The Earl had gently expired in 1881 in Florence and his body was embalmed and taken to Scotland. Bearing in mind the habits of the body-snatchers, the family took the following precautions:

1. The Earl was interred in a granite tomb under the private chapel adjoining Dunecht House.
2. His body was first placed in a leaden shell,
3. then in an inner case of wood,
4. and finally in an outer coffin of carved wood, mounted in silver.

Nevertheless, despite all these precautions, a man named Charles Souter and others somehow gained entry to the tomb, unscrewed the outer case of the Earl's coffin, forced open the inner case and cut open the leaden shell. Then the Earl was submitted to the indignity of being dragged out, feet first, and kidnapped. A letter was sent with a ransom demand but the family apparently were not desperate enough for the return of the Earl's body—and refused to pay under any circumstances. Some time later the body was discovered in a shallow grave, some five hundred yards from the mansion, wrapped ignominiously in a blanket. Souter, who had drunkenly led some companions to the body, protested his innocence vigorously when he had sobered up. Nevertheless he was accused of complicity, sentenced to five years' penal servitude and died still claiming his own innocence.

The most famous case of traditional body-snatching was that of Burke and Hare (1827). A popular street song of the time ran:

> Up the close and down the stair,
> But and ben with Burke and Hare,
> Burke's the butcher, Hare's the thief,
> Knox the boy that buys the beef.

The song defined the trio all too well. Hare was the landlord of a squalid Edinburgh boarding house and Burke was one of his guests. Together they decided that digging up corpses was too much like hard work and it would be more practical to murder their guests. Experimentally they smothered one lodger with a pillow, taking the corpse to a Dr Robert Knox who paid £7 10s. for it. This suited everybody (except the victim) and a large number of people were enticed to the Burke and Hare establishment, there to be murdered in their beds. Knox paid £10 in winter and £8 in summer for each corpse—corpses that included the sick, the lame, prostitutes, *etcetera*. Finally Burke, seemingly in a fit of remorse, confessed and Hare quickly turned King's Evidence. They were probably only one jump ahead of arrest, anyway, for suspicion had long hung over the grisly trio. Dr Knox denied all, despite Hare's accusations, but they all seemed to be heading for the gallows. In the end only Burke was hung whilst Hare and Knox eluded the rope over a legal technicality.

Lycanthropy

The *Encyclopedia of Religion and Ethics* gives two definitions for the word lycanthropy:

1. It may indicate merely a form of madness in which the patient imagines that he is an animal, especially a wolf, and acts as such. This disease was common in antiquity and especially in the Middle Ages, doubtless as a result of the widespread belief that transformation into animal form was possible.
2. It indicates the popular belief that on occasion a human being can actually transform himself, or be transformed, into a wolf or some other animal. In this form he slays and eats men. But, if wounded while in his wolf form, it is found that a corresponding wound exists on the human body from which the transformation has taken place. When wounded or killed, the werewolf's human form is restored.

The word lycanthropy is derived from the Greek word *λυκος*, which means wolf and *ανθρωπος* which means man. The werewolf superstition is worldwide and is very similar to the vampire superstition. Whilst the werewolf is more a type of shape-shifting, the vampire is actually a member of the undead. Yet according to popular belief a werewolf, on death, will become a vampire.

Throughout the Middle Ages many theologians considered lycanthropy to be a form of sorcery. The doctrine was that 'by the help of Satan, sorcerers could transform themselves into noxious animals, particularly wolves, for purposes inimical to others'. In his treatise *De Magorum Demonomania* J. Bodin writes:

> Theological opinion thus coincided with popular superstition, and many of the instances cited as proofs are little better than the popular tales referred to above—eg, where a wolf is wounded and a human being is found with a similar wound soon after. The severest measures were therefore taken against lycanthropes, especially on the part of the Inquisition, and this authoritative announcement of the reality of the transformation added to the popular terrorism. People easily imagined the truth of the charges brought against those charged with them, or came forward as witnesses of the alleged facts. Indeed, the prisoners themselves often maintained their truth, showing that insanity and hallucination had much to do with the matter. The peculiarly heinous aspect of the crime is seen in this: H. Boguet, a judge who tried many cases and who wrote many works against sorcery, drew up a code in 1601 in which he stated that, while sorcerers should be first strangled and then burned, the *loups-garous* should be burned alive. The belief in sorcery as well as the theological animus against it often led to epidemics of sorcery; the people in a district, eg, became terrorized by the idea that all around them were sorcerers, or many persons, half crazy, maintained this regarding themselves. At the beginning of the 16th century in Lombardy during such an epidemic, witches were freely accused of having changed into cats and entered houses to suck the blood of children. Reports of many trials of reputed lycanthropes are still extant, and afford sad evidence of human credulity.

The connection between werewolves and vampires is fairly tangible. Suspected werewolves were burnt after death to prevent them from becoming vampires, but it was thought to be possible for the dead to return either as werewolves or vampires. During the last century graves were watched by priests in Normandy during a werewolf scare; the Malaysians believed that the ghosts of dead wizards entered the bodies of tigers. In New Zealand lizards were feared because it was thought that the souls of those whose last rites had been neglected became malignant and entered the lizards, and Ethiopians believed that the king of the devils rode on a fire-breathing wolf and was followed by fiends in the form of wolves.

Eliphas Levi in his book *A History of Magic* (1913) claims that lycanthropy is a process of doubling. The subject sleeps in his own bed, dreaming of being a wolf. At the same time his astral body craves for meat on roads and in graveyards. If the astral body is wounded or killed, then the sleeper is also wounded or killed (providing silver bullets or a silver blade have penetrated the werewolf). Some werewolves were thought to be able to turn their skin inside out—rather like a lining between flesh and skin.

In the sixteenth century, when belief in lycanthropy was particularly widespread, hundreds of innocent victims, suspected of being werewolves, were literally ripped to pieces in an attempt to expose the wolf hair on their inside-out skin. Between 1520 and 1630 30,000 cases were recorded, and according to Ornella Volta, in 1573, the Parliament of Dôle in France ordered a hunt with kitchen spits, halberds, spears, arquebuses, and sticks to hunt, capture, bind and kill the werewolf who infested the district.

The same kind of religious and pagan hysteria surrounds the werewolf myth as surrounds the vampire myth. There is no doubt that the belief was genuine if the transformation itself was not.

Malleus Maleficarum

This was the title of one of the most extraordinarily ambiguous documents ever to receive the papal seal. The authors were appointed by the Pope to write what really amounted to a handbook for the Inquisition as a direct result of a wave of European paranoia concerning witchcraft, vampirism and werewolvery. It became the ultimate authority in the Church's struggle against the Black Arts and provided the justification for crushing evildoers and heretics alike. In the introduction it stated:

> Even preachers of the Divine Word did not hesitate to assure the people that there were no such things as witches; that they had

> no arts by which they could injure men and animals; by which imprudent language the secular arm was not unfrequently restrained from punishing such sorceries; and thus they became amazingly increased, and heresy became enormously strengthened.

The *Maleficarum* was translated into German as *Der Hexenhammer* and into English as *The Witch Hammer*. The title was descriptive. The Pope was determined to lighten the darkness of Europe and to expose its satanists as heretics and evil-doers. This strange document was first published *circa* 1489 and the authors were James Sprenger and Henry Kramer.

The publication took the form of question and answer inquisition and the authors were expressly called *Inquisitores haereticae pravitatis*.

In *The Witch Hammer*, the idea of witchcraft was systematically determined.

> Witches, sorcerers, and sorceresses, are people who deny God, and renounce Him and His grace; who have made a league with the devil; have given themselves up to him body and soul; who attend his assemblies and sabbaths, and receive from him poison-powder, and, as his subjects, receive command from him to injure and destroy men and animals; who, through devilish arts, stir up storms, damage the corn, the meadows, and the fields, and confound the powers of nature.

In *The Witch Hammer*, Part I, Question XV, under the rubric, 'It is Shown that, on account of the Sins of Witches, the Innocent are often Bewitched, yea, Sometimes even for their Own Sins,' the authors relate an instance which came under their own observation. They say:

> Sin, and consequently punishment, can also be passed on through some consent or dissimulation. For when those in authority neglect to reprove sin, then very often the good are punished with the wicked, as St. Augustine says in the first book *De Civitate Dei*. An example was brought to our notice as Inquisitors. A town once was rendered almost destitute by the death of its citizens; and there was a rumour that a certain buried woman was gradually eating the shroud in which she had been buried, and that the plague could not cease until she had eaten the whole shroud and absorbed it into her stomach. A council

was held, and the Podesta with the Governor of the city dug up the grave, and found half the shroud absorbed through the mouth and throat into the stomach, and consumed. In horror at this sight, the Podesta drew his sword and cut off her head and threw it out of the grave, and at once the plague ceased. Now the sins of that old woman were, by Divine permission, visited upon the innocent on account of the dissimulation of what had happened before. For when an Inquisition was held it was found that during a long time of her life she had been a Sorceress and Enchantress.

The Witch Hammer is a valuable document in that it throws a good deal of light on the muddled and narrow thinking of the times. It has, however, become a great source of embarrassment to the Catholic Church and is not referred to in the Catholic Encyclopaedia. The two authors were obviously disturbed and seemed to abhor the entire female sex. They laid the blame for all evil on women and declared that all witchcraft springs from the 'carnal lust' which to their minds was an innate attribute of the female.

There is no doubt that *The Witch Hammer* contributed to superstition. The vampire myth was now in direct conflict with the Church—a battle that could only give the fantasy credence and the mind additional terror and pressure.

Vampire Bats

In Central and South America and the Caribbean, the vampire bat is still a menace—and it was the spread of stories of the vampire bats' activity that further substantiated belief in the undead. On examining the activities of this species of bat it is easy to see the link between them and the legend of the undead.

There are four types of vampire bat although there is little distinction between them: the *Desmodus Rufus*, the *Didemus Yungi*, the *Diphylla Caudata*, and the *Desmodus Rotunda*. All are blood-sucking, all spread rabies and in the main all attack cattle and horses, biting them on the neck.

The bites, similar to a narrow cut made by a razor blade, eventually prove fatal—though rabies is the destructive factor rather than the blood-sucking itself. The vampire bat drinks about 10 ccs of blood per day and experiments are being carried out on them by the Nuffield Research Foundation at the Royal Zoological Society under special conditions. The research is aimed at helping victims of thrombosis, as something in the saliva of the vampire bat prevents and destroys blood clots—the agents of death to the thrombosed patient. This is why the wound made by a vampire bat will not clot and blood can run from the incision, in minute quantities, for hours.

The bat will on occasion attack human beings, incising only at the extremities, ie toes or nose. Once again rabies is the big danger but there is little evidence to indicate that there are many human casualties. The personal habits of vampire bats are pretty diabolical; if overcrowded they will feed on each other. Their cannibalistic habits also apply to attacks on the older, weaker bats by the young and the Nuffield Foundation have often rescued from their cages elderly relatives who are beginning to look bat-pecked. Despite the fact that pregnancy can last up to a year and it is virtually impossible to detect the difference between male and female, the Nuffield Foundation have been successful in breeding young bats, keeping them in captivity and feeding them with fresh blood.

Less scientific evidence has come from a variety of other sources. One explorer, Peter Martyr (who wrote just after the conquest of South America by the Spaniards) claimed that vampire bats were capable of killing men, and Sir Robert Schomburg said that at Wicki, on the river Berlice, no chickens could be kept as a result of the attacks of vampire bats. Charles Darwin relates in his book *Naturalist's Voyage Round The World* that

> We were bivouacking late one night near Coquimbo in Chile, when my servant, noticing that one of the horses was very restive, went to see what was the matter, and fancying he could detect something, suddenly put his hand on the beast's withers, and secured the vampire.

Psychic Vampires

Ross Nichols, a British occult authority and Chief Druid of the Bardic Order, has had wide experience of psychic vampirism. He writes:

> On first thoughts, vampires would seem to be a ghoulish piece of romanticism. However strong the local beliefs in vampirism at one time in the Carpathian Mountains, the only reality corresponding to it seems to be the vampire bat. Move the idea of the vampire to the psychic intellectual plane, however, and it is valid enough, and one begins to speculate whether the Dracula story is not a parable. Blood is a symbol for life, and psychic force and ideas are the life of the mind.
>
> Every public speaker knows the difference between a co-operative interested audience and one which in a passive way wants material given to it but gives nothing in return. The speaker is exhausted, whereas after talking to an actively interested audience he is usually refreshed and satisfied. There are those who suck ideas therefore, and this is a common experience.
>
> Less common, however, is the speaker who knowingly drains the vitality of his audience for psychic uses of his own. A process of mass and individual hypnosis takes place, wherein feelings of sympathy or enthusiasm for the speaker or a cause he represents flow towards him unguardedly. The misuse of sympathy is commonly the main weapon used. The most effective and damaging form of this is that which is learnt from African methods. This presupposes a 'black master' able to absorb the psychic essences from excited and sexually stimulated people; that is, he can travel astrally at will, project himself and know at a distance...
>
> An unbelievable degree of psychic dependence develops, and on a wider national scale it was similar methods, without the actual sexual element, that brought Hitler power. He was able to draw on the vital feelings of vast crowds and so charge himself with a magnetism of personality and a certain intuitive ability about events. The psychic forces of a large part of the nation continually flowing in one direction were absorbed and used by the initiatory black order of the S.S., the Nazi movement's priesthood.

Other than vampires the only bodies that remain uncorrupted in the tomb are those of saints, monarchs or high-grade dignitaries—or so both superstition and the Church dictated. A massive array of evidence has been put forward through the centuries for the incorruptibility of the corpses of the revered. None of it is particularly convincing but it does prove one important point—that for hundreds of years tombs were continuously being opened and shut. This natural curiosity about the dead could be likened to the little boy who discovers the corpse of a bird and with full ceremony conducts a funeral service. Once buried the bird will be dug up time after time 'to see how it is getting on' until interest is eventually lost. Man had more sophisticated motives—to see if life remained after vampire activity, or to ensure that a saint's body was still whole and therefore pure. Another motive was theft—to steal priceless objects buried with the chieftain, or king or high priest. This continuous process of exhumation started legend after legend about the dead walking, particularly at the time when tomb despoliation was rife.

Bernard Puckle, in *Funeral Customs, Their Origin and Development* (1926), describes how the tomb of Edward I was opened in 1774 in the presence of the Dean of Westminster, and accurate descriptions of the royal vestments and of the inner coverings of fine cerecloth were noted down for the behoof of the inquisitive in such matters. The body was found in a state of complete preservation, having on two robes, one of gold and silver tissue, the other of crimson velvet, a sceptre in each hand, a crown on his head, and many still bright jewels.

In the *Gentleman's Magazine* for May 1834, there is an account of the private opening of the tomb of King Henry IV, who died in the Jerusalem Chamber, Westminster, and was buried at Canterbury. His countenance was unchanged except in colour, but after a few minutes' exposure to the air collapsed.

The coffin of Thomas Grey, Marquis of Dorset, who was buried in the chancel at Astley, in Warwickshire, was opened about the year 1607. Though he had been then interred for more than a hundred years, his corpse, in colour, proportion, and softness, was like one newly interred. The same is said of the body of William the Conqueror, after an inhumation of above four hundred years, on the opening of his tomb at Caen in 1522.

Puckle gives two ghoulish accounts of despoliation.

> A strange zeal for this gloomy kind of knowledge, more honoured, we think, in the breach than the observance, was exhibited at Danbury Church, Essex, in the year 1779. In a shell, enclosed in an elm coffin, and that again in a leaden one, under a mossy stone—substantial barriers, one would have thought, against spoilation—was a body in good preservation, in a pickle which had somewhat the appearance of mushroom-catsup. One of the discoverers, writing to the *Gentleman's Magazine*, says, 'As I never possessed the sense of smelling, and was willing to ascertain the flavour of the liquor, I tasted it.' *De gustibus*, say we. The adventurous experimentalist found it 'aromatic, though not very pungent, partaking of the taste of catsup and of the pickles of Spanish olives.' Here indeed the zeal for scientific analysis might perchance form some extenuation, but it must have been the excess of depraved curiosity which, when the coffin of 'Good Duke Humphrey' was opened, caused the multitude to press forward and taste the liquor in which the body was preserved, until the corpse was left bare and dry, and of course soon mouldered away.

The theft of saints' relics was a practice adopted by the Monarchy, the Church and the population at large. One fascinating story concerns a Mr Thompson of Worcester who 'baited his angling-hook with part of the corrupted form of King John, and carried the fish he caught in vulgar and brutal triumph through the streets'. The tomb, which had been opened for repairs in 1797, was hurriedly closed by the Dean and Chapter—but not before someone else had stolen one of the King's finger bones and sent it to London to be tipped with silver.

The remains of King Stephen, disinterred from Faversham Abbey, were flung into the river for the lead which lined the coffin. In 1562 the Calvinists broke open the tomb of Matilda, Queen of the Conqueror, and stole a ring off one of her fingers, and in 1505 the tomb of St Dunstan (who had been buried for over 500 years) was opened by the Archbishop and the Prior of Canterbury who took part of his crown. Perhaps one of the most famous of the relic thieves was Henry VIII who broke into Becket's tomb to obtain a jewel placed in the coffin by a wealthy pilgrim.

One particularly unpleasant example that combines both preservation and despoliation is the sad case of Saint Teresa of Avila. In 1583 the nuns of Alba discovered that a strange scent was coming from the tomb of this future saint. They opened the coffin and discovered Sister Teresa to be in a remarkable state of preservation. Everyone wept with delight at this true sign of utter sanctity. The body was then transferred to a vastly superior coffin but the wily priest in charge of this operation, Father Graziano, cut off one of Sister Teresa's hands saying that he would carry it, with due pomp and reverence, to Avila, Sister Teresa's home town. He actually hid it in his own house. In 1585 the decision was taken to transfer the body to Avila. In the process the priest in charge of the removal, Father Gregorio, cut off, as a souvenir for the Monastery, Teresa's left arm. And so it went on. The body was shifted several times and in 1592 Teresa's heart was stolen by the Mother Superior of the convent, St Catalina di Sant'-Angelo, where the body then rested. The body was continuously exhumed—and it continuously travelled. On the way, apart from losing small portions of flesh, Teresa lost her right foot and a rib. At last in 1760 (the body at this stage being 178 years old) what was left of Sister Teresa was locked away in a casket—to protect her from the indignity of the souvenir hunters.

The real origins of the vampire lie in the minds of men. Certainly there was, in the Middle Ages, enough physical terror in the world to convince Man that the tragedies of life were projected by an unseen force: the powers of darkness. Once the Church had accepted these powers of darkness as Satan then the underworld sprang into greater and more powerful visibility. The dead walked, empowered by Satan to persecute man. But they walked in the mind and the real-life vampires—those who actually drank blood—were men across whose minds were imprinted not just the vampire myth but all the savagery of their cannibalistic, totèm-worshipping forebears.

It is appropriate to conclude this section with the curse sequence from Lord Byron's demonic poem *The Giaour* which he wrote in 1813.

But first on earth, as Vampyre sent,
Thy corpse shall from its tomb be rent;
Then ghastly haunt thy native place,
And suck the blood of all thy race;
There from thy *daughter, sister, wife,*
At midnight drain the stream of life;
Yet loathe the banquet, which perforce
Must feed thy livid living corse,
Thy victims, ere they yet expire,
Shall know the demon for their sire;
As cursing thee, thou cursing them,
Thy flowers are withered on the stem.
But one that for *thy crime* must fall,
The youngest, best beloved of all,
Shall bless thee with a *father's* name—
That word shall wrap thy heart in flame!
Yet thou must end thy task and mark
Her cheek's last tinge—her eye's last spark,
And the last glassy glance must view
Which freezes o'er its lifeless blue;
Then with unhallowed hand shall tear
The tresses of her yellow hair,
Of which, in life a lock when shorn
Affection's fondest pledge was worn—
But now is borne away by thee
Memorial to thine agony!
Yet with thine own best blood shall drip
Thy gnashing tooth, and haggard lip;
Then stalking to thy sullen grave
Go—and with Ghouls and Afrits rave,
Till these in horror shrink away
From spectre more accursed than they.

Part Two

Vampire Traits and Practice

The vampire, throughout the world, can be divided into two basic manifestations. The spirit of a dead person is the first and the second is a corpse, re-animated by his own spirit or alternatively by a demon, who returns to suck at the life of the living, depriving them of blood or some vital organ in order to maintain its own vitality. Those in line for vampirism include wizards, witches and sorcerers, suicides, excommunicants, those who died an untimely death, an unhappy death or an unavenged death, murderers, robbers and villains, the accursed and those who ran into a strange variety of sinister taboos.

This section is concerned with vampire practice—and prevention. Vintage vampire practice was mainly recorded amongst Slavic peoples, in China, and in Greece. But more 'spiritual' vampirism can be found in the Middle East, in India, in Malaya and in Africa, whilst the Slavic vampire legends later translated themselves to the rest of Europe, to Russia, to America and to Britain. But this chapter is not concerned just with mythical vampirism, powerful as it was, but with real-life vampires such as Gilles de Rais, Elizabeth of Bathory, Peter Kürten, Sawney Beane, Fritz Haarmann, Victor Ardisson, Sergeant Bertrand and a dark host of others—all of whom perpetrated far more horrific crimes than their mythical cousins. Admittedly, the Penanggalan of Malaya, the Rákshasa of India, the boneless, fungoid Bulgarian vampire, the Greek Vrykolakas, the Stigoi, Moroii and Varcolaci of Rumania and the traditional Hungarian vampire were not nice people to be with, but *they* were myths. Man-made myths, however, of such magnitude and of such power that they terrified thousands of people to death. They also made a great deal of money for a number of bodies and individuals—bodies like the Church, who traded on mass ignorance and hysteria as a way of keeping the faithful faithful, and individuals such as the Dhampir—the so-called vampire's son who could exorcise his father and relatives for a fat fee. Protection against vampirism varied from area to area and methods employed ranged from transfixing the corpse with a stake (made of aspen, maple, blackthorn or hawthorn, depending on local belief) to lopping off the head, and from burning the corpse to ashes to tearing out the heart and throwing boiling water or oil on to the grave. Small wonder that the desecration of graves was frequent in Central and Eastern Europe and that innocent living victims of the vampire scare were repeatedly attacked. One particularly strange and haunting means of discovering a vampire's grave in Serbia was related to Dom Calmet, a seventeenth-century chronicler, by an officer quartered in Wallachia.

> At the time when we were quartered at Temeswar in Wallachia, there died of this disorder two dragoons of the company in which I was cornet, and several more who had it would have died also, if the corporal of the company had not put a stop to it, by applying a remedy commonly made use of in that country. It is of a very singular kind, and, though infallibly to be depended on, I have never met with it in any Dispensatory.

> They pick out a boy, whom they judge to be too young to have lost his maidenhead, and mount him bare upon a coal-black stone-horse, which has never leaped a mare. This virgin-pair is led about the church-yard, and across all the graves, and wherever the animal stops, and refuses to go on, in spite of all the whipping they can give him, they conclude they have discovered a vampire. Upon opening the grave, they find a carcass as fleshy and fair as if the person were only in a slumber. The next step is to cut off his head with a spade, and there issues from the wound such a quantity of fresh and florid blood, that one would swear they had cut the throat of a man in full health and vigour. They then fill up the pit, and it may be depended on that the disorder will cease, and that all who were ill of it will gradually get strength, like people that recover slowly after a long illness. Accordingly this happened to our troopers, who were attacked with the distemper.

There also existed in vampire belief a very strong love motive which involved the vampire in having intercourse with a living woman. This belief probably grew up via the occasional erotic stimulant of blood-letting in intercourse, the breaking of virginity, and, on a more mystic level, the mediaeval succuba, an erotic demon who preyed upon and destroyed man's virility.

Finally, recognition of the vampire type was all-important and in Europe sniffing out a vampire was a practised art. Before I analyse vampire activity throughout the world area by area, the following check-list of characteristics may help the reader. These, of course, only apply to the mythical vampire type; psychotic persons who relish the spilling and drinking of blood look like you and me.

Characteristics to be Determined on Disinterment of Suspected Vampire

1. Are there a number of holes (about the breadth of a man's finger) in the soil above the grave?
2. Does the revealed corpse have any of the following:
   A. wide-open eyes
   B. a ruddy complexion
   C. no signs of corruption
3. Have the nails and hair grown as in life?
4. Are there two small livid marks on the neck?

5. Is the shroud partially devoured?
6. Is there blood in the veins of the corpse?
7. Is the coffin full of blood?
8. Does the body look well-fed?
9. Are the limbs fully flexible?

If the answer to these questions is 'yes' refer to your neighbourhood Dhampir, priest or witch to provide exorcism recipe. Or alternatively read on.

Africa

Practice: Blood is deeply sacred amongst primitive peoples, and as the Church had always treated blood with extreme reverence this was reaffirmed by the wave of missionaries. Unfortunately, when interpreted literally, the symbolic drinking of the blood of Christ during the Communion Service becomes a cannibalistic feast, so it is not very strange that primitive peoples ate the men of God from time to time. The missionaries drank Christ's blood and ate his body so why shouldn't their native students drink the missionaries' blood and eat their bodies?

Cannibals and non-cannibals alike were continuously persecuted by malignant spirits, usually emanating from the totem structure of ancestor worship. Vengeful ancestors, irrationally annoyed, would return from the dead, leaving death and destruction in their wake. They also lusted after blood, at all times anxious to take it in great draughts so that their underworld-defying revenge-bent return could continue for as long as possible. Revenant fathers, mothers, aunts, cousins, grandfathers, great-grandfathers and great-great-grandfathers, unappeased by sacrifice and antagonised by some insignificant family crime, would spread a wave of terror and pillage about them—until finally they mercifully and wearily returned to their eyries of jaundiced observation.

Other *revenants* include sorcerers, monarchs, suicides, witch-doctors, dead children, dead mothers, gods and spirits. No one is safe from the vengeful departed and this fear, linked with blood taboo and the blood sanctity of Christianity, carried primitive superstition to a zenith.

Here are a few examples of vampirism, blood taboo and so on, throughout the continent of Africa.

Rhodesia

Type: Gods and Spirits.

Activity: The Bantu in Northern Rhodesia are representative of a vast number of tribes all over Africa, including the Awemba, the Herero and the Ovambo amongst many others, who worship spirits of departed chiefs (publicly worshipped by the entire tribe) and the spirits of relations (privately worshipped by the family). Often the family spirits are worshipped inside the hut by means of animal sacrifice. A sheep or goat is killed, the blood is poured on the ground and the family eat the flesh. The family believe that the spirit drinks the blood from the floor. So here is a prime example of a spirit imbibing the traditional vampire's feast of blood. Should the family spirit *not* be honoured then it is likely that he or she will cause illness or death to a member of the family—another vampire-like tendency.

Origin: Universal ancestor worship.

Loango

Type: Ex-Sorcerers.

Activity: This particular species is said to be ten times as strong as the moon and is able, at will, to turn itself into a bat. This is, strangely, an unusual manifestation as, contrary to popular belief, there is no real association between the blood-seeking corpse of vampiredom and the blood-sucking habits of vampire bats.

Origin: The death and burial of a witch, wizard or sorcerer was not considered to be the end of him or her.

Ashantiland

Type: Asanbosam.

Activity: The three varieties of this vampire type (men, women and children) suck blood from the thumbs of a sleeping person.

Origin: Possible association with the vampire bat (usually found in South America) which will occasionally nip at the extremities of sleeping humans, despite its normal concentration on cattle or poultry. There could well have been a local equivalent of this kind of bat.

Guinea

Type: Owenga.

Activity: Vengeful ancestors, bad spirits or dead magicians might return in tangible form, taking lives or at least searching for continuous supplies of life-protracting blood.

Origin: Throughout North Africa natives are careful to obliterate any blood that falls to the ground. They will also go to the extent of burning wood or cloth upon which blood falls. If blood falls upon their bodies the most detailed ceremonies are enacted as a purification. In Guinea the natives hold the same fears, and travellers have recorded that blood-stained bandages have been burnt or thrown far into the sea to defeat the needs of the undead.

Hereros Land

Type: Otgiruru.

Activity: General persecution in the typical style of the undead.

Origin: The Herero (a Bantu tribe from South-West Africa) fear their ancestors as the most demonic presence in their lives. At all costs they must be continuously appeased and never angered. The Herero believe that the dead continue not only to live but to menace the living.

Kenya

Type: Mau Mau practice.

Activity: In 1954 vampirism was practised by the Mau Mau movement during their oath-taking ceremonies (see Part Seven: The Vampire Today). At their mildest the oaths involved drinking sheep's blood, at their most horrific they involved drinking the blood of recently murdered Europeans.

Origin: All candidates for the Mau Mau were expected to divest themselves of European tradition and materialism and to return to the unity of the old tribal régimes.

Madagascar

Type: Ramanga (Living Vampire).

Activity: The Ramanga were a lesser breed within the Betsileo tribe. It was their rôle to eat the nail-parings and drink the spilt blood of the nobles. High-ranking noblemen were inevitably accompanied by the Ramanga but should they not be in attendance it was then necessary for them to collect both spilt blood and nail-parings for their serfs to devour on their return.

Origin: Once again, it was imperative to prevent magical parts of the body falling into the hands of sorcerers who were bound to use them for evil purposes.

Protection: It was absolutely vital not to offend the dead. Despite father's gentle kindliness in life he was quite likely to be transformed into a veritable demon after his death, and as for grandfather—he became even more prickly as his age in death increased. Continuous sacrifices, both human and animal, were the answer—combined with a good deal of lip-service to these neurotic dead. A ready means of protection was to sacrifice, on the floor of the hut, a sheep or a goat. The spirit would then lap up the blood. Ancestor-worship was the concern of each individual family but the honouring of a departed village chieftain was the concern of the whole tribe.

Dead sorcerers and witch-doctors are trickier customers and more difficult to protect oneself from—at least in the African continent. Magicians were liable to achieve ten times the strength of the moon, or to change themselves at will into bats or even dogs. These creatures would suck blood from various parts of the body, would certainly have vampiristic 'undead' characteristics and would regard blood as a supercharger. There are various methods of protection and all are far more complex than the appeasement of ancestors and chieftains. Vampiristic sorcerers or magicians must either be burnt at night when there is no moon, or be nailed to the ground. It is vital when burning them to allow the fire to consume each fragment or the monster will rise again from the smallest scrap of charred flesh and will obviously be anxious for revenge—and above all for blood.

Other vampire-sorcerers include the Asanbosam, who come in three varieties: men, women and children. They are easily recognisable, as for some inexplicable reason they have a pair of books instead of a pair of feet.

As in other continents, menstruating women must at all costs be avoided owing to the blood taboo. It is considered that anything touched by a woman in that condition would immediately be contaminated. The same fear surrounds women who die in childbirth and stillborn babies, all of whom undoubtedly return as malignant spirits.

North and South America

Vampire experience in the Americas is highly diffused. The Kwakiytl Indians of British Columbia were vampiristic, attacking corpses and living people for both flesh and blood.

In New England in 1691 during the Salem witch prosecutions allegations concerning vampirism were made against many of the accused. In 1854, near Norwich, New England, three members of the Ray family died of consumption—of literally wasting away—and when a fourth member died the authorities decided to exhume the other three and cremate them—just in case a vampire was amongst them.

In Mexico, during the time of the Spanish conquest, vampire witches named the Civateteo were rumoured to be abroad. These creatures were fairly traditional in that they held their sabbaths at crossroads and would attack buildings which contained young children. If their attack was successful, the children would then dwindle away. The Civateteo were held responsible for the spread of infantile paralysis and were linked with the Tezcatlipoca—the most powerful and awesome of Mexican gods. The Civateteo were considered to be the evil spirits of noblewomen who had died in childbirth and were out to take their revenge on their little murderers!

In South America the Maya Indians had particularly nasty rites and the death-rites of the tribes in this area were amongst the most savage and repulsive yet recorded. Dripping fat from roasting corpses was caught by priests in buckets and was used for anointing their hands and faces, and the hands and faces of the mourners. Then a baby would be sacrificed, its body slashed open with knives, and its heart removed. After severing the head, the priests would throw the remains of the corpse down the steps to the crowd.

The natives wanted the vitality of the dead person to pass into their own bodies—it compensated for the absence of the visible deceased and helped their feelings of loss. As the mass of the people ate the body, it would appear that they were not acting cannibalistically but were chewing the flesh as a form of communion.

In Peru the blood of children who had been sacrificed to the gods was collected by the priests and kneaded with maize dough into an image of the god Uitzilopochtli.

In Grenada an elderly species of vampire, known as the *loogaroo*, and in the shape of demonic old ladies, forged a pact with the devil and as a result were forced nightly to supply him with large quantities of warm blood. Each night these dear old bodies wended their way to the occult silk-cotton tree, divested themselves of their skin, and went about their ghoulish business. This particular superstition was probably imported from the Congo and from Guinea by African slaves.

In the West Indies, sorcerers were considered to be heart-devourers. Having offended a sorcerer or sorceress one would soon find oneself with a dried-up heart and liver. The medical origin of this superstition is most relevant here, bearing in mind the many disease-ridden tribes of the area.

Finally, in Brazil there are two kinds of vampire: the Jaracaca (in the shape of a snake) and the Lobishomen. The conveniently-shaped Jaracaca attacks mothers when they are breast-feeding their children. The child is hurled to one side and the tail of the snake is lodged in its mouth. Meanwhile the Jaracaca sucks the milk from the mother's breast. Blood and milk are inextricably linked as both are basic donors of the life-stuff. The only recorded activity of the Lobishomen that I have found is that this species attacks women who, on recovery, become nymphomaniacs.

Asia

China

Practice: Willoughby-Meade in his book *Chinese Ghouls and Goblins* (1928) points out that the demonic vampires of China had a very close link with their East European cousins.

> The malevolence and strength of the monster, and its power of assuming various forms, are manifested between sunset and sunrise; and it is not represented as attacking only the weak-minded or the wicked, but as entirely and gratuitously hostile to all comers.

The Chinese vampire is reputed to be a demon—a demon who inhabits a corpse and prevents it from decaying by feeding on other corpses or alternatively on living bodies. If a skeleton remains undecayed, or even just the skull, the *P'o* (or lower soul) has become a vampire.

The Chinese are more afraid of the vampire than of any other supernatural form, which considering their appearance and abilities is not surprising.

The features of the Chinese vampire are quite startling. The body is covered with white or greenish-white hair, and it has glaring eyes and long claws—a fantasy demon figure that, if of some experience or standing, will master the art of flying.

Protection: Certain precautions must be observed to prevent the *P'o* becoming a vampire. A cat, for instance, must never be allowed to be in the same room as the corpse for if the animal took it into its head to jump over the corpse it might 'impart to the body (still containing the lower soul) a modicum of the tiger nature and the corpse may become a vampire' (Willoughby-Meade). It is essential that rays from the sun or moon should not be allowed to shine directly on to the unburied body, for if they do the corpse will become catalysed by a generous shot of *Yang Cor* positive force. This means that the lower soul would then be strengthened and able to go out and supply the corpse with fresh blood so that it could remain undecayed. From this rite probably springs the European habit of pulling down the blinds when there is a death in the house.

Luckily the gods took a hand from time to time and occasionally destroyed a member of the flying variety of vampire with a well-timed flash of lightning. Apparently there was a degree of antagonism between the vampires and such early Vedic gods as Agni, Indra and other purveyors of good and bad weather.

The following stories collected by Willoughby-Meade indicate a strong similarity to European or Near Eastern counterparts.

Liu, tutor to a family living some distance from his home, obtained a holiday at Ch'ing Ming time in order to tend his ancestral tombs. On the day of his return to duty his wife, entering his room to call him in the early morning, found his headless body on the bed, but no trace of blood.

The woman gave the alarm, but was arrested on suspicion of having murdered her husband, and remanded in gaol for further enquiries to be made. Then, one day, a neighbour gathering firewood on an adjoining hill saw a good, sound coffin, its lid partly raised, lying near a neglected grave. Suspecting robbery, he called some people together, and they approached and took off the lid. Within was a corpse with the face of a living man, its body covered with white hair. Between its arms it held the missing head of Liu! The corpse held the head so tightly that its arms had to be chopped off to release the head; fresh blood gushed from its arms, but the head of Liu was dry and bloodless. The magistrate ordered the corpse to be burnt, and Liu's widow to be set free.

Outside the Southern Gate of Tan Yang Kiang Su, a certain Lu had an orchard, which brought him a fair profit every year. Naturally he kept watch, with his sons' help, night and day, when the fruit was ripe. One moonlight night he was seated, watching, upon a stone, when he suddenly saw among the trees a head, covered with disordered hair, appear out of the ground. He called his sons, and they all went to see what it was. A woman, dressed in red, rose before them; whereupon the old man fainted, and the sons ran away terrified. The woman pursued them to the door of their house; there she stopped with one foot inside the threshold and the other outside. At the cries of the sons, a number of people ran to the rescue; but the icy breath of the spectre kept them back. The woman entered, glided under a bed and disappeared. Then the sons went to their father and brought him round with a strong decoction of ginger; but after that they were afraid to guard their fruit-trees, and a thief entered the orchard one night. Next morning he was found, lying on the ground, almost frightened to death. He said he had seen a man without a head. Thereupon they dug in the garden in the place where the manifestations had taken place, and discovered a red coffin, containing the body of the woman whose ghost had appeared, and a black one, containing the corpse of a decapitated man. Both bodies were perfectly preserved. They were burnt, and thereafter all was quiet.

A Mr Ch'ien lived outside the I-Fêng gate of the town of T'ung Ch'êng. One night he returned very late from a party, although his friends tried to persuade him to spend the night with them, and not risk meeting anything uncanny. Ch'ien, however, had been enjoying himself, and was merry with wine; so he seized a lantern, mounted his horse, and stoutly set out for home. On the way he had to cross a flat space covered with graves. Suddenly he saw a spectre rise out of a cutting in the earth, and come leaping towards him. It had straggly hair, bare feet, and a face as white as chalk. The horse was frightened and refused to move; the lantern burned dimly, giving out a pale greenish glow. Ch'ien, reckless with drinking, stood his ground; and when the Thing reached him he gave it a buffet on the cheek that turned its head completely round. It retreated, but wishing to make a fresh attack, its face glared at Ch'ien, while its legs carried it away from him. Again and again it repeated these antics, and eventually re-entered the cutting and disappeared.

Next morning, Ch'ien noticed that the hand with which he had struck the vampire was as black as ink, and it did not regain its colour for four years. When he asked the neighbours what they thought of the manifestation, they said it was a newly-made vampire, which did not yet know its business!

In 1761, a government courier called Chang Kuei was sent from Peking with an urgent dispatch. One night after passing Liang Hsiang, he was caught in a storm and his lantern was blown out. Thinking he saw a small rest-house by the road, he made his way to it. A girl of about eighteen ushered him into a cottage, gave him hospitality, and looked after his horse. Next day, at dawn, he failed to wake up; but some hours later, pierced with the cold and disturbed by the wind in the trees, he came to himself, and found that he was lying on a tomb in dense undergrowth, with his horse tied to a tree close by. When he delivered his dispatch, over twelve hours late, he was questioned, and related what had happened. The authorities made enquiries on the spot, and learned that a girl named Chang, of evil repute, had hanged herself there, and had treated several people in the same way as she had the courier. Her tomb was opened, and the body was found to be fresh and rosy; so it was burnt by order of the authorities.

All these stories represent the more traditional type of Chinese vampire. Here is a particularly beautiful passage from the *T'ien Kung Kai Wuh* which concerns the wills-o'-the-wisp—which in China are regarded as fire and disease devils. Wills-o'-the-wisp are vampiristic by nature and are reputed to arise from spilt blood. Their behaviour recalls in some ways the appearance of the vampires of Eastern Europe in the form of whirling specks of luminous matter. In China, beside being harbingers of illness, they are bad for the harvests.

> When, after the ears of corn have sprouted, spectral lights flit about in the dark and singe it, it is a sixth catastrophe. These lights are emitted from the interior of decaying wood, so that wood is their mother, and the lights are her children ... Whenever the year is rainy so that in the graves on the lonely plains —sapped and ruined by foxes as so often they are—the coffins

> are soaked and in a rotten condition, their wood decays and the lights detach themselves from it and fly about. Being lights produced by Yin, they can endure no Yang (sun) light, and await the twilight after sunset to burst forth ... lacking power to rise in the air, they move about irregularly over short distances; and when ears and blades of corn come in contact with them, these are at once cut off, singed and burnt. The men who chase away these lights, whenever they see roots of trees emit them, fall upon them and beat them ... When spectre-light sees lamp-light, it vanishes of its own accord.

Willoughby-Meade, who made a study of Chinese vampirism, concluded that the vampire belief came about for a number of reasons. Firstly, the Chinese believe that the dead 'carry over to their other life the loves and hatreds of their life on earth'. Secondly, ghosts undergoing the Buddhist purgatory of hunger and penury may well be considered to have enough reason to seek alleviation from their privations by devouring human flesh and drinking human blood. Other origins, he considered, could well include cannibalism and its attendant blood-drinking, malarial fever producing fantasy and delusion, thought-transference, hypnotism and so on. China was and still is a superstition-imbued society and therefore it is hardly surprising that the power of the vampire should be so strong in this ancient, fatalistic land.

Malaysia

> Oh ye mosquito fry at the river's mouth, when yet a great way off ye are sharp of eye; When near, ye are hard of heart. When the rock in the ground opens of itself then (and then only) be emboldened the hearts of my foes and opponents! When the corpse in the ground opens of itself, then (and then only) be emboldened the hearts of my foes and opponents! May your heart be softened when you behold me, by grace of this prayer that I am called Silam Bayan.
>
> A *Charm for laying Langsuirs*

There are quite a number of highly malignant Malayan spirits—all of which have vampiristic qualities.

1. *Bâjang Practice*

The *Bâjang* is said to be a male spirit. Its shape is normally that of a polecat which mews outside the door of its victim. Sir Frank Swettenham writes in *Malay Sketches* (1895):

> The hereditary *bâjang* comes like other evils, the unsought heritage of a dissolute ancestry, but the acquired *bâjang* is usually obtained from the newly-buried body of a stillborn child, which is supposed to be the abiding-place of a familiar spirit until lured therefrom by the solicitations of someone who, at dead of night, stands over the grave and by potent incantations persuades the *bâjang* to come forth.

Protection against the Bâjang: Certain diligent measures had to be taken against the *bâjang*. Sir Frank Swettenham writes:

> Someone in the village falls ill of a complaint the symptoms of which are unusual; there may be convulsions, unconsciousness, or delirium, possibly for some days together or with intervals between the attacks. The relatives will call in a native doctor, and at her (she is usually an ancient female) suggestion, or without it, an impression will arise that the patient is the victim of a *bâjang*. Such an impression quickly develops into certainty, and any trifle will suggest the owner of the evil spirit. One method of verifying this suspicion is to wait till the patient is in a state of delirium, and then to question him or her as to who is the author of the trouble. This should be done by some independent person of authority, who is supposed to be able to ascertain the truth.
>
> A further and convincing proof is then to call in a *Pawang* skilled in dealing with wizards (in Malay countries they are usually men), and if he knows his business his power is such that he will place the sorcerer in one room, and, while he in another scrapes an iron vessel with a razor, the culprit's hair will fall off as though the razor had been applied to his head instead of to the vessel! That is supposing he *is* the culprit; if not, of course, he will pass through the ordeal without damage.
>
> I have been assured that the shaving process is so efficacious that, as the vessel represents the head of the person standing his trial, wherever it is scraped the wizard's hair will fall off in a corresponding spot. It might be supposed that under these circumstances the accused is reasonably safe, but this test of guilt is not always employed. What more commonly happens is that when several cases of unexplained sickness have occurred in a village, with possibly one or two deaths, the people of the place lodge a

formal complaint against the supposed author of these ills, and desire that he be punished.

Before the advent of British influence it was the practice to kill the wizard or witch whose guilt had been established to Malay satisfaction, and such executions were carried out not many years ago.

I remember a case in Perak less than ten years ago, when the people of an up-river village accused a man of keeping a *bâjang*, and the present Sultan, who was then the principal Malay judge in the State, told them he would severely punish the *bâjang* if they would produce it. They went away hardly satisfied, and shortly after made a united representation to the effect that if the person suspected were allowed to remain in their midst they would kill him. Before anything could be done they put him, his family, and effects on a raft and started them down the river. On their arrival at Kuala Kangsar the man was given an isolated hut to live in, but not long afterwards he disappeared...

There are plenty of people living in Perak who have seen more than one ancient Malay dame taken out into the river and, despite her protestations, her tears, and entreaties, have watched her, with hands and feet tied, put into the water and slowly pushed down out of sight by means of a long pole with a fork at one end which fitted on her neck. Those who have witnessed these executions have no doubt of the justice of the punishment, and not uncommonly add that after two or three examples had been made there would always ensue a period of rest from the torments of the *bâjang*. I have also been assured that the *bâjang*, in the shape of a lizard, has been seen to issue from the drowning person's nose. That statement no doubt is made on the authority of those who condemned and executed the victim.

It is generally accepted that the *bâjang*'s presence implies some impending disaster but there is some possibility of having this spirit as a kind of pet. The *bâjang* can be enslaved to man and become his familiar spirit. Long-standing familiars were often regarded as heirlooms which were kept imprisoned by the master of the house in a *tabong* (a vessel made from a bamboo joint and closed by a stopper made from the leaves of a certain plant). The *bâjang* is fed, babylike, on milk and can be commanded at will to prey upon defaulting neighbours, friends or members of the family who have incurred the *bâjang* master's wrath.

2. *Langsuir Practice*

The *Langsuir* is a far more demonic proposition than the *Bâjang*, who is a mere mischievous sprite in contrast to this sinister lady who adopts the shape of a night owl. W. W. Skeat, who wrote *Malay Magic* in 1900, described her as being a woman of dazzling beauty, who died from the shock of hearing that her child was stillborn, and had taken the shape of the *Pontianak* (a cousin of the *Mati-anak* described later in this section). On hearing this terrible news, she 'clapped her hands', and without further warning 'flew whinnying away to a tree, upon which she perched'. She may be known by her robe of green, by her tapering nails of extraordinary length (a mark of beauty), and by the long jet-black tresses which she allows to fall down to her ankles—only, alas! in order to conceal the hole in the back of her neck through which she sucks the blood of children!

In their wild state these woman-vampires are exceedingly fond of fish, and may be seen 'sitting in crowds on the fishing-stakes at the river mouth awaiting an opportunity to steal the fish'.

The popular superstition about the *Langsuir* is described by Sir William Maxwell: *

> If a woman dies in childbirth, either before delivery or after the birth of a child, and before the forty days of uncleanness have expired, she is popularly supposed to become a *langsuyar*, a flying demon of the nature of the 'white lady' or 'banshee'. To prevent this a quantity of glass beads are put in the mouth of the corpse, a hen's egg is put under each armpit, and needles are placed in the palms of the hands. It is believed that if this is done the dead woman cannot become a *langsuyar*, as she cannot open her mouth to shriek (*ngilai*) or wave her arms as wings, or open and shut her hands to assist her flight.

Protection against the Langsuir: There is only one way of protecting oneself against this species and it is more than a little difficult and certainly no way to treat a lady. She has to be caught and physically suppressed. Whilst she is lying prone her nails must be cut short, her long, luxurious hair must be cut

* *Journal of the Straits Branch of the Royal Asiatic Society*, Singapore (1878-1899).

short and both nail parings and hair clippings must be stuffed into the hole in the back of her neck.

Cases apparently have been known where the *Langsuir* became a respectable wife and mother and lived, albeit somewhat uneasily, in conventional Malay native society. In one such case, however, her guardians slipped up by allowing the rehabilitated *Langsuir* to dance at a village merry-making. Seizing her opportunity, the *Langsuir* became reprobate, reverted to her ghostly form and flew off cackling into the depths of the forest.

3. *Mati-anak* (or *Pontianak*) *Practice*

This stillborn child of the *Langsuir* is similar to its mother—a ghostly night-owl. However, the stillborn child was able to rise to Djinn or Genie status and was known as the *Pontianak*. A charm for laying the *Pontianak* runs:

> O Pontianak the Stillborn,
> May you be struck dead by the soil from the grave-mound.
> Thus we cut the bamboo-joints, the long and the short,
> To cook therein the liver of the Djinn Pontianak,
> By the grace of 'There is no god but God'.

Mati-Anak (or *Pontianak*) *Prevention*: To prevent a stillborn child becoming a monster a hen's egg is put under each armpit, a needle in the palm of the hand and glass beads in its mouth. This, together with a charm, is quite foolproof.

4. *Pĕnanggalan Practice*

The *Pĕnanggalan* is a very fine vampire specimen and far more magnificent in its outrageous behaviour than the mischievous *Bâjang*, the approachable *Langsuir* or the ineffective *Mati-anak*. Skeat describes this remarkable creature as

> a soul of monstrous vampire which delights in sucking the blood of children. The story goes that once upon a time a woman was sitting, to perform a religious penance (*dudok bĕrtapa*), in one of the large wooden vats which are used by the Malays for holding the vinegar made by drawing off the sap of the thatch-palm (*mĕnyadap nipah*). Quite unexpectedly a man came in, and finding her sitting in the vat, asked her, 'What are you doing there?' To this the woman replied, 'What business have you to ask?'

but being very much startled she attempted to escape, and in the excitement of the moment, kicked her own chin with such force that the skin split round her neck, and her head (with the sac of the stomach depending from it) actually became separated from the trunk, and flew off to perch upon the nearest tree. Ever since then she has existed as a spirit of evil, sitting on the roof-tree whinnying (*mĕngilai*) whenever a child is born in the house, or trying to force her way up through the floor on which the child lies, in order to drink its blood.

Another account of the *Pĕnanggalan* is more precise. She was originally a woman, who used the magic arts of a devil in whom she believed, and she devoted herself to his service night and day until the period of her agreement with her teacher had expired and she was able to fly. Her head and neck were then loosened from the body, the intestines being attached to them, and hanging down in strings. The body remained where it was. Wherever the person whom the *Pĕnanggalan* wished to injure happened to live, thither flew the head and bowels to suck his blood, and the person whose blood was sucked was sure to die. If the blood and water which dripped from the intestines touched any person, serious illness immediately followed and his body broke out in open sores. The *Pĕnanggalan* likes to suck the blood of women in childbirth.

The person who has the power of becoming a *Pĕnanggalan* always keeps at her house a quantity of vinegar in a jar or vessel of some kind. This is used to soak the intestines in, for when they issue forth from the body they immediately swell up and cannot be put back, but after being soaked in vinegar they shrink to their former size and enter the body again. There are many people who have seen the *Pĕnanggalan* flying along with its entrails dangling down and shining at night like fire-flies.

Protection against the Pĕnanggalan: The *Pĕnanggalan* is a worthier enemy than her contemporaries. But the *Pĕnanggalan*'s penchant for sucking the blood of women in childbirth can be used to her disadvantage. At all times, in all Malaysian houses when a birth occurred, the custom was to hang up Jenyu leaves at the doors and windows. This prickly foliage had an even more violent effect on the *Pĕnanggalan* than garlic does on its European counterpart, for she had a dread of thorns becoming caught in her trailing intestines—ever since one of her kind, out on a night's blood-drinking spree, became inextricably entangled in a thorny hedge. There she stayed, until daylight, mercilessly impaled, and was killed by local villagers.

5. Polong Practice

The *Polong* is a vampiristic bottle imp or familiar spirit. In shape the *Polong* resembles a tiny mannikin or female figure (about the size of the top joint of the little finger). It is capable of flying and is linked with a demonic house-cricket called the *Pĕlĕsit*. When the *Polong* wishes to enter a victim's body it sends the *Pĕlĕsit* before it to burrow its way in. It enters tail foremost, chirps encouragingly—and the *Polong* quickly follows. The origin of the *Polong* is said to be as follows:

> The blood of a murdered man must be taken and placed in a bottle (a bottle having a spherical or wide body and a long narrow neck). Then prayers are said over it, and something or other is read, I don't know what, but it has to be learnt. After seven days of this worship, according to some people, or after twice seven days according to others, a sound is heard in the bottle like the chirping of young birds. The operator then cuts his finger and inserts it into the bottle and the *Polong* sucks it. The person who thus supports the *Polong* is called his father, or, if it happens to be a woman, she is his mother. Every day the parent feeds it with his (or her) blood. The object of doing this and the advantages to be gained from it are these: if he entertains a feeling of anger against anyone he orders the *Polong* to go and afflict him, that is to say, to cause him pain or sickness; or if a third person is at enmity with another he goes in secret to the person who keeps the *Polong*, and gives him a sum of money to send the *Polong* to attack the person against whom he bears ill-will. This is the use of it. The person who is tormented by the *Polong*, whether a virgin, or a married woman, or a man, cries out and loses consciousness of what he (or she) is doing, and tears and throws off his (or her) clothing, biting and striking the people near, blind and deaf to everything, and does all sorts of other things. Wise men are called in to prescribe remedies; some come and chant formulas over the head of the patient, others pinch his

thumb and apply medicines to it. When the remedy is successful the sick person cries out, 'Let me go, I want to go home.' The doctor replies, 'I will not let you go if you do not make known who it is that has sent you here, and why you have come, and who are your father and mother.' Sometimes he (the *Polong* in the patient) remains silent and will not confess or give the names of his parents; sometimes he confesses, and says 'Let me go, my father is such-a-one and lives at such-and-such a *kampong*, and my mother is so-and-so. The reason that I have come here is that such-a-one came to my parents and asked for their aid, and gave them a sum of money because he bore ill-will against this person' (or whatever the reason may have been). Sometimes he makes a false statement, and mentions entirely wrong persons in order to conceal the names of his parents. As soon as the people know the name of the person who contrived the attack and the reason, they let him go, and the sick person at once recovers his consciousness, but he is left weak and feeble. When a *Polong* attacks a person and will confess nothing, the person who is attacked shrieks and yells in anger, and after a day or two he dies. After death blood pours forth bubbling (*ber-kopak-kopak*) from the mouth, and the whole body is blue with bruises.

Protection against the Polong: The Polong can be caught and imprisoned in a bottle of special dimensions where its evil impulses can be restrained—or alternatively be used as an influence of evil against one's enemies.

6. *Pĕlĕsit Practice*

This plaything of the *Polongs* flies to and fro till it finds the body its master or mistress wishes it to enter. Malay women are reputed to be the most subtle capturers of the *Pĕlĕsit*. Once caught, the cricket-like spirit is fed on saffron-stained rice or blood drawn from the tip of the fourth finger.

Protection against the Pĕlĕsit: If a sick person is infected with the *Pĕlĕsit* he or she will generally rave uncontrollably about cats—although there seems to be very little link between the two. This, however, is a well-known symptom and at least the doctor now knows that the patient is housing the *Pĕlĕsit* and maybe its mentor, the *Polong*, as well. The doctor then asks the inhabitants of the body:

'Who is your mother?'

The *Pĕlĕsit* betrays her, speaking with the patient's voice but in a high falsetto. Measures are then taken to deal with the malignant owner.

Finally here is a recipe, drawn from Skeat's research, for securing a *Pĕlĕsit*:

> Go to the graveyard at night and dig up the body of a first-born child whose mother was also first-born, and which has been dead less than forty days. On digging it up, carry it out to an ant-hill in the open ground, and there dandle it (*di-timang*). After a little while, when the child shrieks and lolls its tongue out (*tĕrjĕlir lidah-nya*), bite off its tongue and carry it home. Then obtain a coconut shell from a solitary 'green' coconut palm (*niyor hijau*), and carry it to a place where three roads meet, light a fire and heat the shell till oil exudes, dip the child's tongue in the oil, and bury it in the heart of the three crossroads (*hati sempang tiga*). Leave it untouched for three nights, then dig it up and you will find that it has turned into a *Pĕlĕsit*.

India

Village legends were predominant in India and tree spirits, primitive totemism, taboos and good-luck symbols abounded—curiously similar to the superstitions which flourished in rural England. Here were gods, ghouls, ghosts, sorcerers, saints, demons and ogres—all competing in equal strength and all held in equal fear. Certain animals were worshipped, ancestors were vengeful and Man was still an amoebic being over which huge forces dominated. One much-credited monster was the *Rákshasa*—an omnipotent sub-being, far more powerful than the destructive spirits of China and Malaya. He was dreaded by the peasants, and William Crooke wrote the following description of the devilish *Rákshasas* in *Folklore of Northern India*:

> The *Rákshasas* misled night travellers like the will-o'-the-wisp; they hid treasures of gold and jewels in the earth as did the Irish fairies; they vanished at dawn, in the manner of Hamlet's ghost and the night spirits that ravished Sodom; they abducted ill-protected new babies as did the Hedley Kow in northern England;

> and their giant fossil bones suggested Orestes' bones in the gigantic coffin described by Herodotus.

He goes on to describe the *Rákshasa*'s varied activities.

> He goes about at night, haunts cemeteries, disturbs sacrifices and devout men, animates dead bodies, ensnares and even devours human beings, and is generally hostile to the human race. He is emphatically a devourer of raw flesh, and eats carrion. Some have long arms; some are fat; some thin; some dwarfish; others enormously tall or hump-backed. Some have only one eye, others only one ear; some have enormous paunches, projecting teeth, and crooked thighs; others can on occasion assume noble forms and are beautiful to look at. He is the great *Deus ex machina* of folklore. He can change into almost any form as he pleases, his breath is a roaring wind, he can lengthen his arms to eighty miles, and he can smell out human beings like Giant Blunderbore.

Amongst the more outstanding Indian vampiristic witches and demons is a Northern Indian witch called the *Jigar-Khor*, or Liver-Eater, who is believed to possess the power of being able to steal other people's liver by incantations and piercing looks. There are the group of witches known as the *Bhûts* with their extraordinary fondness for fish, the *Hánh Sàburo*, spirits that chase men into the forest with the help of dogs in order to drink their blood, the *Hánt-Pare* who clings like a leech to the wound of an injured person and sucks his blood, the *Pisâchâs*, a complete race of flesh-eaters, and the *Hántu-Dor Dong* who lives in caves or crevices and drinks the blood of dogs and wild hogs. Hugh Clifford in his book *In Court At Kampong* refers to a further three manifestations: the *Pênangal* (our old friend from Malaya whose activities are equally rife in India), the *Mah'ânah*, a strange and very small white animal that makes indescribable noises over the graves of children, and the familiar spirits that 'men raise up from the corpses of babes who have never seen the light, the tips of those whose tongues they bite off and swallow, after the child has been brought back to life by magic agencies'. Finally there is the *Vetala*, which looks like an old hag and sucks the blood of sleeping women, providing they are mad or drunk or both.

The master of demonry in India is a very sinister figure known as *Mmbyu*, who is also Death. *Mmbyu*'s older name, *Pacu Pati* (lord of the herd), soon gained the dread meaning of 'Master of Human Cattle'. He is chief of all mischievous spirits, of ghouls, of vampires and of all creatures that frequent places of execution and graveyards. Normally *Mmbyu* prowls with his dark host during the tyranny of the night.

Finally there is the legend of the *Baital-Pachisi*, which is a huge bat, vampire or evil spirit which inhabits and reanimates dead bodies. Sir Richard Burton documented the legend in *Vikram and the Vampire, or Tales of Hindu Devilry* (1832), and in the preface his wife Isabel Burton writes:

> It is an old, and thoroughly Hindú, legend composed in Sanskrit, and is the germ which culminated in the Arabian Nights, and which inspired the *Golden Ass* of Apuleius, Boccaccio's *Decamerone*, the *Pentamerone*, and all that class of facetious fictitious literature.
>
> The story turns chiefly on a great king named Vikram, the King Arthur of the East, who in pursuance of his promise to a *Jogi* or Magician, brings to him the *Baital* (Vampire), who is hanging on a tree. The difficulties King Vikram and his son have in bringing the Vampire into the presence of the *Jogi* are truly laughable; and on this thread is strung a series of Hindú fairy stories, which contain much interesting information on Indian customs and manners. It also alludes to that state, which induces Hindú devotees to allow themselves to be buried alive, and to appear dead for weeks or months, and then to return to life again; a curious state of mesmeric catalepsy, into which they work themselves by concentrating the mind and abstaining from food.

The Balkans

Bulgarian Vampire Practice

Both the Balkans and Central Europe were a hotbed of traditional vampire lore—lore far different and essentially more realistic than the spiritual devilry of China, India and Malaysia. From the twelfth to the fourteenth century waves of hysterical fear swept across Europe—waves of fear aided and abetted by the Church with its penalties of excommunication and its condemnation of suicides (see Part Four). Bulgaria was a typical example of a backward country very much a prey to bouts of terror concerning the undead. In 1863, for instance, there was a voracious epidemic of vampirism amongst the remoter villages. Villagers burnt candles at night and collected together in public places, in unity against their spectral enemy. They claim to have been besieged by *Obours* (vampires) who, according to Dudley Wright in *Vampires and Vampirism* (1914),

> lit up the streets with their sparkles. Some of the most enterprising of them threw their shadows on the walls of the rooms where the peasants were assembled through fear, while others howled and shrieked and swore outside the door, entered the abandoned houses, spat blood on the floors, turned everything topsy-turvy, and smeared everything, even the pictures of the saints, with cow-dung, until an old lady, suspected of witchcraft, discovered and laid the troublesome spirit, and afterwards the village was free.

Bulgaria was exceptional in the intensity of its beliefs and the unmentionable tortures inflicted upon those suspected of vampirism. The power of the Church in Bulgaria was limited, and the country was a good example of what can happen during the course of a pagan holocaust. People's imaginations ran riot, scapegoats were found and ignorance summoned forth the most amazing spectres. There was no question of official exorcism, or of holy artifacts negating the threat. Vampires had to be banished by their own contemporaries and accessories—the witches.

Here are two extracts from *Twelve Years' Study of the Eastern Question in Bulgaria* (published in London in 1877) by St Clair and Brothy, a pompous but fearful work that accurately conveys the flavour of the prevalent superstition.

> We will now give the unadulterated Bulgarian superstitions, merely prefacing that we ought to be well acquainted with it, inasmuch as a servant of ours is the son of a noted Vampire, and is doing penance during this present Lent by neither smoking, nor drinking wine or spirits, in order to expiate the sins of his father and to prevent himself inheriting the propensity.
>
> When a man who has Vampire blood in his veins—for this

condition is not only epidemic and endemic, but hereditary—or who is otherwise predisposed to become a Vampire, dies, nine days after his burial he returns to upper earth in an aeriform shape. The presence of the Vampire in this his first condition may be easily discerned in the dark by a succession of sparks like those from a flint and steel; in the light, by a shadow projected upon a wall, and varying in density according to the age of the Vampire in his career. In this stage he is comparatively harmless, and is only able to play the practical jokes of the German Kobold and Gnome, of the Irish Phooka, or the English Puck; he roars in a terrible voice, or amuses himself by calling out the inhabitants of a cottage by the most endearing terms, and then beating them black and blue.

When the Bulgarian Vampire has finished a forty days' apprenticeship to the realm of shadows, he rises from his tomb in bodily form, and is able to pass himself off as a human being, living honestly and naturally. Thirty years since a stranger arrived in this village, established himself, and married a wife with whom he lived on very good terms, she making but one complaint, that her husband absented himself from the conjugal roof every night and all night. It was soon remarked that (although scavengers were, and are, utterly unknown in Bulgaria) a great deal of scavengers' work was done at night by some unseen being, and that when one branch of this industry was exhausted, the dead horses and buffaloes which lay about the streets were devoured by invisible teeth, much to the prejudice of the village dogs; then the mysterious mouth drained the blood of all cattle that happened to be in any way sickly. These occurrences, and the testimony of the wife, caused the stranger to be suspected of Vampirism; he was examined, found to have only one nostril, and upon this irrefragable evidence was condemned to death. In executing this sentence, our villagers did not think it necessary to send for the priest, to confess themselves, or to take consecrated halters or daggers; they just tied their man hand and foot, led him to a hill a little outside Derekuoi, lit a big fire of wait-a-bit thorns, and burned him alive.

The Bulgarian vampire was not a dead body possessed by a demon but a soul in revolt against the inevitability of death. Its physical attributes included a boneless frame and fungoid-like flesh, and, even more sinister, it did not always cast a shadow.

Between Christmas and Epiphany there was a period known

in Bulgaria (and other parts of Europe) as the 'Unclean Days' during which the forces of evil ruled the world. Therefore any birth or death during this period was subject to the influence of the vampire.

Protection against Bulgarian Vampires: It was considered that the only really safe method of extermination of the vampire species was by witchcraft. All other forms of prevention or execution were ineffective. Medicine had to be administered by a local witch, providing she could discover the vampire's resting place. On discovery the entrance had to be blocked with human excrement (a dish much loved by the Bulgarian vampire) mixed with poisonous herbs.

There were other, even more doubtful methods. For instance, as the process of vampire creation involved the swelling up of the corpse, the body was often punctured by a sharp instrument in order to liberate the noxious vampiristic gases within. Also, the powers of evil sometimes adopted the shape of a pig, a bird or a domestic animal which were able to approach the corpse and claim possession of the body, so to prevent this a fence was built around the grave and death-lights were burnt for six days. Burning was another means of destruction, as was bottling. This is discussed by St Clair.

> The belief that spirits and evil entities could be enclosed in vessels of glass would appear to be of Oriental origin, and amongst other fantasies to have been introduced into Spain by the Morisco. Owing to the notorious trial for witchcraft of Doctor Eugenio Torralda in 1531, the Grand Inquisitor, Don Alfonso Manriquez, promulgated certain articles detailing various offences connected with demonolatry which every good Christian was bound to denounce to the Holy Office, and among these appears the following inquiry: 'If any person made or caused to be made mirrors, rings, phials of glass or other vessels in order thereby to control or therein to contain some spirit who should reply to his demands and aid his projects,' such a one must be delated to the proper ecclesiastical authorities.

In Bulgaria the bottling process is a skilled craft and those who dabbled in witchcraft made considerable sums of money out of their vampire-bottling expertise. The recipe was as follows: The sorcerer, armed with the picture of some saint, ambushes the unsuspecting passing vampire. The vampire, observing the icon with some trepidation, makes for the nearest tree or roof. Undaunted the sorcerer clambers after him waving the icon threateningly. Gradually the vampire, unable to gain sanctuary, wanders in the direction of the bottle that the sorcerer has prepared. Once the vampire is in, there is no escape and a cork is rammed home, on the interior of which there is a fragment of the icon. Then with a wild cry of exultation the sorcerer throws bottle and vampire into a roaring fire where they are immediately consumed. The sorcerer, having accomplished, or claiming to have accomplished, his task, then goes and claims his fee.

Another method of prevention is discussed by the intrepid Gordon Cooper, who wrote a book in 1940 entitled *I Searched the World for Death*.* Cooper, in his travels, researched a variety of death rites and claimed to be a witness to a Bulgarian Second Burial service.

> At Razlog I had a rather interesting experience. Apparently the word had gone round that I was interested in death ceremonies. While I was scouting around trying to find out how to reach the monastery, a man approached me and asked whether I would be interested in viewing a ceremony known as the 'Second Burial'. Naturally I wanted to know more about this strange rite. I knew that primitive people have a great terror of the dead and that the inhabitants of these mountains possessed many peculiar beliefs.
>
> He told me that five years before a man had died during the 'Unclean Days', which fall between Christmas and Epiphany. During these days the world is ruled by the forces of evil. Anybody who dies then is in danger of being turned into a vampire. Knowing this the old man had made his relations swear to give him a second burial on his saint's day, five years later. Thus he would escape the terrible fate. If his relatives broke their oath terrible calamities would befall them. He swore to come back and haunt them. It was a common custom in this part of the world to bury the dead a second time.
>
> Now the five years were up and the relatives of the dead man had gathered together to carry out their oath. The ceremony was to take place in a small village some distance from Razlog...
>
> At sundown we all went to the churchyard. As we entered the

* Published in London by John Long.

gate the sexton threw holy water over each member of the party. Then we made our way to the dead man's grave. It was just an overgrown mound of earth with a wooden cross at one end. The men stood on one side of the grave, the women and children on the other.

The priest came out of the church. He carried a spade, a cross, and a lighted candle. He began the ceremony by saying a short prayer. Then the grave was opened. The coffin lid was removed and the bones lifted out. They were placed on a sheet beside the grave. There were still pieces of hair adhering to the skull.

Four young men took hold of the sheet by the corners and marched solemnly round the church three times. Then suddenly they turned and ran out of the graveyard with their burden. It was as if they had suddenly sighted the devil. Everybody else went into the church, where the priest said another prayer.

I went back to have a look at the grave. The bones had been placed in a cotton bag and left there. The skull had been placed on a little mound of earth. A priest washed the skull with wine and then wiped it dry with the shroud. Another priest came out of the church carrying two earthenware jars. One contained oil, the other wine. He poured some of each into the grave. Then the bag of bones was replaced and the grave was filled again. The ceremony of the 'Second Burial' was over, and nobody need fear the dead man's wrath.

Greek Vampire Practice and Protection

Both the vampire and werewolf legends were brought into Greece by the Slavs. The Greek word, *vrykolakas*, originally meant a *revenant* but later came to mean a vampire. Before the Slavs introduced the more familiar brutal vampire the Greeks had believed in the incorruptibility and the re-animation of the bodies of certain types of men—but these men returned from their graves with dignity and had no such vampiristic notions as revenge, or a thirst for blood. Admittedly a *revenant* might seek revenge, but only where revenge was just. The Greeks had to some extent believed in the vampire, assuming him to be a more vicious version of the *revenant*, but were not particularly afraid of him as his activities were obscure. A change occurred in this thinking when it was discovered, with some consternation, that werewolves became vampires after death. The werewolf legend was considered to be infinitely more panic-making and therefore, once this link was established, the vampire image took on a more sinister colour. Gradually public memory forgot the former gentle personality of the *revenant* and replaced it with a monster —and by the seventeenth century the situation was beginning to get out of control.

The Church, of course, was placed in an extremely awkward position. The word *revenant* had acquired a new and sinister meaning—and there was now a marked difference between the popular and clerical uses of the word. The sentence of excommunication was totally binding and theoretically, having received it, a man would not rot in his grave. He would remain uncorrupted, his soul would lurk within him and he would be forever damned. The last thing the Church wanted was to be held responsible for the resuscitation of the vampire, although they were equally unwilling to diminish the terrors of excommunication—an act that was their most powerful weapon. A statement was issued to the following effect: that although excommunicants remained uncorrupt and their bodies took on a drum-like look, they were not, like the *vrykolakas,* subject to demonic re-animation. Needless to say, the Church's statement had absolutely no effect and utter confusion reigned. Therefore excommunication (see Part Four) was immediately, in Greece and elsewhere, set down as one of the direct causes of vampirism.

The Slavonic vampire's hostility was directed almost entirely at his next of kin. It was therefore much feared that a member of one's own family would become a vampire. In spite of this, the Greek habit of cursing the dead seems to almost invite this event. A popular favourite was 'May the earth not receive him'. Others included 'May the ground not consume him', 'May the earth not digest thee', 'May the black earth spew thee up', 'Mayst thou remain incorrupt', 'May the earth not lose thee', and 'May the ground reject thee'. These are interestingly linked with formal excommunicative phrases and incantations including 'And after death thou shalt be bound eternally, even as stone and iron' or 'And after death bound and indissoluble'.

There are certain likely candidates for vampirism apart from ex-communicants and those who had been subjected to a curse. They are as follows:

1 Those who do not receive the full and due rites of burial.
2 Those who meet any sudden or violent death (including suicides) or those who have been murdered and have remained unavenged.
3 Children conceived or born on one of the great Church festivals and stillborn children.
4 Those who died unbaptised or apostate.
5 Those over whose dead body a cat or other animal has passed.
6 Those who have eaten the flesh of a sheep that was killed by a wolf.
7 Those who lived an evil, immoral life.
8 Those who dabbled in the Black Arts.

It was difficult to avoid falling into one of these categories and it brought the vampire far nearer home than the Chinese, Indian and Malayan vampires—far nearer even than the untamed and almost unlayable Bulgarian breed.

Leo Allatius, a seventeenth-century Greek folklorist, produced a treatise on the *vrykolakas*: *

> The *vrykolakas* is the body of a man of evil and immoral life—very often of one who has been excommunicated by his bishop. Such bodies do not like those of other dead men suffer decomposition after burial nor turn to dust, but having, as it appears, a skin of extreme toughness become swollen and distended all over, so that the joints can scarcely be bent; the skin becomes stretched like the parchment of a drum, and when struck gives out the same sound. Into such a body the devil enters, and issuing from the tomb goes about, chiefly at night, knocking at doors and calling one of the household. If such a one answer, he dies next day; but a *vrykolakas* never calls twice, and so the inhabitants of Chios [whence Allatius' observations and information were chiefly taken] secure themselves by always waiting for a second call at night before replying. This monster is said to be so destructive to men, that appearing actually in the daytime, even at noon—and that not only in houses but in fields and highroads and enclosed vineyards—it advances upon them as they walk along, and by its mere aspect without either speech or touch kills them.

* *De Graecorum hodie Quorundam Opinionatibus*, published in Cologne in 1645.

> Hence, when sudden deaths occur without other assignable cause, they open the tombs and often find such a body. Thereupon it is taken out of the grave, the priests recite prayers, and it is thrown on to a burning pyre; before the supplications are finished the joints of the body gradually fall apart; and all the remains are burnt to ashes. This belief is not of fresh and recent growth in Greece; in ancient and modern times alike men of piety who have received the confessions of Christians have tried to root it out of the popular mind.

Here is an account of the *vrykolakas* written by a monk in 1888:

> It is popularly believed that most of the dead, those who have lived bad lives or those who have been excommunicated by some priest become *vrykolakes*; that is to say, after the separation of the soul from the body there enters into the latter an evil spirit, which takes the place of the soul and assumes the shape of the dead man and so is transformed into a *vrykolakas* or man demon. In this guise it keeps the body as its dwelling-place and preserves it from corruption, and it runs swift as lightning wherever it lists, and causes men great alarms by night and strikes all with panic. And the trouble is that it does not remain solitary, but makes everyone, who dies while it is about, like to itself, so that in a short space of time it gets together a large and dangerous train of followers. The common practice of the *vrykolakes* is to seat themselves upon those who are asleep and by their enormous weight to cause an agonising sense of oppression. There is great danger that the sufferer may expire, and himself too be turned into a *vrykolakas*, if there be not someone at hand who perceives his torment and fires off a gun, thereby putting the blood-thirsty monster to flight; for fortunately it is afraid of the report of fire-arms and retreats without effecting its purpose.

A hotbed of Greek vampire superstition was and still is the island of Santorini. Santorini has an extremely antiseptic soil which lends itself to the preservation of corpses. Therefore undecayed bodies were often found, particularly as it was the custom of the Church in Greece to exhume corpses after three years. Relatively whole bodies were discovered and an outbreak of vampire mania began on the island in the seventeenth century. Santorini was supposed to be the home of the *vrykolatios*—a vampire-ghoul combination. This sub-human was meant to have the power of raising the dead from the graves and 'sending them forth to banquet on the living'. (Montague Summers, *The Vampire in*

Europe.) The inhabitants of Santorini became experts at exterminating vampires and many vampire corpses were carried to Santorini, there to be dealt with.

An eye-witness account of Greek vampire practice was observed by the French botanist Joseph Pitton de Tournefort who travelled through Greece between 1700 and 1702. His book *Relations d'un Voyage du Levant* was translated into English in 1741.

> In the island of Mycona we witnessed a very singular scene, being the alleged return of a deceased person after interment. In northern Europe those who come back in this manner are called vampires, while the Greeks designated them under the name of *Broucolaques*. The case in question was that of a peasant of Mycona who was naturally gloomy and quarrelsome. It is a circumstance worthy of note, on account of parallel instances. He was killed in the countryside, no one knew why or by whom. Two days after his burial in a church of the city, a report went abroad that he was seen nightly wandering about at a great pace. He also visited houses, turned over the furniture, put out the lights, embraced people from behind and performed innumerable other tricks. At first it was a laughing matter, but it took a serious turn when reliable people began to complain. The priests themselves certified to the fact, and no doubt they had their reasons. Recourse was had to masses, said for the purpose, but the peasant continued the same course with no sign of amendment. After several meetings of the chief persons, priests and monks of the town it was concluded to wait for the expiration of nine days after the interment, following I know not what ancient procedure. On the tenth day a mass was said in the church wherein the body had been buried, for the purpose of expelling the demon who was thought to have entered into it. The mass over, the corpse was disinterred and the heart removed. It was necessary to burn incense owing to the evil smell, but the combination made bad worse and almost stifled those present. It was testified that a thick smoke exhaled from the corpse, and we who were present at the operations did not venture to suggest that it was really the smoke of the incense. There was also those who affirmed that the blood of the unfortunate person was abnormally scarlet, while yet others declared that the flesh was still warm, whence it was concluded that the deceased person was seriously wrong in not being properly dead, or rather in allowing himself to be brought

to life by the devil. This is precisely the idea which obtains concerning the vampire, and that word began to be repeated persistently. A crowd assembled, loudly protesting that the body was obviously not rigid when it was carried to the church for burial and that it was therefore a veritable vampire.

Appeal being made to us, we expressed the opinion that the person was undoubtedly dead, and as for the supposed scarlet blood, it was easy to see that it was only bad-smelling slime. For the rest, we attempted to cure or at least not provoke further their excited imaginations by explaining the fumes and warmth attributed to the corpse. Such arguments notwithstanding, it was determined to burn the heart of the deceased person, but after this had been done he was not more amenable than formerly and indeed created greater stir. He was accused of beating people at night, of breaking down doors and windows, tearing garments and emptying pitchers and bottles. Altogether, the deceased made himself highly objectionable. There is reason to believe that he spared no house save that of the consul, in which we happened to be lodging. Every imagination was overwrought, people of good sense being affected as much as others. A disease of the brain seemed abroad, as dangerous as that of madness; entire families abandoned their houses and carried their pallets to the outskirts, there to pass the night. Even then they complained of fresh insults, and the most sober retired into the country. Citizens who were imbued with a sense of public zeal decided that one essential detail had been missed, so far, in the observance; from their point of view, the mass should have been celebrated after, and not before, removing the heart from the body. With this precaution it was pretended that the devil would have been taken by surprise and would not have attempted to return; but unfortunately they began with the mass, which gave him time to depart, and he was able to come back at his ease. These considerations left matters in their original state of difficulty. There were meetings and still meetings, both evening and morning; there were processions for three days and three nights; fasts were imposed on the priests; houses were visited by them, *aspergillus* in hand; there was sprinkling with holy water and doors were purified. Even the mouth of the miserable vampire was filled with holy water.

In the midst of such prepossessions our course was to say nothing; we should have been regarded as jesters and infidels. What, however, was to be done to help the inhabitants? Every morning brought a fresh scene in the comedy by the recital of new pranks of this nightbird, who was even accused of committing the most abominable crimes. We did, however, represent more than once to the governor of the town that in our country, under such circumstances, a watch would not fail to be set, to take note of what passed. The precaution was ultimately taken, and led to the arrest of some vagabonds who were undoubtedly at the bottom of the disorder. It was, of course, relaxed too soon, and two days subsequently, to atone for the fast which the said wastrels had undergone in prison, they betook themselves to emptying the wine jars in some of the abandoned houses. After driving in numberless drawn swords over the grave of the body, people now returned to their prayers, combined with disinterring the corpse as caprice led them, when an Albanian, who happened to be there, pointed out in an authoritative tone that it was highly ridiculous, in a case of the kind, to make use of the swords of Christians; these being cross-handled effectually prevented the devil from leaving the body, and his recommendation was therefore to substitute Turkish sabres. The advice of this expert came to nothing; the vampire was not more tractable, and they knew not what saint to invoke, when all with one voice, as if a word of command had been given, cried out through the whole town that the vampire must be burned completely, after which they might defy the devil, and that certainly it was better to have recourse to this extremity rather than that the island should be deserted. As a fact, certain families were preparing already for their departure.

The vampire was therefore carried by order of the governors to the extremity of the isle of St. George, where a great pyre had been prepared with tar, lest even dry wood should not kindle quickly enough. What remained of the miserable body was cast therein and speedily consumed. This was on the first day of January, 1701. Henceforth there were no complaints against the vampire; it was agreed that the devil had that time been overreached and songs were made to deride him.

Eastern Europe

Even the demonic outbreaks of vampirism in the Balkans were minor compared to the outbreaks of mass hysteria in Eastern Europe throughout the centuries. The very word vampire is a derivation of the Magyar word *vampir*—a word of Slavonic origin occurring in varying forms in Russia, Poland, Czechoslovakia, Serbia, Bulgaria and Russia. The Balkans have already established the real power of the Slavonic vampire—that most traditional and bestial of all *revenants.* Joseph Ennemoser, the German historian of magic, pointed out in his book *History of Magic* (1854) that:

> Towards the end of the seventeenth century the belief in witchcraft grew more wavering, and men began to oppose it with keenness and vigour; and this even in Germany, which had hitherto swarmed with witches, and where the smoke of the death fires had choked all genuine Christianity. But that which this mock-faith lost in Germany, France, and Italy, is gained in the far north and in the east of Europe, in Livonia, in Poland and Russia, in Servia and Wallachia, where the blood-sucking vampire hovered the longest—a superstition of the most revolting kind. 'A vampire-ghost', says an official document quoted by Horst, 'is a dead person who continues to live on in the grave; who in the night ascends from his tomb as an apparition, in order to suck the blood of the living, by which he maintains his body in the earth unemaciated, and incapable of decay.'
>
> This vampirism had a different kind of penal trial from that of witches, for here the dead bodies were examined and burnt. It is said in the above-mentioned statement, which being official may stand as the type of many others, that 'after P. Plagoymitz had been interred a few days, several persons at once fell ill, and within eight days nine people died. All these on their deathbeds protested that the said Plagoymitz was the sole cause of their deaths, because he had come by night as they slept, had seized them by their throats, and sucked their blood. In order to put an end to this general calamity in the village, it was determined to open the grave, when, to the astonishment of all the spectators, the body, although it had lain three weeks in the grave, gave forth not the slightest odour of death, and, except that his nose was somewhat fallen in, the whole was perfectly fresh and sound. They took the body out of the grave, sharpened a stake, and drove it through the heart of the vampire, upon which fresh blood gushed from the mouth and ears. They then burnt the body, and turned him, thus pierced through, to dust and ashes.' This account is drawn up from the surgeon of the place, who himself directed the inquiry.

Austrian Vampire Practice

A particularly vivid description of the Austrian vampire type comes from the pen of the director of the Gymnasium of Essen, Henry Zopfius, who during the mid-seventeenth century wrote an illuminating little dissertation on Austrian vampire practice.

> The vampyres, which come out of their graves in the night-time, rush upon people sleeping in their beds, suck out all their blood, and destroy them. They attack men, women, and children, sparing neither age nor sex. The people attacked by them complain of suffocation, and a great interception of the spirits; after which, they soon expire. Some of them, being asked at the point of death what is the matter with them, say they suffer in a manner just related from people lately dead, or rather the spectres of those people; upon which their bodies, from the description given of them, by the sick person, being dug out of the graves, appear in all parts, as nostrils, cheeks, breast, mouth, *etcetera*, turgid and full of blood. Their countenances are fresh and ruddy; and their nails, as well as hair, are very much grown. And, though they have been much longer dead than many other bodies, which are perfectly putrified, not the least mark of corruption is visible upon them. Those who were destroyed by them, after their deaths, become vampyres; so that to prevent so spreading an evil, it is found requisite to drive a stake through the dead body, from whence, on this occasion, the blood flows, as if the person was alive. Sometimes the body is dug out of the grave, and burnt to ashes; upon which, all disturbances cease. The Hungarians call these spectres Pamgri and the Serbians, Vampyres; but the etymon or reason of these names is not known.

Cataleptic or semi-cataleptic situations were fairly common in Austria. In 1893, in a small Austrian town, a young woman died. She was pregnant. After the normal three-day waiting period she was buried, but an exhumation took place shortly afterwards owing to a proliferation of rumours which suggested that the young wife might well have been poisoned by the husband. To the horror of the authorities it was discovered that not only had she been buried alive in a trance-like or cataleptic condition but she had put up the most incredible struggle within the coffin. During the course of this she had given birth to a child. Both had suffocated to death.

Another incident concerned a Mrs Zeller who lived—and purportedly died—in the town of Salzburg during the 1860s. The death warrant having been signed, the wealthy Mrs Zeller was buried with due pomp and ceremony. On her finger she wore a ring of some value. An undertaker's assistant took quiet note of this fact during the funeral and returned that night to exhume the corpse—and steal the ring. As he roughly pulled open the coffin lid he broke Mrs Zeller's cataleptic trance, she stirred, he fled and she later returned home in her shroud. The shattering event was commemorated by a plaque which is still in existence today.

One well-documented Austrian vampire case, of a far less rational nature, was described in the September 1909 edition of the *Occult Review*:

> On 10 June, 1909, there appeared in a prominent Vienna paper (*The Neues Wiener Journal*) a notice saying that the castle of B— had been burned by the populace, because there was a great mortality among the peasant children, and it was generally believed that this was due to the invasion of a Vampire, supposed to be the last Count B—, who died and acquired that reputation. The castle was situated in a wild and desolate part of the Carpathian Mountains, and was formerly a fortification against the Turks. It was not inhabited, owing to its being believed to be in the possession of ghosts; only a wing of it was used as a dwelling for the caretaker and his wife.
>
> Now it so happened that, when I read the above notice, I was sitting in a coffee-house at Vienna in company with an old friend of mine who is an experienced occultist and editor of a well-known journal, and who had spent several months in the neighbourhood of the castle. From him I obtained the following account, and it appears that the Vampire in question was probably not the old Count, but his beautiful daughter, the Countess Elga, whose photograph, taken from the original painting, I obtained. My friend said: 'Two years ago I was living at Hermannstadt, and being engaged in engineering a road through the hills, I often came within the vicinity of the old castle, where I made the acquaintance of the old *castellan*, or caretaker, and his wife, who occupied a part of the wing of the house, almost separate from the main body of the building. They were a quiet old couple and rather reticent in giving information or express-

ing an opinion in regard to the strange noises which were often heard at night in the deserted halls, or of the apparitions which the Wallachian peasants claimed to have seen when they loitered in the surroundings after dark. All I could gather was that the old Count was a widower and had a beautiful daughter, who was one day killed by a fall from her horse, and that soon after the old man died in some mysterious manner, and the bodies were buried in a solitary graveyard belonging to a neighbouring village. Not long after their death an unusual mortality was noticed among the inhabitants of the village; several children and even some grown people died without any apparent illness; they merely wasted away; and thus a rumour was started that the old Count had become a Vampire after his death. There is no doubt that he was not a saint, as he was addicted to drinking, and some shocking tales were in circulation about his conduct and that of his daughter; but whether there was any truth in them, I am not in a position to say.

'Afterwards the property came into the possession of —, a distant relative of the family, who is a young man and officer in a cavalry regiment at Vienna. It appears that the heir enjoyed his life at the capital and did not trouble himself much about the old castle in the wilderness; he did not even come to look at it, but gave his directions by letter to the janitor, telling him merely to keep things in order and to attend to repairs, if any were necessary. Thus the *castellan* was actually master of the house, and offered its hospitality to me and my friends.

'One evening I and my two assistants, Dr E—, a young lawyer, and Mr W—, a literary man, went to inspect the premises. First we went to the stables. There were no horses as they had been sold; but what attracted our special attention was an old, queer-fashioned coach with gilded ornaments and bearing the emblems of the family. We then inspected the rooms, passing through some halls and gloomy corridors, such as may be found in any old castle. There was nothing remarkable about the furniture; but in one of the halls there hung in a frame an oil-painting, a portrait, representing a lady with a large hat and wearing a fur coat. We were all involuntarily startled on beholding this picture—not so much on account of the beauty of the lady, but on account of the uncanny expression of her eyes; and Dr E—, after looking at the picture for a short time, suddenly exclaimed: "How strange. The picture closes its eyes and opens them again, and now it begins to smile."

'Now Dr E— is a very sensitive person, and has more than

once had some experience in spiritism, and we made up our minds to form a circle for the purpose of investigating this phenomenon. Accordingly, on the same evening, we sat around a table in an adjoining room, forming a magnetic chain with our hands. Soon the table began to move and the name *Elga* was spelled. We asked who this Elga was, and the answer was rapped out: "The lady whose picture you have seen."

'"Is the lady living?" asked Mr W—. This question was not answered; but instead it was rapped out: "If W— desires it, I will appear to him bodily to-night at two o'clock." W— consented, and now the table seemed to be endowed with life and manifested a great affection for W—; it rose on two legs and pressed against his breast, as if it intended to embrace him.

'We inquired of the *castellan* whom the picture represented; but to our surprise he did not know. He said that it was the copy of a picture painted by the celebrated painter Hans Markart of Vienna, and had been bought by the old Count because its demoniacal look pleased him so much.

'We left the castle, and W— retired to his room at an inn a half-hour's journey distant from that place. He was of a somewhat sceptical turn of mind, being neither a firm believer in ghosts and apparitions nor ready to deny their possibility. He was not afraid, but anxious to see what would come of his agreement, and for the purpose of keeping himself awake he sat down and began to write an article for a journal.

'Towards two o'clock he heard steps on the stairs and the door of the hall opened; there was the rustling of a silk dress and the sound of the feet of a lady walking to and fro in the corridor.

'It may be imagined that he was somewhat startled; but taking courage, he said to himself: "If this is Elga let her come in." Then the door of the room opened and Elga entered. She was most elegantly dressed, and appeared still more youthful and seductive than the picture. There was a lounge on the other side of the table where W— was writing, and there she silently posted herself. She did not speak, but her looks and gestures left no doubt in regard to her desires and intentions.

'Mr W— resisted the temptation and remained firm. It is not known whether he did so out of principle or timidity or fear. Be this as it may, he kept on writing, looking from time to time at his visitor and silently wishing that she would leave. At last, after half an hour, which seemed to him much longer, the lady departed in the same manner in which she came.

'This adventure left W— no peace, and we consequently arranged several sittings at the old castle, where a variety of uncanny phenomena took place. Thus, for instance, once the servant-girl was about to light a fire in the stove, when the door of the apartment opened and Elga stood there. The girl, frightened out of her wits, rushed from the room, tumbling down the stairs in terror with the lamp in her hand, which broke, and came very near to setting her clothes on fire. Lighted lamps and candles went out when brought near the picture, and many other "manifestations" took place which it would be tedious to describe; but the following incident ought not to be omitted.

'Mr W— was at that time desirous of obtaining the position as co-editor of a certain journal, and a few days after the above-narrated adventure he received a letter in which a noble lady of high position offered him her patronage for that purpose. The writer requested him to come to a certain place the same evening, where he would meet a gentleman who would give him further particulars. He went, and was met by an unknown stranger, who told him that he was requested by the Countess Elga to invite Mr W— to a carriage drive, and that she would await him at midnight at a certain crossing of two roads, not far from the village. The stranger then suddenly disappeared.

'Now it seems that Mr W— had some misgivings about the meeting and drive, and he hired a policeman as detective to go at midnight to the appointed place, to see what would happen. The policeman went and reported next morning that he had seen nothing at all but the well-known old-fashioned carriage from the castle, with two black horses, standing there as if waiting for somebody, and that as he had no occasion to interfere, he merely waited until the carriage moved on. When the *castellan* of the castle was asked, he swore that the carriage had not been out that night, and in fact it could not have been out, as there were no horses to draw it.

'But that is not all, for on the following day I met a friend who is a great sceptic and disbeliever in ghosts, and always used to laugh at such things. Now, however, he seemed to be very serious: "Last night something very strange happened to me. At about one o'clock this morning I returned from a late visit, and as I happened to pass the graveyard of the village, I saw a carriage with gilded ornaments standing at the entrance. I wondered about this taking place at such an unusual hour, and being curious to see what would happen, I waited. Two elegantly dressed ladies issued from the carriage. One of these was very young and pretty, but threw at me a devilish and scornful look as they both passed by and entered the cemetery. There they were met by a well-dressed man, who saluted the ladies and spoke to the younger one, saying: 'Why, Miss Elga! Are you returned so soon?' Such a queer feeling came over me that I abruptly left and hurried home."

'This matter has not been explained; but certain experiments which we subsequently made with the picture of Elga brought out some curious facts.

'To look at the picture for a certain time caused me to feel a very disagreeable sensation in the region of the solar plexus. I began to dislike the portrait and proposed to destroy it. We held a sitting in the adjoining room; the table manifested a great aversion to my presence. It was rapped out that I should leave the circle, and that the picture must not be destroyed. I ordered a Bible to be brought in, and read the beginning of the first chapter of St John, whereupon the above-mentioned Mr E— (the medium) and another man present claimed that they saw the picture distorting in face. I turned the frame and pricked the back of the picture with my penknife in different places, and Mr E—, as well as the other man, felt all the pricks, although they had retired to the corridor.

'I made the sign of the pentagram over the picture, and again the two gentlemen claimed that the picture was horribly distorting its face.

'Soon afterwards we were called away and left that country. Of Elga I heard nothing more.'

Hungarian Vampire Practice

Hungary, the traditional seat of vampiredom (called here the *Pamgri*), is also the best-documented country in this respect. Here the European vampire was at his most typical and indeed at his most violent. Calmet, the French theologian and historian, brought out a document in 1746 called *Traité sur les Apparitions des Esprits, et sur les Vampires* in which he says:

> In this present age and for about sixty years past, we have been the hearers and the witnesses of a new series of extraordinary incidents and occurrences. Hungary, Moravia, Silesia, Poland, are the principal theatre of these happenings. For here we are told that dead men, men who have been dead for several months,

I say, return from the tomb, are heard to speak, walk about, infest hamlets and villages, injure both men and animals, whose blood they drain thereby making them sick and ill, and at length actually causing death. Nor can men deliver themselves from these terrible visitations, nor secure themselves from these horrid attacks, unless they dig the corpses up from the graves, drive a sharp stake through these bodies, cut off the heads, tear out the hearts; or else they burn the bodies to ashes. The name given to these ghosts is *Oupires*, or Vampires, that is to say, blood-suckers, and the particulars which are related of them are so singular, so detailed, accompanied with circumstances so probable and so likely, as well as with the most weighty and well-attested legal deposition, that it seems impossible not to subscribe to the belief which prevails in these countries that these Apparitions do actually come forth from their graves and that they are able to produce the terrible effects which are so widely and so positively attributed to them....

The Apparitions (*Revenants*) of Hungary, or Vampires ... are men who have been dead for some considerable time, it may be for a long period or it may be for a shorter period, and these issue forth from their graves and come to disturb the living, whose blood they suck and drain. These vampires visibly appear to men, they knock loudly at their doors and cause the sound to echo throughout the whole house, and once they have gained a foothold death generally follows. To this sort of Apparition is given the name Vampire or *Oupire*, which in the Slavonic tongues means a blood-sucker.

Gradually paranoia developed amongst the Hungarian peasantry over a period of two centuries and the following account by Calmet illustrates the phenomena.

An Official Vampire Investigation in 1732

The Prince (Duke Charles Alexander of Würtemberg, governor of Serbia) sent a deputation from Belgrade consisting of both civil and military officials, with the Public Prosecutor of the kingdom, to a village where a notorious vampire, dead many years since, was ravaging his kinsmen; for it is notable that the blood-suckers only seek to destroy their own families. This deputation was composed of respected persons, both civil and military, well known for their experience and respectability; they were put on oath, and accompanied by a lieutenant of the

Grenadiers of Prince Alexander of Würtemberg's regiment and twenty-four of his men.

Many reputable citizens accompanied the deputation, even the Duke himself, who happened to be in Belgrade at the time, in order to have visible proof of the strange occurrences.

When they reached the village they discovered that the vampire had already dispatched three of his nieces and nephews and one of his own brothers within the past fortnight. He had just commenced on his fifth victim, his young and beautiful niece, and had sucked her blood twice when the tragedy was arrested in the following manner.

At dusk some members of the deputation went to the grave in the presence of a crowd of people. My informant was unable to tell me precisely at what time the previous victims were sucked nor the details. The pangs are so violent that after his blood has been sucked the victim remains in a pitiful state of weakness and lassitude. The vampire had been buried three years ago; now they saw a light over his tomb like a flickering lamp.

The grave was opened and a man was revealed, as whole and apparently as healthy as anyone present; his hair, and the hair on his body, his nails, teeth and eyes (which were half-open) were all firmly attached as in life, and his heart was beating.

He was taken from his coffin; the body was not truly flexible, but no particle of bone or flesh was missing; his heart was then pierced through with a species of sharp iron bar; a whitish fluid issued, mixed with blood, but the blood predominating, and the whole without any bad odour; next the head was cut off with a sort of axe such as is used in England for executions: the same fluid and blood issued as before, but more abundantly.

The body was put into the ground, covered with quicklime to consume it as rapidly as possible, and from this time onwards the girl who had been sucked twice began to recover. A bluish patch forms on the spot where these people have been sucked; but the spot is not precise, it shows in different places at different times.*

Elizabeth of Bathory, 1611

Opinions vary as to how many young women were slaughtered by Countess Bathory. Some say three hundred—others claim it

* From a letter to a friend of Don Calmet, published in *The Vampire, An Anthology*, by Ornella Volta and Valeria Riva (Neville Spearman, 1963).

is more like six hundred. Sufficient to say that this psychotic middle-aged noblewoman, widow of the Count Nadasay, killed hundreds of young girls by draining them of their blood by various methods. One method, as documented by the court records of the time, was to 'put a terrified naked girl in a narrow iron cage furnished with pointed nails turned inward, hang it from the ceiling and sit beneath it enjoying the rain of blood that came down'.* Another little gimmick was

> an automat beautifully made by a German clock-smith, which was shaped like a girl and covered with red hair, and wearing red teeth torn from the mouth of some servant; the robot would clutch anyone that came near it in a tight embrace and then transfix them with a series of sharp points that came out of her metal breasts. The blood ran down into a channel so that it could be collected, warmed over a fire and used for the Countess's bath.

There is a strange similarity between Elizabeth Bathory and Gilles de Rais (see French Vampire Practice) who lived a couple of centuries before her. Bathory was lesbian; de Rais was homosexual. Bathory was highly aristocratic, as was de Rais. And all Bathory's servants colluded with her in her blood-bath, as did the servants of de Rais.

Bathory's psychotic mania was connected with her own beauty. She believed that the blood of virgins (or if not that, the blood of young women in general) would act as an excellent skin conditioner and she literally bathed in their blood. But

> on December 30th, 1610, Count Gyorsy Thurzo, her own cousin, the governor of the province, accompanied by soldiers, gendarmes and the village priest, raided the castle and arrested everybody in it. They had interrupted an orgy of blood. In the main hall of the castle they found one girl drained of blood and dead, another living girl whose body had been pierced with tiny holes, another who had just been tortured. In the dungeons and cellars they found and liberated a number of other girls, some of whose bodies had already been pierced and 'milked', others intact, plump, well-fed, like well-kept cattle in their stalls. The dead bodies of some fifty more were subsequently exhumed.†

* From *The Vampire* by Ornella Volta (Tandem, 1965).
† From *Witchcraft* by William Seabrook (Sphere, 1970).

The trial was held at Bitcse in 1611. The Countess refused to attend. Her servants were put to death and the Countess's life hung in the balance. Finally King Matthias II of Hungary commuted her sentence to life imprisonment, walled up in her own castle.

The Hungarian Soldier

About fifteen years ago a soldier who was billeted at the house of a Haidamaque peasant, on the frontiers of Hungary, as he was one day sitting at table near his host, the master of the house, saw a person he did not know come in and sit down to table also with them. The master of the house was strangely frightened at this, as were the rest of the company. The soldier knew not what to think of it, being ignorant of the matter in question. But the master of the house being dead the very next day, the soldier inquired what it meant. They told him it was the body of the father of the host, who had been dead and buried for ten years, who had thus come to sit down next to him, and had announced and caused his death.

The soldier informed the regiment of it in the first place, and the regiment gave notice of it to the general officers, who commissioned the Count de Cabreras, captain of the regiment of Alandetti infantry, to make information concerning this circumstance. Having gone to the place with some other officers, a surgeon and an auditor, they heard the depositions of all the people belonging to the house, who decided unanimously that the ghost was the father of the master of the house, and that all the soldier had said and reported was the exact truth, which was confirmed by all the inhabitants of the village.

In consequence of this the corpse of the spectre was exhumed and found to be like that of a man who had just expired, and his blood like that of a living man. The Count de Cabreras had his head cut off and caused him to be laid again in the tomb. He also took information concerning other similar ghosts: among others, of a man dead more than thirty years who had come back three times to his house at meal-time. The first time he had sucked the blood from the neck of his own brother, the second time from one of his sons, and the third time from one of the servants in the house; and all three died of it instantly and on the spot. Upon this deposition the commissary had this man taken out of his grave, and finding that, like the first, his blood was in a fluidic state like that of a living person, he ordered them to run a large nail into his temple and then to lay him again in the grave.

He caused a third to be burned who had been buried more than sixteen years and had sucked the blood and caused the death of two of his sons. The commissary having made his report to the general officers, was deputed to the Emperor, who commanded that some officers both of war and of justice, some physicians and surgeons and some learned men should be sent to examine the causes of these extraordinary events. The person who related these particulars to us had heard them from the Count de Cabreras at Friborg in 1730. (Calmet)

Protection against Hungarian Vampires

At the beginning of the eighteenth century the Bishop of Olmutz, unable to bear the total ineffectiveness of the authorities, ordered a series of detailed vampire investigations. As a result the superstition intensified, for the Bishop chose to accept fully the evidence that was put before him. Here is an extract from one of his commissioned reports, published at Naples in 1744.

> The ministers received exact information and, forming a juridical assembly, pronounced a final sentence against the so-called Vampire, by which, according to all due forms, it was solemnly and legally decreed that the public Executioner should go to the place where the vampire was, open the tomb, and with a saw or long sword, and in sight of all the public spectators, should cut off the vampire's head and then open his chest with a lance and transfix the vampire's heart with an iron stake, striking through the breast, and then closing the tomb again. In this way, the Cardinal told me, the Vampire would cease to appear, while many others who had not yet been judged or executed were still appearing and producing calamitous results like the first. But what was worth noticing, and marvelling at, according to the same author, was that many of these adjudged vampires were found full of colour, rosy-cheeked, eyes open and full of living blood, as though they were actually alive and in good health, so that when they were struck with a lance, as sentence was being inflicted upon them, they uttered a horrifying shriek, and a copious stream of blood shot out from their chest that not only filled the grave but spurted outside and soaked the nearby ground.

Pope Benedict XIV read the report with 'pleasure and admiration', which illustrates the collusion of the Church in this field.

Polish Vampire Practice

Public records of 1693 and 1694 give a detailed description of vampire sightings during that period. The activity of the Polish and the Russian vampires differs slightly from that of the vampires of Eastern Europe, who emerge from their tombs after midnight and retire before dawn. But in Poland and Russia the vampires emerge only between midday and midnight. They have enormous thirsts and drink the blood of men and animals in such vast quantities that it continuously pours down their mouths. They float in blood in their coffins and are so hungry that they consume their winding sheets as a matter of course.

Protection against Polish Vampires

The only efficient method of eliminating the Polish vampire is to pierce its heart or cut off its head. When slaughtered a great deal of blood pours from this voracious vampire, which is mixed with flour and made into bread. If this bread is eaten then one is free from vampire persecution. Preventive treatment includes burying the body with a cross made of willow under its armpits, chin and chest, or burying it face downwards, well covered by earth.

Rumanian Vampire Practice

> There was once a time when Vampires were as common as blades of grass, or berries in a pail, and they never kept still, but wandered round at night among the people.
>
> *Old Folk Tale*

> In Rumania the vampire tradition extends back far into the centuries, and there is perhaps no supernatural belief which is so strongly prevalent both in city and market-town as in the villages and remoter country districts. Moreover the tradition is amplified and complicated by local legends and peculiarly romantic ideas of rustic fancy, which often proves poetical enough and not without a certain macabre beauty, but often exhibits itself as materially gross and saturnine. It is hardly too much to say that in Rumania we find gathered together around

> the Vampire almost all the beliefs and superstitions that prevail throughout the whole of Eastern Europe. Although a certain species of vampire may tend to merge into a mere mythical imagination (the *vârcolac*), and again although he may be at times identified with the witch who in her turn is frequently no more than the *baba* or wise woman of some hamlet, yet when he preserves his own horrid qualities he is a being much dreaded and feared throughout the whole country even at the present day.*

The Rumanian peasant mind believed that, after death, the soul was not finally separated from the body and could not enter Paradise until forty days had passed. So naturally, should the deceased have pretensions to vampirism, this period is one of extreme anxiety. As in Greece, all bodies were exhumed three years after death to ensure that the corpse was putrified and the spirit had ascended.

There are many categories of people who might become vampires in Rumania, some of which are as follows:

1. The suicide.
2. The witch.
3. An unbaptised child (will become vampiristic after seven years have passed and the spot where it was buried will become unhallowed ground).
4. Perjurers or those who bear false witness.
5. A seventh son. This curious idea is in complete contradiction to the Gaelic belief in the seventh son being a symbol of good luck and accredited with powers of healing. However in Rumania the seventh son is definitely a bad omen. This may well have some connection with the idea that offerings to the dead had to be seven in number or a multiple of seven.
6. A man born with a caul (another contradiction to a normally lucky affliction).
7. 'If a vampire cast his cold grey eyes upon a pregnant woman, especially if she be past her sixth month, and the spell be not undone by the blessing of the Church, the child she carries will become a vampire. If a pregnant woman does

* Montague Summers, *The Vampire in Europe.*

not take sick she is big with vampire.' (Montague Summers, *The Vampire in Europe.*)

8. Should a cat jump over a corpse, a nun step over the corpse, or the shadow of a living man fall over the corpse, then that corpse will assuredly become a vampire.

In addition the Rumanians believed that some people are doomed to become vampires and are unable to escape their destiny. According to Summers, whilst they sleep the soul escapes from the mouth in the form of a fly.

> In the account of a trial for witchcraft at Mühlback in the year 1746 it appeared that a woman had engaged two men to work in her vineyard. About noon all took the usual repose from the heat of the day. After an hour had passed the labourers got up and tried to wake the woman so that they might duly proceed to work. However, she was stretched out motionless and stark with her mouth wide open. Towards eventide when the sun was setting they returned but she still lay inert, scarce seeming to breathe, as though she were dead. Just then a large fly buzzed past and this was caught by one of the men who put it in his leather pouch. Then they again endeavoured to wake the woman but without success. Afterwards they released the fly which flew straight into the woman's mouth and she instantly awoke. Upon seeing this the men could no further doubt that she was indeed a witch.

This soul-slipping belief was widespread, occurring in Serbia (the soul of a sleeping witch leaves her body in the shape of a butterfly), in Transylvania (where the soul of a child slips out in the shape of a mouse), in East India (as a cricket), in Germany (as a white or red mouse), and in Scotland (as a bee).

There are three main types of vampire in Rumania:

1. Dead Vampire Type (*Stigoi*).

A re-animated corpse, made live again by the return of the soul.

2. Live Vampire Type (*Moroii*).

People who will become vampires after death are able, in life, to send out their souls and bodies, to meet with reanimated corpses (the Dead Vampire Type).

3. Mythical Vampire Type (*Vârcolaci*).

Called the *vârcolac*, this mystical vampire eats the sun and the moon and is thus able to cause eclipses. Two definitions, the first from Ciauşanu's *Superstitüle poporului Român* and the second from Otescu's *Beliefs of the Roumanian Peasant Concerning the Sky and the Stars*, romantically illustrate the activities of the *vârcolac*.

> In Valcea there are said to be beings who are called *vârcolaci*, because their spirit is *vârcolaci*. They are recognized by their pale faces and dry skin, and by the deep sleep into which they fall when they go to the moon to eat it. But they eat it only during an eclipse, and when the disc of the moon is red or copper-coloured. The redness is the blood of the moon, escaping from the mouths of the *vârcolaci* and spreading over the moon.
>
> When the spirit of the *vârcolaci* wants to eat the moon, the man to whom the spirit belongs begins to nod, falls into a deep sleep as if he had not slept for weeks, and remains as if dead. If he is roused or moved sleep becomes eternal, for, when the spirit returns from its journey, it cannot find the mouth out of which it came, and so cannot go in again...
>
> Some say that God orders the *vârcolaci* to eat the moon so that men may repent and turn from evil.

Vârcolaci are supposed to be different from any beings on the earth. They cause eclipses of the moon, and even of the sun, by mounting up to heaven and eating the moon or sun. Some think that they are animals smaller than dogs. Others that they are dogs, two in number ... They have different origins; some say that they are the souls of unbaptized children, or of children of unmarried parents, cursed by God and turned into *vârcolaci*.... Others again say that *vârcolaci* originate from the air of heaven, when women spin at night, especially at midnight, without a candle, particularly if they cast spells with the thread they spin. Hence it is never good to spin by moonlight, for vampires and *vârcolaci* get up to the sky by the thread and eat the sun and the moon. They fasten themselves to the thread, and the thread makes itself into a road for them. As long as the thread does not break the *vârcolaci* have power, and can go wherever they wish. They attack the heavenly bodies, they bite the moon, so that she appears covered with blood, or till none of her is left. But if the thread is broken their power is broken and they go to another part of the sky...

In Rumania both 'live vampires' and 'dead vampires' indulge in a unique form of witchcraft. 'Live vampires' meet 'dead vampires' on certain nights in forgotten cemeteries or in some forest depths. There, the 'live vampires' learn from their dead compatriots the runes of black magic. As a result the 'live vampires' form covens —in the true tradition of witchcraft. In Mihalcea the vampires were chiefly supposed to be women—witch-women who could control the power of both animals and objects for their own ulterior motives. Normally this power was used for selfish but non-malicious ends. Vampire witches were able to make their hens plump and prolific egg-layers; they were able to draw vitality from bees and fowls, and they were even able to bake better and lighter bread than their neighbours.

Endless superstitions clung around the vampire-witches. They were able to control the rain, to sell the power of beauty, and to assume animals' shapes. Their influence over climatic conditions was of vital importance—and landowners would compel their employees to bathe in the river, hoping that there might be a vampire amongst them, because when a vampire washes, rain quickly follows.

Here are two stories which illustrate the Rumanian vampire's activities. The first is a beautiful and strangely haunting folk tale:

> There was an old woman in a village. And grown-up maidens met and span, and made a 'bee'. And the young sparks came and laid hold of the girls, and pulled them about and kissed them. But one girl had no sweetheart to lay hold of her and kiss her. And she was a strapping lass, the daughter of wealthy parents; but for three whole days no one came near her. And she looked at the big girls, her comrades. And no one troubled himself with her. Yet she was a pretty girl, a prettier was not to be found. Then came a fine young spark, and took her in his arms and kissed her, and stayed with her until cock-crow. And when the cock crowed at dawn he departed. The old woman saw he had cock's feet. And she kept looking at the lad's feet, and she said, 'Nita, my lass, did you see anything?'
>
> 'I didn't notice.'
>
> 'Then didn't I see he had cock's feet?'
>
> 'Let be, mother, I didn't see it.'

And the girl went home and slept; and she arose and went off to the spinning, where many more girls were holding a 'bee'. And the young sparks came, and took each one his sweetheart. And they kissed them, and stayed a while, and went home. And the girl's handsome young spark came and took her in his arms and kissed her and pulled her about, and stayed with her till midnight. And the cock began to crow. The young spark heard the cock crowing, and departed. Then said the old woman who was in the hut, 'Nita, did you notice that he had horse's hoofs?'

'And if he had, I didn't see.'

Then the girl departed to her home. And she slept and arose in the morning, and did her work that she had to do. And night came, and she took her spindle and went to the old woman in the hut. And the other girls came, and the young sparks came, and each laid hold of his sweetheart. But the pretty girl looked at them. Then the young sparks gave over and departed home. And only the girl remained neither a long time nor a short time. Then came the girl's young spark. Then what was the girl to do? She took heed, and stuck a needle and thread in his back. And he departed when the cock crew, and she knew not where he had gone. Then the girl arose in the morning and took the thread, and followed up the thread, and saw him in a grave where he was sitting. Then the girl trembled and went back home. At night the young spark that was in the grave came to the old woman's house and saw that the girl was not there. He asked the old woman, 'Where's Nita?'

'She has not come.'

Then he went to Nita's house, where she lived, and called, 'Nita, are you at home?'

Nita answered, 'I am.'

'Tell me what you saw when you came to the church. For if you don't tell me I will kill your father.'

'I didn't see anything.'

Then he looked, and he killed her father, and departed to his grave.

Next night he came back. 'Nita, tell me what you saw.'

'I didn't see anything.'

'Tell me, or I will kill your mother, as I killed your father. Tell me what you saw.'

'I didn't see anything.'

Then he killed her mother, and departed to his grave.

Then the girl arose in the morning. And she had twelve servants. And she said to them, 'See, I have much money and many oxen and many sheep; and they shall come to the twelve of you as a gift, for I shall die tonight. And it will fare ill with you if you bury me not in the forest at the foot of an apple-tree.'

At night came the young spark from the grave and asked, 'Nita, are you at home?'

'I am.'

'Tell me, Nita, what you saw three days ago, or I will kill you, as I killed your parents.'

'I have nothing to tell you.'

Then he took and killed her. Then, casting a look, he departed to his grave.

So the servants, when they arose in the morning, found Nita dead. The servants took her and laid her out decently. They sat and made a hole in the wall and passed her through the hole, and carried her, as she had bidden, and buried her in the forest by the apple-tree.

And half a year passed by, and a prince went to go and course hares with greyhounds and other dogs. And he went to hunt, and the hounds ranged the forest and came to the maiden's grave. And a flower grew out of it, the like of which for beauty there was not in the whole kingdom. So the hounds came on her monument, where she was buried, and they began to bark and scratched at the maiden's grave. Then the prince took and called the dogs with his horn, and the dogs came not. The prince said, 'Go quickly thither.'

Four huntsmen arose and came and saw the flower burning like a candle. They returned to the prince, and he asked them, 'What is it?'

'It is a flower, the like was never seen.'

Then the lad heard, and came to the maiden's grave, and saw the flower and plucked it. And he came home and showed it to his father and mother. Then he took and put it in a vase at his bed-head where he slept. Then the flower arose from the vase and turned a somersault, and became a full-grown maiden. And she took the lad and kissed him, and bit him and pulled him about, and slept with him in her arms, and put her hand under his head. And he knew it not. When the dawn came she became a flower again.

In the morning the lad rose up sick, and complained to his father and mother, 'Mammy, my shoulders hurt me, and my head hurts me.'

His mother went and brought a wise woman who tended him. He asked for something to eat and drink. And he waited a bit, and then went to his business that he had to do. And he went home again at night. And he ate and drank and lay down on his couch, and sleep seized him. Then the flower arose and again became a full-grown maiden. And she took him again in her arms, and slept with him, and sat with him in her arms. And he slept. And she went back to the vase. And he arose, and his bones hurt him, and he told his mother and his father. Then his father said to his wife, 'It began with the coming of the flower. Something must be the matter, for the boy is quite ill. Let us watch tonight, and post ourselves on one side, and see who comes to our son.'

Night came, and the prince laid himself in his bed to sleep. Then the maiden arose from the vase, and became there was never anything more fair—as burns the flame of a candle. And his mother and his father, the king, saw the maiden, and laid hands on her. Then the prince arose out of his sleep, and saw the maiden, that she was fair. Then he took her in his arms and kissed her, and lay down in his bed, and slept till day.

And they made a marriage and ate and drank. The folk marvelled, for a being so fair as that maiden was not to be found in all the realm. And he dwelt with her half a year, and she bore a golden boy, two apples in his hand. And it pleased the prince well.

Then her old sweetheart heard it, the vampire who had made love to her, and had killed her. He arose and came to her and asked her, 'Nita, tell me, what did you see me doing?'

'I didn't see anything.'

'Tell me truly, or I will kill your child, your little boy, as I killed your father and mother. Tell me truly.'

'I have nothing to tell you.'

And he killed her boy. And she arose and carried him to the church and buried him.

At night the vampire came again and asked her, 'Tell me, Nita, what you saw.'

'I didn't see anything.'

'Tell me, or I will kill the lord whom you have wedded.'

Then Nita arose and said, 'It shall not happen that you kill my lord. God send you burst.'

The vampire heard what Nita said, and burst. Ay, he died, and burst for very rage. In the morning Nita arose and saw the floor swimming two hand's-breadth deep in blood. Then Nita bade her father-in-law take out the vampire's heart with all speed. Her father-in-law, the king, hearkened, and opened him and took out his heart, and gave it into Nita's hand. And she went to the grave of her boy and dug the boy up, applied the heart, and the boy arose. And Nita went to her father and to her mother, and anointed them with the blood, and they arose. Then, looking on them, Nita told all the troubles she had borne, and what she had suffered at the hands of the vampire.

Another, better-documented account comes from Dr Tudor Panfile, a Rumanian scholar, who published many vampire legends in *Ion Creanda*, a magazine devoted to peasant culture.

Some twenty or thirty years ago (from 1914) in the commune Afumati in Dolj, a certain peasant, Mărin Mirea Ociscisc, died. It was noticed that his relations also died, one after the other. A certain Badea Vrajitor (Badea the wizard) dug him up. Badea himself, going later into the forest up to the frontier on a cold wintry night, was eaten by wolves. The bones of Mărin were sprinkled with wine, a church service read over them, and replaced in the grave. From that time there were no more deaths in the family.

Some fifteen years ago, in Amărăsti, in the north of Dolj, an old woman, the mother of the peasant Dinu Gheorghiţa, died. After some months the children of her eldest son began to die, one after the other, and, after that, the children of her youngest son. The sons became anxious, dug her up one night, cut her in two, and buried her again. Still the deaths did not cease. They dug her up a second time, and what did they see? The body was whole without a wound. It was a great marvel. They took her and carried her into the forest, and put her under a great tree in a remote part of the forest. There they disembowelled her, took out her heart, from which blood was flowing, cut it in four, put it on hot cinders, and burnt it. They took the ashes and gave them to children to drink with water. They threw the body on the fire, burnt it, and buried the ashes of the body. Then the deaths ceased.

Some twenty or thirty years ago, a cripple, an unmarried man, of Cuşmir, in the south of Mehedinţi, died. A little time after, his relations began to die, or to fall ill. They complained that a leg was drying up. This happened in several places. What could it be? 'Perhaps it is the cripple; let us dig him up.' They dug him up one Saturday night, and found him as red as red, and all drawn up into a corner of the grave. They cut him open, and took the customary measures. They took out the heart and liver, burnt them on red-hot cinders, and gave the ashes to his sister and other relations, who were ill. They drank them with water, and regained their health.

In the Cuşmir, another family began to show very frequent deaths, and suspicion fell on a certain old man, dead long ago. When they dug him up, they found him sitting up like a Turk, and as red as red, just like fire; for had he not eaten up nearly the whole of a family of strong, young men. When they tried to get him out he resisted, unclean and horrible. They gave him some blows with an axe, they got him out, but they could not cut him with a knife. They took a scythe and an axe, cut out his heart and liver, burnt them, and gave them to the sick folk to drink. They drank, and regained their health. The old man was re-buried, and the deaths ceased.

Protection against Rumanian Vampires

It was essential that in all circumstances heavy precautions should be taken at burials of suspected vampires. These were roughly the same as those of the rest of Eastern Europe, as follows:

1. At one blow a stake must be driven through the heart or navel.
2. Small stones or grains of incense must be placed in all the extremities so that the vampire would have something to nibble on awakening—thus diverting his attention from more succulent fare.
3. Garlic must be stuffed in his mouth.
4. As another delaying factor millet must be scattered over the vampire's body, as the vampire delays his exit from the tomb until each grain of millet has been eaten or counted.
5. The corpse has to be buried face downwards.
6. Wild, thorny roses must be strung around the outside of the coffin in order to impede the vampire's progress out of the tomb.

These, however, were only the minimum general precautions and more intricate prevention differed from district to district:

a Zârneşti

Iron forks were driven through the heart, eyes and breast of an exhumed female vampire. Then the grave was considerably deepened and the corpse buried face downwards.

b Romanati

In this district the suspected vampire is put naked into a bag. Meanwhile both clothes and artifacts are sprinkled with holy water and returned to the coffin. Then the body is taken away to a remote place, is hacked into sections and cast on to a fire on which every scrap of flesh and bone must be incinerated—lest a scrap be left and a vampire rise from it.

Vampire detection in a churchyard was normally done with the use of a white stallion who was led to the cemetery and led over each grave. If he failed to pass over one, then this was without doubt the vampire's tomb.

The calendar is very relevant to vampirism in Rumania—as indeed it is in the rest of Eastern Europe. Vampires are particularly in season on St Andrew's Eve and on St George's Eve. On these two nights rebellious witches, vampires, warlocks and evil-doers are at their most outrageous and between the twelfth and the seventeenth century the Rumanians protected themselves by lighting bonfires, tolling the church bells, garlanding their houses with flowers, garlic and thistles, hanging the cattle-stalls with roses and putting tar crosses on doors. The happenings on the Eves of St Andrew and St George were a remarkable example of pagan and Christian influence merging. The powers of darkness were abroad and were clamouring at the doors—at a time when the powers of goodness and sainthood were believed to be at their lowest.

Russian Vampire Practice

The dread of the undead—the deceased returning from the grave—has always been very great in the vast and primitive wastes of Russia. Familiar, traditional precautions after funerals were strictly observed. Masks were worn by the mourners, devious routes were taken on the return home and no one looked back.

W. R. S. Ralston writes in his *Russian Folk Tales* (1873):

> The districts of the Russian Empire in which a belief in vampires mostly prevails are White Russia and the Ukraine. But the ghastly blood-sucker, the *Upir*, whose name has become naturalized in so many alien lands under forms resembling our 'Vampire', disturbs the peasant-mind in many other parts of

Russia, though not perhaps with the same intense fear which it spreads among the inhabitants of the above-named districts, or of some other Slavonic lands. The numerous traditions which have gathered around the original idea vary to some extent according to the locality, but they are never radically inconsistent.

Some of the details are curious. The Little-Russians hold that if a vampire's hands have grown numb from remaining long crossed in the grave, he makes use of his teeth, which are like steel. When he has gnawed away with these through all obstacles, he first destroys the babes he finds in a house, and then the older inmates.

The Kashoubes say that when a *Vieszcy*, as they call the Vampire, wakes from his sleep within the grave, he begins to gnaw his hands and feet; and as he gnaws, one after another, first his relations, then his other neighbours, sicken and die. When he has finished his own store of flesh, he rises at midnight and destroys cattle, or climbs a belfry and sounds the bell. All who hear the ill-omened tones will soon die. But generally he sucks the blood of sleepers. Those on whom he has operated will be found next morning dead, with a very small wound on the left side of the breast, exactly over the heart. The Lusatian Wends hold that when a corpse chews its shroud or sucks its own breast, all its kin will soon follow it to the grave. The Wallachians say that a *murony*—a sort of cross between a werewolf and a vampire, connected by name with our nightmare—can take the form of a dog, a cat, or a toad, and also of any blood-sucking insect. When he is exhumed, he is found to have long nails of recent growth on his hands and feet, and blood is streaming from his eyes, ears, nose and mouth.

Russian vampires (called *Vieszcy* or *Upierczi*), like Polish vampires, have the odd trick of appearing from noon to midnight only. Apart from the more traditional activities mentioned above, the vampire also has mythical attributes—such as heart-devouring. A hero, if touched by an aspen or another twig credited with magical properties, will awake with the heart of a hare and remain a coward for the rest of his life. Other mischievous vampiristic traits included giving inoffensive peasants cocks' hearts, resulting in a crowing obsession.

Many Russian legends about vampires have been passed on from generation to generation, and two are recounted here.

1. *Documented by Madame Blavatsky in* Isis Unveiled (1910)

About the beginning of the nineteenth century there occurred in Russia one of the most frightful cases of vampirism on record. The governor of the province of Tch— was a man of about sixty years of age, of a cruel and jealous disposition. Clothed with despotic authority, he exercised it without stint, as his brutal instincts prompted. He fell in love with the pretty daughter of a subordinate officer. Although the girl was betrothed to a young man whom she loved, the tyrant forced her father to consent to his having her marry him; and the poor victim, despite her despair, became his wife. His jealous disposition soon exhibited itself. He beat her, confined her to her room for weeks together, and prevented her seeing anyone except in his presence. He finally fell sick and died. Finding his end approaching, he made her swear never to marry again, and with fearful oaths threatened that if she did he would return from his grave and kill her. He was buried in the cemetery across the river, and the young widow experienced no further annoyance until, getting the better of her fears, she listened to the importunities of her former lover, and they were again betrothed.

On the night of the customary betrothal feast, when all had retired, the old mansion was aroused by shrieks proceeding from her room. The doors were burst open, and the unhappy woman was found lying on her bed in a swoon. At the same time a carriage was heard rumbling out of the courtyard. Her body was found to be black and blue in places, as from the effects of pinches, and from a slight puncture in her neck drops of blood were oozing. Upon recovering, she stated that her deceased husband had suddenly entered her room, appearing exactly as in life, with the exception of a dreadful pallor; that he had upbraided her for her inconstancy, and then beaten and pinched her most cruelly. Her story was disbelieved; but the next morning the guard stationed at the other end of the bridge which spans the river reported that just before midnight a black coach-and-six had driven furiously past without answering their challenge.

The new governor, who disbelieved the story of the apparition, took nevertheless the precaution of doubling the guards across the bridge. The same thing happened, however, night after night, the soldiers declaring that the toll-bar at their station near the bridge would rise of itself, and the spectral equipage would sweep past them, despite their efforts to stop it. At the same time every night the watchers, including the widow's family and the servants, would be thrown into a heavy sleep; and every morning the young victim would be found bruised, bleeding, and swooning as before. The town was thrown into consternation. The physicians had no explanations to offer; priests came to pass the night in prayer, but as midnight approached, all would be seized with the same terrible lethargy. Finally the archbishop of the province came and performed the ceremony of exorcism in person. On the following morning the governor's widow was found worse than ever. She was now brought to death's door.

The governor was finally driven to take the severest measures to stop the ever-increasing panic in the town. He stationed fifty Cossacks along the bridge, with orders to stop the spectral carriage at all hazards. Promptly at the usual hour it was heard and seen approaching from the direction of the cemetery. The officer of the guard and a priest bearing a crucifix planted themselves in front of the toll-bar and together shouted: 'In the name of God and the Czar, who goes there?' Out of the coach was thrust a well-remembered head, and a familiar voice responded: 'The Privy Councillor of State and Governor C— !' At the same moment the officer, the priest, and the soldiers were flung aside, as by an electric shock, and the ghostly equipage passed them before they could recover breath.

The archbishop then resolved as a last expedient to resort to the time-honoured plan of exhuming the body and driving an oaken stake through its heart. This was done with great religious ceremony in the presence of the whole populace. The story is that the body was found gorged with blood, and with red cheeks and lips. At the instant that the first blow was struck upon the stake a groan issued from the corpse and a jet of blood spouted high into the air. The archbishop pronounced the usual exorcism, the body was reinterred, and from that time no more was heard of the vampire.

2. *Documented by Ralston in* Russian Folk Tales

A certain soldier was allowed to go home on furlough. Well, he walked and walked, and after a time he began to draw near to his native village. Not far off from that village lived a miller in his mill. In old times the soldier had been very intimate with him: why shouldn't he go and see his friend? He went. The miller received him cordially, and at once brought out liquor; and the two began drinking, and chattering about their ways and doings. All this took place towards nightfall, and the soldier stopped so long at the miller's that it grew quite dark.

When he proposed to start for his village, his host exclaimed:

'Spend the night here, trooper! It's very late now, and perhaps you might run into mischief.'

'How so?'

'God is punishing us! A terrible warlock has died among us, and by night he rises from his grave, wanders through the village, and does such things as bring fear upon the very boldest! How could even you help being afraid of him?'

'Not a bit of it! A soldier is a man who belongs to the crown, and "crown property cannot be drowned in water nor burnt in fire". I'll be off: I'm tremendously anxious to see my people as soon as possible.'

Off he set. His road lay in front of a graveyard. On one of the graves he saw a great fire blazing. 'What's that?' thinks he. 'Let's have a look.' When he drew near, he saw that the warlock was sitting by the fire, sewing boots.

'Hail, brother!' called out the soldier.

The warlock looked up and said:

'What have you come here for?'

'Why, I wanted to see what you're doing.'

The warlock threw his work aside and invited the soldier to a wedding.

'Come along, brother,' says he, 'let's enjoy ourselves. There's a wedding going on in the village.'

'Come along!' says the soldier.

They came to where the wedding was; there they were given drink, and treated with the utmost hospitality. The warlock drank and drank, revelled and revelled, and then grew angry. He chased all the guests and relatives out of the house, threw the wedded pair into a slumber, took out two phials and an awl, pierced the hands of the bride and bridegroom with the awl, and began drawing off their blood. Having done this, he said to the soldier:

'Now let's be off.'

Well, they went off. On the way the soldier said:

'Tell me; why did you draw off their blood in those phials?'

'Why, in order that the bride and bridegroom might die. To-morrow morning no-one will be able to wake them. I alone know how to bring them back to life.'

'How's that managed?'

'The bride and bridegroom must have cuts made in their heels, and some of their own blood must then be poured back into those wounds. I've got the bridegroom's blood stowed away in my right-hand pocket, and the bride's in my left.'

The soldier listened to this without letting a single word escape him. Then the warlock began boasting again.

'Whatever I wish,' says he, 'that I can do!'

'I suppose it's quite impossible to get the better of you?' said the soldier.

'Why impossible? If anyone were to make a pyre of aspen boughs, a hundred loads of them, and were to burn me on that pyre, then he'd be able to get the better of me. Only he'd have to look out sharp in burning me; for snakes and worms and different kinds of reptiles would creep out of my inside, and crows and magpies and jackdaws would come flying up. All these must be caught and flung on the pyre. If so much as a single maggot were to escape, then there'd be no help for it; in that maggot I should slip away!'

The soldier listened to all this and did not forget it. He and the warlock talked and talked, and at last they arrived at the grave.

'Well, brother,' said the warlock, 'now I'll tear you to pieces. Otherwise you'd be telling all this.'

'What are you talking about? Don't you deceive yourself; I serve God and the Emperor.'

The warlock gnashed his teeth, howled aloud, and sprang at the soldier—who drew his sword and began laying about him with sweeping blows. They struggled and struggled; the soldier was all but at the end of his strength. 'Ah!' thinks he, 'I'm a lost man—and all for nothing!' Suddenly the cocks began to crow. The warlock fell lifeless to the ground.

The soldier took the phials of blood out of the warlock's pockets, and went on to the house of his own people. When he had got there, and had exchanged greetings with his relatives, they said:

'Did you see any disturbance, soldier?'

'No, I saw none.'

'There now! Why, we've a terrible piece of work going on in the village. A warlock has taken to haunting it!'

After talking awhile, they lay down to sleep. Next morning the soldier awoke, and began asking:

'I'm told you've got a wedding going on somewhere here?'

'There was a wedding in the house of a rich *moujik*,' replied his relatives, 'but the bride and bridegroom have died this very night—what from, nobody knows.'

'Where does this *moujik* live?'

They showed him the house. Thither he went without speaking a word. When he got there, he found the whole family in tears.

'What are you mourning about?' said he.

'Such and such is the state of things, soldier,' said they.

'I can bring your young people to life again. What will you give me if I do?'

'Take what you like, even were it half of what we've got!'

The soldier did as the warlock had instructed him, and brought the young people back to life. Instead of weeping there began to be happiness and rejoicing; the soldier was hospitably treated and well rewarded. Then—left about, face. Off he marched to the Starosta, and told him to call the peasants together and to get ready a hundred loads of aspen wood. Well, they took the wood into the graveyard, dragged the warlock out of his grave, placed him on the pyre, and set it alight—the people all standing round in a circle with brooms, shovels, and fire-irons. The pyre became wrapped in flames, the warlock began to burn. His corpse burst, and out of it crept snakes, worms, and all sorts of reptiles, and up came flying crows, magpies, and jackdaws. The peasants knocked them down and flung them into the fire, not allowing so much as a single maggot to creep away! And so the warlock was thoroughly consumed, and the soldier collected his ashes and strewed them to the winds. From that time forth there was peace in the village.

The soldier received the thanks of the whole community. He stayed at home some time, enjoying himself thoroughly. Then he went back to the Tsar's service with money in his pocket. When he had served his time, he retired from the army, and began to live at his ease.

Both witches and wizards were feared after death. At midnight they were supposed to rise, hungry for the flesh of the watchers around the bier. To prevent this happening the supposed witch, wizard (or extreme sinner) was manacled in his coffin by means of steel bands, and scriptures were read over him all night. A magic circle was drawn on the door in which the reader would stand, clutching in one hand a sledgehammer which symbolised the weapon of the thunder-god. Dudley Wright, in his book *Vampires and Vampirism*, draws this old tale from the records of the Kharkov Government:

Once, in the days of old, there died a terrible sinner. His body was taken into the church, and the sacristan was told to read psalms over him. The sacristan took the precaution to catch a cock, and carry it with him. At midnight, when the dead man leapt from his coffin, opened his jaws wide, and rushed at his victim, the sacristan gave the bird a pinch. The cock uttered his usual crow, and at that very moment the dead man fell backwards to the ground a numb, motionless corpse.

Protection against Russian Vampires

The stake with which the vampire's corpse must be pierced should be driven in at a single blow—a repetition of the blow would soon prove fatal to the deliverer and would restore the vampire to life. It is interesting to note that this idea is often referred to in the Russian *shezki* and other Slavonic stories in which it is usual for the hero to be warned that he must strike a monster once—and once only. Other methods of vampire extermination include destruction by fire or execution with a gravedigger's shovel.

Yugoslavian Vampire Practice and Protection

The *dhampir*, an interesting vampire phenomenon, is not necessarily unique to this area but is basically of Serbian origin. *Dhampir* is the Serbian name for a vampire's son, and he has the advantage of being able to see his father—an advantage indeed as the true Serbian vampire is invisible to the mortal eye. However, popular tradition has it that the *dhampir* was far from faithful to his parent and was quite happy, in return for some kind of settlement, to exterminate father. Having arrived at the suspected haunt of his father or his father's brother or father's cousin the *dhampir* goes through a strange exorcism. Looking at the sky, the *dhampir* blows his nose and closely observes the four cardinal points. He then goes to a public meeting-place where an audience has gathered. They are looking forward to the show but at the same time they keep at a respectful distance from the *dhampir's* activities—for if one drop of blood splashes on them they will immediately go mad and die. The ritual begins with the traitorous *dhampir* making contact with his unfortunate relative. Ornella Volta, in her book *The Vampire*, explains the ritual as follows:

> The *dhampir* begins to whistle like a hunter, then behaves as though he were seeing someone with difficulty through a fog, and he plays hide and seek behind various objects, and takes off his clothes, remaining in his underwear and looking through the sleeves of his shirt as though it were a telescope. The onlookers ask him what form the vampire has assumed and he either answers 'It is human' or 'It is a serpent' (or a chicken, or something of the kind). Then, the *dhampir* begins a true and proper hand-to-hand fight with the vampire, struggling against the invisible enemy, hitting it and writhing as though he were tearing it to pieces, and finally emitting a long, curious whistle, to express his satisfaction at having k.o.'d the vampire, and exclaiming 'I have killed it'. Lately, however, *dhampirs* prefer using a gun to bodily struggling with the vampire.

This incredible piece of showmanship was practised, to great financial advantage, throughout Serbian countries, and the last known *dhampir* activity was recorded in 1959 at Vrbrica, a village in the province of Kosovo-Metohija. Payments the *dhampir* has been known to accept include oxen, a cow, buffalo, a trousseau of clothes or a fee of between a thousand and one thousand eight hundred dinars.

A more disturbing and serious example of mass vampire hysteria occurred in the strange case of Arnold Paole, a dangerous vampire whose extermination warranted a delegation from Belgrade (on the orders of Charles VI) which was composed of both soldiers and civic dignitaries. The expedition was commanded by Charles Alexander of Würtemberg, who was Governor of the kingdom of Serbia. In all twelve hundred people came to Meduegna (Paole's village) to deal with the outbreak. This is probably the most detailed and best-attested vampire history of all time, and it was signed, in January 1732, by three army surgeons, a lieutenant-colonel and a sub-lieutenant. The legend is recounted in *The History of Magic* by Ennemoser.

> In the spring of 1727 there returned from service in the Levant to his native village Meduegna, a young man named Arnold Paole, who although he had seen military service but a few years

had, according to his own accounts, met with many and varied adventures in that part of the world, a career which afforded him opportunity to save enough to purchase a good cottage and an acre or two of land in his native place, whence he was determined not to stir for the remainder of his days. It appeared a little remarkable to some that a man in the early prime of life, far from ill-looking, one who must have seen the rough as well as the smooth and companied with many a good fellow, should settle down so early in a quiet and out-of-the-way village. Yet his scrupulous honesty in all business transactions, his disciplined habits of work, his steady conduct, soon showed that the adventures with which he must have met in his travels had not, as is only too often the case with young soldiers, affected his probity and self-control. Nevertheless some noticed a certain uneasiness, a certain strangeness in his manner, which gave them food for suspicions, although they could not exactly tell whither these suspicions tended. It seemed as though he almost systematically avoided meeting Nina, the daughter of a rich farmer whose land ran along his own. And yet, as the gossips of the village said, what more equal match could there be? He was young; he had a decent property which in time would greatly improve; he had health, he was obviously of industrious habits, and he himself had been heard to declare that he had formed no connexions and had no ties in other lands.

As time passed on Arnold could not always avoid the society of his neighbours, and no surprise was felt when it was announced that he had been formally betrothed to Nina. And yet, as she often told her friends, the maiden felt that there was a shadow between them. At last she resolved to tackle him on the subject and she boldly asked what trouble so continuously oppressed him. After a while he consented to tell her, and having informed her that he was always haunted by the fear of an early death he related a strange adventure which had befallen him at Kostartsa near Granitsa whilst he was on active service. He said that in those parts of Greece the dead returned to torment the living. By some evil chance they had been stationed in a terribly haunted spot, and he had experienced the first visitation. Immediately he sought the unhallowed grave and executed summary vengeance upon the vampire. He had then, in spite of the persuasion of his superiors, sent in his resignation from the army, and had literally fled to his native village. It was true that so far he had experienced no ill effects, and he trusted that he might have been able to counteract the evil.

It so happened that during the harvest-home Arnold fell from the top of a loaded hay-wagon and was picked up insensible from the ground. They carried him to bed but he had evidently received some serious injury, for after lingering a short time he died. In a few days his body was laid to rest, as they thought, in the village churchyard.

About a month later, however, reports began to be circulated that Arnold had been seen wandering about the village after nightfall, and several persons, whose names are entered upon the official report, complained that they were haunted by him, and that after he had appeared to them they felt in a state of extraordinary debility. After only a short time several of these persons died, and something like a panic began to spread through the neighbourhood. As the dark winter nights approached no man dared to venture outside his doors when once dusk had fallen, yet it was whispered that the spectre was able easily to penetrate closed windows and walls, that no locks or bars could keep him out if he wished to enter. Throughout the whole winter the wretched village seems to have lived in a state of frantic terror and dismay. The evil, as we may well imagine, was aggravated by the cold hungry nights of a snow-tossed December and January. At length some ten weeks, or rather more, after his funeral it was resolved that the body of Arnold must be disinterred with a view to ascertaining whether he was indeed a vampire. The party consisted of two officers, military representatives from Belgrade, two army surgeons, *Unterfeldscherern*, a drummer boy who carried their cases of instruments, the authorities of the village, the old sexton and his assistants. Dr Mayo thus reconstructs the scene.

'It was early on a grey morning that the commission visited the quiet cemetery of Meduegna, which, surrounded with a wall of unhewn stone, lies sheltered by the mountains that, rising in undulating green slopes, irregularly planted with fruit trees, ends in an abrupt craggy ridge, feathered with underwood. The graves were, for the most part, neatly kept, with borders of box, or something like it, and flowers between; and at the head of most a small wooden cross, painted black, bearing the name of the tenants. Here and there a stone had been raised. One of considerable height, a single narrow slab, ornamented with grotesque Gothic carvings, dominated over the rest. Near this lay the grave of Arnold Paole, towards which the party moved. The work of throwing out the earth was begun by the bent crooked old sexton, who lived in the Leichenhaus beyond the great crucifix.

He seemed unconcerned enough.' But, as might well be supposed, the young drummer-boy was gazing intently, fascinated by horror and suspense. Before very long the coffin was rather roughly dragged out of the ground, and the grave-digger's assistant soon knocked off the lid. It was seen that the corpse had moved to one side, the jaws gaped wide open and the blue lips were moist with new blood which had trickled in a thin stream from a corner of the mouth. All unafraid, the old sexton caught the body and twisted it straight. 'So,' he cried, 'you have not wiped your mouth since last night's work.' Even the officers accustomed to the horrors of the battlefield and the surgeons accustomed to the horrors of the dissecting room shuddered at so hideous a spectacle. It is recorded that the drummer-boy swooned upon the spot. Nerving themselves to their awful work they inspected the remains more closely, and it was soon apparent that there lay before them the thing they dreaded—the vampire. He looked indeed, as if he had not been dead a day. On handling the corpse the scarfskin came off, and below there were new skin and new nails. Accordingly they scattered garlic over the remains and drove a stake through the body, which it is said gave a piercing shriek as the warm blood spouted out in a great crimson jet.

When this dreadful operation had been performed they proceeded to exhume the bodies of four others who had died in consequence of Arnold's attacks. The records give no details of the state in which these were found. They simply say that whitethorn stakes were driven through them and that they were all five burned. The ashes of all were replaced in consecrated ground.

It might have been thought that these measures would have put an end to vampirism in the village, but such unhappily was not the case, which shows that the original vampire at Kostartsa must have been of an exceptionally malignant nature. About half-a-dozen years after the body of Arnold Paole had been cremated the infection seems to have broken out afresh and several persons died apparently through loss of blood, their bodies being in a terribly anaemic and attenuated condition. This time the officials did not hesitate immediately to cope with the danger, and they determined to make a complete examination of all the graves in the cemetery to which any suspicion attached. Accordingly several surgeons of eminence were summoned from Belgrade and a very thorough investigation took place which yielded the most extraordinary results. The medical reports from which the following cases of vampirism are quoted were officially signed on 7 January, 1732, at Meduegna by three distinguished army surgeons, Johannes Flickinger, Isaac Siedel, and Johann Friedrich Baumgartner, and formally countersigned by the lieutenant-colonel and a sub-lieutenant then in residence at Belgrade.

The most remarkable examples were the following:

A woman by name Stana, twenty years of age, who had died three months before, after an illness which only lasted three days and which followed directly after her confinement. Upon her deathbed she confessed that she had anointed herself with the blood of a vampire to liberate herself from his persecutions. Nevertheless, she, as well as her baby, had died. The body of the child, owing to a hasty and careless interment, had been half scraped up and devoured by wolves. The body of the woman, Stana, was untouched by decomposition. When it was opened the chest was found to be full of fresh blood, the viscera had all the appearance of soundest health. The skin and nails of both hands and feet were loose and came off, but underneath was a clean new skin and nails.

A woman of the name of Miliza, who had died after an illness lasting three months. The body had been buried nearly one hundred days before. In the chest was liquid blood, and the bowels were sound and entirely healthy. The corpse was declared by a *heyduk* who recognized it to look better and to be far plumper than during life.

The body of a child eight years old, that had likewise been buried ninety days. It was in the vampire condition.

The son of a *heyduk* named Milloc, a lad some sixteen years old. The body had been buried ninety days; it was rosy and flabber, wholly in the vampire condition.

One Joachim, a boy of seventeen, who was likewise the son of a *heyduk*. He had died after a short illness of three days, and had lain buried for eight weeks and four days. His complexion was fresh, and the body unmistakably in the vampire condition.

A woman, named Ruscha. She had died after a sickness lasting ten days. She was buried six weeks before. New blood and warm was found in her chest and in *fundo uentriculi.*

A young girl ten years of age, who had died two months before. Her body was in the vampire condition, and when pierced with a stake a great quantity of hot blood poured forth and swilled the grave.

The wife of a villager named Hadnuck, who had been buried seven weeks before; and that of her babe, eight weeks old, who had lain interred only twenty-one days. It was remarked that these corpses although buried in the same ground and hard by the others were far gone in decomposition.

A serving-man, Rhade, who was twenty-three years old. He had ailed for some three months before his death, and the body which had been buried for five weeks was much tainted with corruption.

A woman and a child who had been buried five weeks, and whose bodies were entire, showing every trace of vampirism.

A *heyduk* named Stanko, a much-respected and important character in the village. He had died six weeks previously at the age of sixty. In the chest and abdomen there was found to be a quantity of rich new blood, and the whole body was in the vampire condition.

Millock, a *heyduk*, twenty-five years old. The body, which bore every trace of vampirism, had been in the earth six weeks.

Stanjoika, the wife of a *heyduk*, twenty years old. She died after a brief illness of three days and had been buried more than a fortnight before. Her face was full and florid; the limbs supple and without any cadaverous coldness. There was a quantity of new blood in her chest and in *uentriculo cordis*. The viscera were sound and healthy. The skin appeared fresh and comely as in life.

Western Europe

French Vampire Practice

France has a most prolific record of case-histories relating to vampirism and numbers amongst its 'living' vampires such monsters as Gilles de Rais (mass murderer), Martin Dummolard and Madame Lafayette (murderers on a more limited scale), Sergeant Bertrand (corpse-violator), Henri Blot (the same), the Marquis de Sade, Jean Grenier, the Papin sisters, and a host of others. All exhibited vampiristic symptoms, and together they exerted more evil influence and carnage than any of their more mythical Eastern European cousins.

Gilles de Rais

He would contemplate those who had the most beautiful heads or members and have their bodies cruelly opened so that he might take delight in the sight of their internal organs; and, very often, when the said children died, he would sit on their stomachs and take pleasure in seeing them thus die and laugh at them... after which he had them burnt and converted into dust.

(*Confessions of Gilles de Rais*, 1440)

De Rais's answer to his judges' questions about his deeds was 'that he had done them and perpetrated them following his own imagination and his own thought, without acting on anyone's advice and according to his own bent, purely for his own pleasure and carnal delectation and not for any other purpose or end.'

Gilles de Rais was in the amazing position of being both a national hero and an archetype villain. Around him he generated total insularity—which meant that the members of his court, rather like that of Elizabeth of Bathory, were heavily involved in their overlord's misdoings.

Gilles was immensely rich; he was both a scholar and a sportsman and had a high intellect. Owing to the death of his parents Gilles came under the influence of his grandfather, Jean de Craon, who was reputed to be unscrupulous and somewhat 'over-permissive'. Yet even de Craon confessed himself shocked by some of his grandson's later activities. The death of de Craon's own son at Agincourt made Gilles one of the wealthiest young men in France and his estates were doubled when he married Catherine de Thouers, a rich heiress. After joining the French court he quickly distinguished himself in action against the English and, in 1429, met Joan of Arc. Gilles fought beside Joan at Orleans and again at Patoy. Finally, when the Dauphin was crowned King of France at Rheims, it was Gilles' task to ride to the Abbey of Saint-Rémy to collect the sacred phial containing the unguent that had been the time-honoured anointment for the kings of France. When he was twenty-four Gilles was appointed a Marshal of France—an incredible feat at such a young age, even in those times.

But after Joan's death Gilles' terrible immaturity began to show itself. He became involved in local feuds, and stretched his own glory to breaking point. Even his enormous fortune was unable to take the strain of financing both his court and army and gradually he began to go bankrupt.

Manoeuvred out of the political field, Gilles retired to his estates where he spent the last of his remaining millions in founding a chapel at Machecoul and equipping it with the full trappings of a cathedral, including a vast choir. In 1435 Gilles made a last public appearance before he retired into the dark shadows of his own self-indulgence. This last appearance was spectacular indeed; Gilles appeared in a full-scale pageant re-enacting the siege and relief of the city of Orleans and the life and times of Joan of Arc. Then he disappeared—only to re-emerge at a later date, on trial for his life. Raymond Rudorff writes in *Monsters*: *

> From the moment he had retired, rumours began to circulate concerning the continual disappearances of young children. In 1432, a twelve-year-old apprentice disappeared for ever from the village of Machecoul, after Gilles' cousin, Gilles de Sillé, had asked the boy's guardians for permission to send the lad on an errand. A nine-year-old boy tending cattle in the fields nearby vanished off the face of the earth after having been seen talking to de Sillé. A widow living in front of the castle complained of the disappearance of her eight-year-old son, 'a comely lad, white of skin and very capable'. Two weeks later, another boy was missing and, after an outcry in the village, Gilles de Sillé came down from the castle and explained that the boys had been taken away as part ransom for his brother, who was being held prisoner by the English who were demanding a number of youths to be trained as pages.

Gilles spent five years committing the most incredible crimes of child murder and sodomy. Gilles also indulged in alchemy and sorcery—pursuits that were inextricably linked with the murder of hundreds of children. He kidnapped, raped and dismembered both young boys and girls. The emphasis was on the boys, for Gilles was a rampant homosexual, using his religion as a kind of aesthetic sensuality. Having lured the children into the castle he and his courtiers would set upon them, abusing them sexually and finally murdering them in the most horrible way. After orgies involving massive blood-letting Gilles would retire to bed, seemingly in a state of coma—and would then return to the carnage with renewed ferocity. Finally, however, rumours grew to such proportions that the Church set up its own investigations,

* Neville Spearman, 1968.

recoiling in horror at the furious necro-sadism of this warrior-prince-turned-vampire. He was arrested, tried and sentenced to death. At first Gilles desperately pleaded his innocence—and then, demonstrating his obvious schizophrenia, admitted everything, recounting in detail his perverted killings, blow by blow. At the same time Gilles clung desperately to his Christian faith, going to the gallows with an apparently peaceful mind.

What caused this young Marshal of France to change from a national hero to a monster is difficult to define. There is no doubt that he had led a violent life during which, in the cause of nationalism, he slaughtered hundreds. Perhaps Gilles found it impossible to give up shedding blood.

Sergeant Bertrand

The most direct case of 'live' vampirism known in France was the unfortunate case of Sergeant Bertrand who, at the time of his trial, was known throughout the country as 'The Vampire'. On July 10th, 1849, an investigation was held before a court-martial headed by Colonel Manselon. For months before, cemeteries in and around Paris had been broken into and the most appalling profanations had taken place, the graves desecrated and their contents strewn around the graveyard. The exhumed corpses were horribly mutilated.

> Every means were taken to discover the criminal; but the only result of the increased surveillance was that the scene of profanation was removed to the cemetery of Mont Parnasse, where the exhumations were carried to such an extent that the authorities were at their wit's ends. Considering, by the way, that all these cemeteries are surrounded by walls and have iron gates, which are kept closed, it certainly seems very strange that any ghoul or vampyre of solid flesh and blood should have been able to pursue his vocation so long undisturbed.*

A trap was laid but the severely wounded vampire escaped, leaving behind him fragments of military clothing. Some soldiers of the 74th Regiment reported that one of their number had been admitted, severely wounded, to the military hospital shortly after midnight. The culprit was discovered. Bertrand was tried

* Summers, *The Vampire in Europe.*

The werewolf, the vampire's first cousin, was addicted to flesh as well as blood. From the engraving by the sixteenth-century German artist Lucas Cranach.

One source of vampire belief was cannibalism;
a group of initiates preparing a cannibal feast in Fiji.

Above. The Great Plague of London, 1665. Mass burial of the dead and undead during outbreaks of plague were another fertile source of vampire belief.

Below. The Resuscitated Corpse. Premature burial, a not uncommon predicament throughout the ages, helped to inspire belief in the undead.

The *Baital,* an Indian variety of vampire, is described in Sir Richard Burton's *Tales of Hindu Devilry*.

A *Baital* disappears into the darkness.

These primitive dolls are the most deadly of Malay vampires.

A bat out of hell;
the blood-sucking South American vampire bat.

The vampire in art; a menacing lady vampire from a drawing by Edvard Munch.

the rush of waters, after which, I distinctly felt some one raising me in their arms. I was dropped again, my limbs felt numbed and chill, an universal spasm shot through my whole system, I opened my eyes, and found myself lying in the open air, by a newly opened grave.

A full moon was sailing through the sky and the cold beams were upon my face ; a voice sounded in my ears, a deep and solemn voice—and painfully distinct was every word it uttered.

"Mortimer," it said, for that was my name, "Mortimer, in life you did one deed which at once cast you out from all hope that anything in that life would be remembered in the world to come to your advantage. You poisoned the pure font of mercy, and not upon such as you can the downy freshness of Heaven's bounty fall. Murderer, murderer of that being sacredly presented to your care by the great Creator of all things, live henceforth a being accursed. Be to yourself a desolation and a blight, shunned by all that is good and virtuous, armed against all men, and all men armed against thee, Varney the Vampyre."

The vampire in Victorian literature; a page from *Varney the Vampire* or *The Feast of Blood* by Thomas Prescott-Prest.

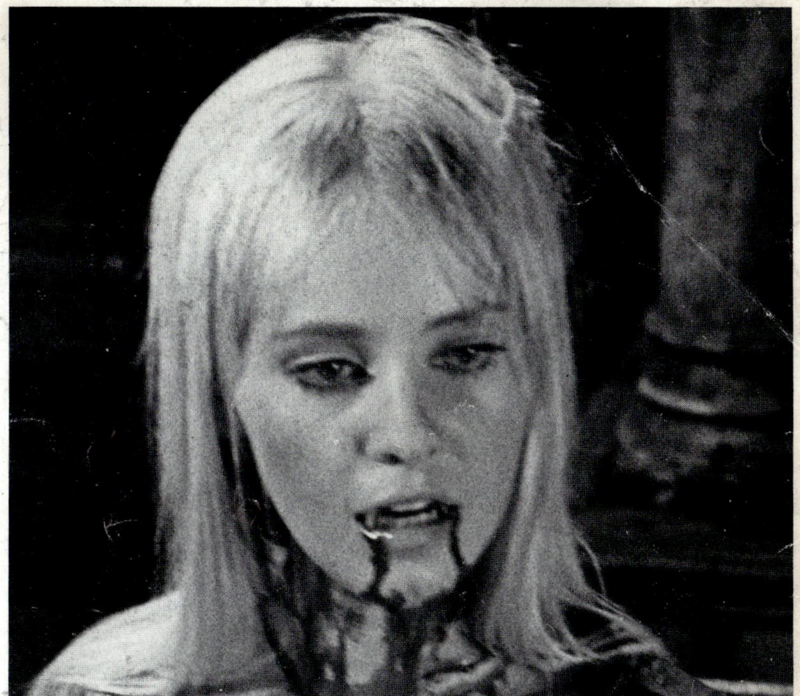

A lovely vampire, gorged with blood, returns to her coffin.

Christopher Lee, the most famous Dracula since Bela Lugosi.

and sentenced to a year in prison. In his defence Bertrand stated that 'he would suddenly feel an irresistible need to destroy and mutilate corpses', after which he would fall into a coma.

In a letter written later from prison Bertrand described his necrophilia in grotesquely matter-of-fact terms:

> If I have sometimes cut male corpses into pieces, it was only out of rage at not finding one of the female sex. Some nights I have had to dig up as many as a dozen men before finding a single woman in the common grave at Montparnasse.

Bertrand would open the corpse's stomach and embrace the corpse, and eventually he would destroy it.

Ornella Volta says of him:

> Bertrand did not recoil before obstacles: when he found an icy moat separating the cemetery of Douai from the city, he swam across it; if he stumbled over one of the man-traps that were set in certain cemeteries as a defence against would-be profaners, he did not let it worry him, but instead dismantled it and took it to pieces with all the aplomb of an expert, and if, during one of his habitual expeditions, he should hear people coming, he would lie perfectly still in the grave next to the corpse; when dogs belonging to the keeper of the cemetery came barking towards him he merely stared them in the eyes. His look must have had a hypnotic power because, like Dracula's, it made animals lower their eyes and tails and slink away in silence.
>
> The act of destroying something that, in any case, was destined to destruction seems to have acted as a tranquillizer for Bertrand's essentially conformist and puritan conscience. In the regiment he would not allow dirty jokes to be told in his presence and used to boast that, although he was not above having the odd affair with a live woman, he had never allowed himself to have relations with a married woman.

The following catalogue of vampiristic incidents show France to be the home of some very strange people:

1. Gilles Gamier (1574) consumed the flesh of the young girls he brutally attacked and killed—taking a prime cut home for his wife's enjoyment.
2. Antoine Leger did the same except he was rather more meth-

odical. Lying in wait for young girls in the wood, Leger raped and killed them as a start. He then tore out their hearts which he ate. On being asked by the judge why he drank the blood of his victims, Leger replied that he was thirsty. He was guillotined in 1824.

3. Necrophile Alexandre Siméon found the sheets on death beds to be particularly erotic. According to Volta 'He ended by passing entire days behind the doors of houses where people were dying, and when the deceased, preferably a woman, was carried away, he would throw himself on the bed, rapturously winding the sheets around himself.'

German Vampire Practice

Traditional vampire activities are recorded in Germany from 1343 to 1820. It is interesting to note that cases of vampirism became numerous in the Tyrol after a visitation of the Black Death (1343-8) and roughly the same occurred at Danzig in 1855 after a particularly vicious outbreak of cholera.

Species of German vampire include the *nachzehrer* (easily recognisable in the tomb by its strange habit of holding the thumb of one hand with the other, always having the left eye open, and emitting a grunting sound whilst gnawing at the shroud), the *neuntöter* which spreads plague, the *drakul*, which moves with the help of a demon, and the *strigoiu*, which lives in abandoned houses. In Kodom in Bavaria the spectres of village herdsmen are reputed to appear to peasants—after which the peasants are doomed to die.

There are several 'living' vampires worth mentioning in Germany.

Clara Geisslerin, 1597

Clara Geisslerin was accused of prostitution in league with three devils who, bored by continuous murder, had dug hundreds of children out of their graves in order to drink their blood. Rudorff describes the witch's trial as follows:

> When she appeared before her judges, she was first made to undergo the torture of the thumb-screws but, despite the excruciating pain, she persisted in denying all the charges brought

against her. Her legs and feet were then enclosed in iron leg vices and crushed to a pulp and she was repeatedly stretched on the rack for *several hours at a time* until she finally confessed to everything that was charged against her. Yes, she had murdered many people, as many as sixty; yes, she had drunk the blood of little children; yes, she had consorted with other witches; yes, she did keep a devil with her in the shape of a cat and, yes, she had prowled about the roofs of the town with it at night, being also in the shape of a cat. But no sooner had she been taken down from the rack than she began to deny everything once again. Revealingly, she declared that she was often ill and muddle-headed, and that what she had said about other witches she had only heard from other people. The 'other witches' were accordingly arrested and brought to the torture where judicious application of the screws and the rack elicited the information that Clara Geisslerin was guilty of even worse things than she had herself admitted under torture. As a result, Clara was hauled back on to the rack and confronted with the new list of charges. She admitted to them all only to deny them again once she was released, screaming that God would prove her innocence to her judges. Again she was racked with even greater severity for several hours until at last her tormentors' patience was rewarded for she finally admitted that for the last forty years she had fornicated with countless devils that had visited her in the shape of cats, dogs, fleas and worms; that she had murdered over two hundred and forty people; had given birth to about seventeen children conceived by her devil lovers, had murdered them, eaten them and drunk their blood; that she had caused storms and set houses on fire and had even wanted to burn up the whole town but had been dissuaded from doing so by one of her devil consorts who wished to spare the population so that he might turn more of them into witches. As the torture went on, she grew gradually feebler and as soon as she was taken down from the rack, presumably having satisfied her inquisitors' curiosity, she fell dead upon the ground. Verdict: she had been strangled by the Devil so that she would reveal no more.

Peter Kürten, the Monster of Dusseldorf (1883-1931)

The most extraordinary and horrible point about Kürten's nocturnal prowling lay in the association with the vampire and werewolf of ancient tradition. It was his habit, and his principal

> satisfaction to receive the stream of blood that gushed from his victim's wounds into his mouth.
>
> (M. S. Wagner, a journalist covering the Kürten case)

Peter Kürten was a very strange man indeed. Totally nondescript. He was a neat dresser, wore horn-rimmed glasses and had a minute moustache. Altogether he committed twenty-nine murders and assaults, causing Dusseldorf years of fear and giving it a reputation of horror that filtered throughout Europe. Kürten suffered from haematodipsia, basically a sexual thirst for blood. He would strangle, rape and cut the throats of his victims whilst he underwent an orgasm of great violence. His father was a near-alcoholic, his mother a homely woman whom Kürten thought a saint. Later in his life he was to marry a mother-figure—a woman who was forced to marry him as he repeatedly threatened her life. She never knew of her husband's crimes until the very end—when he confessed like a naughty child to her—and it was she who went to the police and gave him up.

At the time of his trial Kürten wrote appalling letters to the parents of the young girls and children that he had slaughtered. 'What do you want, Madame? I need blood as others need alcohol,' wrote Kürten to the mother of one of his five-year-old victims. He spent years in prison, but mainly for burglary or theft, and he was not discovered to be the Dusseldorf monster until the end of his murderous career—and until an epileptic named Hans Strausberg had already been arrested in his place.

Ornella Volta says that Kürten was a lorry-driver and a good husband by day and a vampire by night.

> He could only be accused of a certain effeminacy: apart from brilliantine, which is unusual for a Northern European man, he also used face-powder. A witness said of him, 'He speaks of his need to kill as others talk of their habit of smoking.' Fritz Lang, who was a spectator at his trial, was inspired by certain aspects of his career when he made his film M in 1932.

In April 1931 Kürten was sentenced to death nine times over (in accordance with German law).

He did not appeal against his sentence and awaited execution with total calm.

Fritz Haarmann 1879-1923

The London *Daily Express* of April 17th, 1925, printed the following remarkable paragraph:

> VAMPIRE BRAIN.
> PLAN TO PRESERVE IT FOR SCIENCE.
> Berlin, *Thursday, April* 16th.
>
> The body of Fritz Haarmann, executed yesterday at Hanover for twenty-seven murders, will not be buried until it has been examined at Göttingen University.
>
> Owing to the exceptional character of the crimes—most of Haarmann's victims were *bitten to death*—the case aroused tremendous interest among German scientists. It is probable that Haarmann's brain will be removed and preserved by the University authorities.—*Central News.*

Fritz Haarmann was nicknamed the Hanover Vampire. Born in 1879, Haarmann went through military school to the army, and on discharge was arrested for offences against children. As a result of the trial Haarmann was sent to an asylum as he was considered to be unbalanced. On release he returned home to Hanover, became involved in gigantic quarrels with his father, left again and rejoined a crack army unit. Here he served for a period, received excellent reports, was discharged and ran into trouble again through both violence and larceny. Haarmann was jailed several times and in 1918 he was released into a beaten Germany. He began a small cook-shop, hawked meat and made money on the side as a police informer. But Haarmann had one more activity—and a particularly fearsome one.

At night he would wander the halls of the main Hanover railway station and there pick up a variety of youngsters who were either refugees or had run away from one part or another of war-torn Germany. Haarmann won their confidence and invited them back home.

Initially Haarmann was arrested for having indecent relations with an eighteen-year-old runaway. He received nine months' imprisonment. Some years later, whilst Haarmann awaited trial for twenty-seven murders, he stated: 'At the time when the police arrested me the head of the boy Friedel Rothe was hidden under a newspaper behind the oven. Later on I threw it into the canal.'

Haarmann had an accomplice to his carnage—Hans Grans, who met Haarmann in 1919. Hanover was a markedly homosexual town with at least five hundred known homosexuals—all ready for pillaging by Messrs Haarmann and Grans. The Café Kröpcke was at the top end of the homosexual social scale as a rendezvous whilst 'Zur schwülen Guste' (Hot-Stuff Gussie's) was at the lower end. Grans and Haarmann had their pickings here and at other venues, befriending the boys and asking them to return to the cook-shop with them.

The *News of the World* of December 7th, 1924, had the following account of the Haarmann-Grans trial under the heading 'Vampires' Victims':

> The killing of altogether twenty-four young men is laid at his door, the horror of the deeds being magnified by the allegation that he sold to customers for consumption the flesh of those he did not himself eat ... With Haarmann in the dock appeared a younger man, his friend Hans Grans, first accused of assisting in the actual murders but now charged with inciting him to commit them and with receiving stolen property. The police are still hunting for a third man, Charles, also a butcher, who is alleged to have completed the monstrous trio ... the prosecuting attorney has an array of nearly 200 witnesses to prove that all the missing youths were done to death in the same horrible way ... He would take them to his rooms, and after a copious meal would praise the looks of his young guests. Then he would kill them after the fashion of a vampire. Their clothes he would put up on sale in his shop, and the bodies would be cut up and disposed of with the assistance of Charles. In open court, however, Haarmann admitted that Grans often used to select his victims for him. More than once, he alleged, Grans beat him for failing to kill the 'game' brought in, and Haarmann would keep the corpses in a cupboard until they could be got rid of, and one day the police were actually in his rooms when there was a body awaiting dismemberment. The back of the place abutted on the river, and the bones and skulls were thrown into the water. Some of them were discovered, but their origin was a mystery until a police inspector paid a surprise visit to the prisoner's home to inquire into a dispute between Haarmann and an intended victim who escaped.

Another *News of the World* account on December 21st states:

> The details of the atrocious crimes for which Haarmann will shortly pay with his life were extremely revolting. All his victims were between 12 and 18 years of age, and it was proved that the accused actually sold the flesh for human consumption. He once made sausages in his kitchen, and, together with the purchaser, cooked and ate them ... Some alienists hold that even then the twenty-four murders cannot possibly exhaust the full toll of Haarmann's atrocious crimes, and estimate the total as high as fifty. With the exception of a few counts, the prisoner made minutely detailed confessions and for days the court listened to his grim narrative of how he cut up the bodies of his victims and disposed of the fragments in various ways. He consistently repudiated the imputation of insanity, but at the same time maintained unhesitatingly that all the murders were committed when he was in a state of trance, and unaware of what he was doing. This contention was specifically brushed aside by the Bench, which in its judgment pointed out that according to his own account of what happened, it was necessary for him to hold down his victims by hand in a peculiar way before it was possible for him to inflict a fatal bite on their throats. Such action often necessarily involved some degree of deliberation and conscious purpose.

Skulls and bones found in the river during the months of May, June, and July 1924, together with an open confrontation with a boy who accused him of indecency, put the finger of suspicion on Haarmann. There is no doubt that Haarmann's behaviour was vampire-like, particularly as he bit at the throats of his victims. He was executed in 1923 whilst Grans received twelve years' imprisonment. In 1924, the newspapers recorded that six hundred people had disappeared in Hanover. Of these many were boys between 14 and 18—and a good proportion of these may well have been butchered by Haarmann and Grans.

Protection against German Vampires

There are some particularly vicious real-life vampires in German history but the traditional mythical vampire was also much feared. In the nineteenth century Mark Twain visited a building in a small Bavarian village. Here the dead were kept for several days to ensure that they really were dead—and not in a state of suspended animation or cataleptic trance. The room was equipped with both food and drink and there was a bell-rope for those who awoke from a trance-like condition to summon immediate assistance. This suggests quite a sophisticated awareness of some of the real reasons behind the undead.

On a more primitive level, food was buried with the corpse—presumably to assuage any immediate pangs of hunger and satisfy the corpse within its own grave. In Dielsdorf, money was placed in the corpse's mouth at burial, and the corpse's name cut from his shirt. If these preventive measures were not taken it was thought that the ghost of the corpse would leave the grave in the shape of a pig. Another method of prevention was to break the corpse's neck before burial.

The vampiristic herdsmen-spectres at Kodom in Bavaria were dealt with in a different way. The corpse was pinned to the ground by a stake. Then the body was burnt by the village executioner—a process during which the corpse was meant to both kick and squirm. Traditionally, the apparitions of the spectre only ceased after the corpse had been reduced to ashes.

Burning was the most effective means of protection from vampires in Germany. There is an account, dating back to 1345, of a dead witch who wandered about at night in the shape of an animal. In order to dispose of her she was cast into a ditch. This, however, was an ineffective measure and she arose in a vinegary mood and continued to create death and havoc—this time clad in the guise of a huge, unclean beast. On exhumation the witch was discovered to be a vampire and a stake was thrust through her breast. But even this more forceful action failed to have the desired effect and the witch continued to spread mayhem—using the stake as a weapon against her victims. Eventually she was burnt to dust and only then did her activities cease.

Vampire Practice and Protection in the Remainder of Western Europe

Although there have been no actual outbreaks of major mythical vampirism in *Italy* there have been plenty of living vampires and necrophiles. Gaetano Mammore, a notorious brigand, drank the blood of his enemies or victims to gather their life-power.

In *Sardinia* the *vendetta* caused thousands of deaths; it was based on the belief that murdered people could not rest in their tombs until vengeance had been taken by a member of their family on the assassin or his kin.

Amongst the peasantry, however, the main threat was vampiristic witchcraft. Children were the victims and mothers watched helplessly as their children wasted away. The Church, when approached, produced a complex remedy which went as follows:

1. The Holy Gospel is recited over the child's head, and the head itself lies on the stole of the Priest.
2. A cross of wax, blessed on Ascension Day, is then hung over the doorway of the house.
3. A linen bag, containing a pinch of salt, is hung around the child's neck.
4. The child's hair is cut and a lock is cast on the fire in the hope that the smoke will sidetrack the witch-vampire and send her far afield on a demonic wild goose chase.
5. The hinges of all doors in the house are sprinkled with holy water.
6. The Credo is recited aloud three times.
7. The husband does a seven-night watch in order to trap the vampire-witch, who can be seized by the hair.

Additional precautions include laying a dead dog or cat across the threshold. The witch then cannot enter until she has counted every hair on the animal's coat. Even working with feverish energy she will be unable to complete the task by dawn, which means that she will be trapped by the sunrise, will be unable to escape and will be discovered stark naked, still desperately counting, outside the house.

The midnight ride of the vampire-witch as she rides to her coven is spectacular. Having rubbed magic salve into her body, she will emit a wild cry of 'Away, away, through snow and storm, carry me to the nut tree of Benevento'. Then she leaps astride a large goat and sets off for the Sabbath. However, en route, she might pause from time to time to sup the blood of babies.

In *Spain* vampire-witches were also a menace; they tended to hunt in packs or covens. They were reputed to raid houses in an attempt to steal away the children, or at least to suck their blood. The local priest often confronted them clad in a stole, with a thurifer in one hand and the Bible in the other. He would sprinkle holy water liberally at the cackling crowd of vampire-witches and tell all the young children in the village to remain firmly at home and preferably in bed. At one stage some of the witches would mount the roof of a house, tear off tiles, howl with manic laughter but fail to get at the throats of the children.

Finally, there is the alarming *Portuguese* female vampire—the *Bruxsa*. Richard Andrée described her in his *Ethnographicte Parallelen und Vergleiche* (1878):

> At night she leaves her resting place and flies from home in the form of some gigantic night bird. The *Bruxsas* keep tryst with their diabolical lovers and seduce, terrify, and torment lonely travellers. On returning from their nocturnal journeys of pleasure they suck the blood of their own children.

Vampire Practice in Australasia

Very little is recorded here and what is recorded relates mainly to cannibalism, ancestor worship or blood taboo. Evil spirits, rather like the vampires of Europe, will attempt to draw away the soul of a tribesman who has died the previous day. Generally speaking, the evil spirit is reckoned to be the ghost of a slain enemy.

In *Fiji* living vampire types were recorded as late as 1846. The war between the Bau and the Rewe was at an end. But the losers were to suffer an alarming fate. Garry Hogg, in his book, *Cannibalism and Human Sacrifice*,* recorded that:

> When the ovens were ready, they cut their victims up very carefully, placing dishes under every part to catch the blood. If a drop fell, they licked it up off the ground with the greatest greediness. While the poor wretches were being cut in pieces, they pleaded hard for life; but all was of no avail, all were devoured.

* Robert Hale, 1958.

This rite emanated from typical cannibalistic belief, which dictated that spilled blood spells immediate misfortune, and the nourishment gained from eating the flesh and drinking the blood of an enemy is akin to transmitting his strength to the soul of the devourer.

In *New Zealand* belligerent ancestors were much feared. The head of each house was worshipped by the children of that house. When dead, the father became a great treasure, and it was supposed that the protection he showed whilst alive would still encompass his family when he was dead. However, the recently dead ancestor was often demanding, easily aggravated and continuously sacrificed to. Summers, in *The Vampire: His Kith and Kin*, pointed out that

> in nearly every case we find recognized the existence of a supreme being, who is certainly a high spiritual power that had never been a man, and the homage paid to whom (in those very rare instances where such worship is conceived of as desirable or even possible) differs entirely from the cult of the dead, be they family ancestors or some line of ancient kings.

In *New Guinea*, if a drop of blood came into the hands of a sorcerer or magician, there was little doubt that he or she would make doubtful use of it. At the same time, should they ever pass this blood to an evil spirit it was then possible for the spirit to achieve a corporate body. Once again blood contains the very soul-stuff of life. Passing even a fragment of this on could be infinitely dangerous.

Finally, in *Polynesia* a more complex version of the vampire belief existed. In the Banks Islands, men or women who sought communion with a ghost would eat a portion of the relevant corpse. As a result, the ghost of the dead person would become a close friend of the man or woman who had eaten a portion of his dead flesh.

English Vampire Practice and Protection

In the twelfth century, England was rife with vampire tradition. But this tradition seemingly died out after this century and, with only rare exceptions, does not reappear until the nineteenth century when there was a revival in occultism.

The Norse legends that the dead were alive in their burrows probably began English vampire belief. An eleventh-century chronicler, William of Malmesbury, recorded that in England the dead walked, providing they were men who had led evil lives. The reanimation was the work of the Devil, who also ordained their activities. But it was not until William of Newburgh came along that the vampire legends of England were chronicled in detail. Newburgh was an Augustinian canon in the priory of Newburgh, in the North Riding of Yorkshire. He lived between 1136 and 1208 and wrote *Historia Rerum Anglicarum*. Chapters XXII and XXIII are reproduced here.

Of the extraordinary happening when a dead man wandered abroad out of his grave

About that time in the county of Buckinghamshire a most remarkable event took place, and this I first heard of from some people who lived in that very district, and it was afterwards told me in fullest detail by Stephen, the highly respected and most worthily esteemed Archdeacon of that diocese. A certain man having died, according to the course of nature, was by the seemly care of his wife and relations decently buried on the Eve of Ascension Day (29th May). But on the following night he suddenly entered the room where his wife lay asleep and, having awakened her, he not only filled her with the greatest alarm but almost killed her by leaping upon her with the whole heaviness of his weight and overlying her. On the second night, also, he tormented the trembling woman in just the same way. Wherefore in the extremity of dread she resolved that on the third night she would remain awake and that then and thenceforth she would protect herself from this horrible attack by providing a company of persons to watch with her. Nevertheless, he visited her; but when he was driven away by the shouts and cries of those who were keeping watch, so that he found he could do her no harm, he swiftly departed. Having been thus baffled and repulsed by his wife, he proceeded in exactly the same manner to harass and annoy his brothers who resided in the same town. But they, taking pattern from the excellent precautions employed by their sister-in-law, passed several nights of wakefulness, surrounded by their household all on guard, and all ready to receive and repel the onset of the dead man. He made his appearance, indeed, but it seemed as though he were only wishful, or only had the power, to molest those who were asleep, and he was kept at bay by the vigilance and the courage of any who were on their guard and waking. Next, then, he roved about and beset animals who were either in the houses or resting near the houses. This was discovered by the unusual panic and disturbances of the terrified beasts. So eventually, since he proved so terrible and continual a danger both to friends and neighbours alike, there was nothing for it save that they should pass their nights in watching and being continually on their guard. Accordingly throughout the town in every house there were certain of the family who kept awake and mounted guard all night long, whilst everybody was anxious and fearful lest they should be subjected to some sudden and unforeseen attack. Now when for a good while he had harried people during the night alone, he began to wander abroad in plain daylight, dreaded by all, although actually he was seen by but a few. Very often he would encounter a company of some half-a-dozen and he would be quite clearly discerned by but one or two of the number, although all of them very perceptibly felt his horrible presence. Well-nigh scared out of their senses, the inhabitants at last determined that they must seek counsel from the church; and accordingly with many piteous lamentations, they laid the whole matter from first to last before Archdeacon Stephen, whom I have mentioned above, in his public and official capacity as president of a diocesan synod which was then convened. The Archdeacon forthwith wrote a letter to that venerable prelate, His Lordship the Bishop of Lincoln (S. Hugh), who happened to be at London. The screed related all these extraordinary circumstances in regular order, and he requested His Lordship to give directions as to what must be done to remedy so intolerable an evil, since he felt that the matter should be dealt with by the highest authority. When the Bishop heard of this he was greatly amazed, and forthwith he consulted with a number of learned priests and reverend theologians, from certain of whom he learned that similar occurrences had often taken place in England, and many well-known instances were quoted to him. They all agreed that the neighbourhood would never obtain any peace until the body of this miserable wretch had been disinterred and burned to ashes. However, such a method seemed extremely undesirable and unbecoming to the holy Bishop, who forthwith wrote out with his own hand a chartula of absolution and sent this to the Archdeacon ordaining that, whatever might be the reason why the man wandered from his grave, the tomb should be opened, and when the chartula of absolution had been laid upon the breast of the corpse, all should be once again fastened up as before. Therefore they opened the tomb, and the body was found therein uncorrupt, just as it had been laid upon the day of his burial. The chartula of episcopal absolution was placed upon his breast, and after the grave had again been fast closed, the dead man never wandered abroad, nor had he the power to injure or frighten anybody from that very hour.

Concerning a similar occurrence which happened at Berwick

It has come to our knowledge that about the same time a similar and no less great wonder took place in the extreme north of England. There is a fine and flourishing town at the mouth of the river Tweed, called Berwick, which comes under the jurisdiction of the King of Scotland. Here then there dwelt a certain man who was indeed surpassing rich in this world's goods, but, as later only too clearly came to light, a most infamous villain. Now, after he was buried, at night he used by the power of Satan, as we may very well believe, continually to issue forth from his grave, and to rush up and down the streets of the town, whilst the dogs howled and bayed in every direction what time this evil thing was abroad. Any citizen who chanced to meet him was distraught with terror, and then just before daybreak he returned to his grave. When this had been going on for some little time nobody dared to step outside his door after nightfall, so terribly did they all dread to meet this fatal monster. Accordingly the authorities, as well as men of poor estate, earnestly discussed what steps had best be taken to rid themselves of so sore a visitation, for even the most thoughtless and irresponsible of them were extremely apprehensive lest, if by some unlucky chance they met this living corpse, they would be fearfully assaulted and injured by the dead man; whilst those who were more sagacious and far-sighted were afraid lest, unless some speedy remedy were found, owing to the fact that black decomposition of this foul body horribly infected the air with poisonous pollution as it rushed to and fro, the plague or another fatal disease might break out and sweep away many, a disaster which had not infrequently been known to happen in circumstances similar to this. Accordingly they chose among them ten young men of singular bravery and strength and bade them exhume this accursed corpse. It was then to be hewn member from member and cut into small pieces, and thrown into a blazing furnace so that it might be entirely burned up and consumed. When this had been done the prevailing panic was calmed, 'and the slaughter ceased' (*Psalm* cv. 30). For the monster, while he was roving abroad by the power of Satan as we have explained, is said to have announced to certain persons whom he encountered that the people should have no rest until his body was consumed to ashes. Therefore, when he had been burned it seemed in truth as though the people had a certain period of rest, but there very shortly broke out a terrible pestilence which carried off the greater part of that town. And nowhere else did the plague rage so fiercely, although certes, about the same time there was an epidemic in several districts of England.

Here are all the components of vampire practice: foraging abroad, priestly intervention, exhumation, burning and the wretched vampire blamed not just for blood-sucking—but plague and pestilence.

Walter Map, who was born in 1140, wrote the *De Nugis Curialium*, which lightens the darker side of the Middle Ages, and recounts many legends and stories.

In one of his chapters Map tells the alarming story of a kind of vampire demon. A knight, having married a devout and religious woman, made a tragic discovery on the morning of the birth of his first child. The baby had had its throat cut from ear to ear as it lay in the cradle. The same tragic circumstances took place with his second and third children. The fourth time, when the Knight's wife had just given birth, a massive vigil was kept, the house was lit with torches and the child was strictly observed. During the course of all this a stranger arrived, seeking hospitality in God's name, as was the custom of the times. In order to repay them for their hospitality the stranger decided to keep the vigil too and in fact he was eventually the only person to remain awake. Halfway through the vigil the stranger saw the child being attacked by 'a most worthy and honourable matron' who had the baby by its throat. The stranger grabbed the woman and alerted the sleeping household who all 'declared that she was the noblest of the most respected matrons of that great city, not only by her birth, but by her splendid way of living, as well as owing to her great wealth, and that she enjoyed a high repute and was universally held in the greatest esteem.' No one could believe that this incredible reputation should be hollow, yet the stranger hung grimly on to her nevertheless. However, as the confrontation grew more embarrassing another lady turned up—the exact replica of the so-called demon, who was still struggling in the stranger's grasp. Suddenly all became clear to the stranger who, addressing the assembled household, said:

> There can be no doubt that the lady who has now come is very virtuous and very dear to heaven, and that by her good works she has stirred hell and provoked the anger of devils against her, and so this evil messenger of theirs, this loathsome instrument of their wrath, has been fashioned as far as possible in the likeness of this noble lady, that this demon may cause this noble soul to be accused of the guilt of her heinous deeds. And in order that you may believe, see what she will do after I release her.

With that the demon flew bellowing through the window.

A more recent example of English vampirism occurred at Croglin Grange in Cumberland, and the following account was related by a Captain Fisher to Augustus Hare and later published in his memoirs.

The Story of My Life

> 'Fisher', said the Captain, 'may sound a very plebian name, but this family is of a very ancient lineage, and for many hundreds of years they have possessed a very curious old place in Cumberland, which bears the weird name of Croglin Grange. The great characteristic of the house is that never at any period of its very long existence has it been more than one storey high, but it has a terrace from which large grounds sweep away towards the church in the hollow, and a fine distant view.
>
> 'When, in lapse of years, the Fishers outgrew Croglin Grange in family and fortune, they were wise enough not to destroy the long-standing characteristic of the place by adding another storey to the house, but they went away to the south, to reside at Thorncombe near Guildford, and they let Croglin Grange.
>
> 'They were extremely fortunate in their tenants, two brothers and a sister. They heard their praises from all quarters. To their

poorest neighbours they were all that is most kind and beneficent, and their neighbours of a higher class spoke of them as a most welcome addition to the little society of the neighbourhood. On their part, the tenants were greatly delighted with their new residence. The arrangement of the house, which would have been a trial to many, was not so to them. In every respect Croglin Grange was exactly suited to them.

'The winter was spent most happily by the new inmates of Croglin Grange, who shared in all the little social pleasures of the district, and made themselves very popular. In the following summer there was one day which was dreadfully, annihilatingly hot. The brothers lay under the trees with their books, for it was too hot for any active occupation. The sister sat in the veranda and worked, or tried to work, for in the intense sultriness of that summer day, work was next to impossible. They dined early, and after dinner they still sat out on the veranda, enjoying the cool air which came with the evening, and they watched the sun set, and the moon rise over the belt of trees which separated the grounds from the churchyard, seeing it mount the heavens till the whole lawn was bathed in silver light, across which the long shadows from the shrubbery fell as if embossed, so vivid and distinct were they.

'When they separated for the night, all retiring to their rooms on the ground floor (for, as I said, there was no upstairs in that house), the sister felt that the heat was still so great that she could not sleep, and having fastened her window, she did not close the shutters—in that very quiet place it was not necessary—and, propped against the pillows, she still watched the wonderful, the marvellous beauty of that summer night. Gradually she became aware of two lights, two lights which flickered in and out in the belt of trees which separated the lawn from the churchyard, and, as her gaze became fixed upon them, she saw them emerge, fixed in a dark substance, a definite ghastly *something*, which seemed every moment to become nearer, increasing size and substance as it approached. Every now and then it was lost for a moment in the long shadows which stretched across the lawn from the trees, and then it emerged larger than ever, and still coming on. As she watched it, the most uncontrollable horror seized her. She longed to get away, but the door was close to the window, and the door was locked on the inside, and while she was unlocking it she must be for an instant nearer to *it*. She longed to scream, but her voice seemed paralysed, her tongue glued to the roof of her mouth.

'Suddenly—she could never explain why afterwards—the terrible object seemed to turn to one side, seemed to be going round the house, not to be coming to her at all, and immediately she jumped out of bed and rushed to the door, but as she was unlocking it she heard scratch, scratch, scratch upon the window, and saw a hideous brown face with flaming eyes glaring in at her. She rushed back to the bed, but the creature continued to scratch, scratch, scratch upon the window. She felt a sort of mental comfort in the knowledge that the window was securely fastened on the inside. Suddenly the scratching sound ceased, and a kind of pecking sound took its place. Then, in her agony, she became aware that the creature was unpicking the lead! The noise continued, and a diamond pane of glass fell into the room. Then a long bony finger of the creature came in and turned the handle of the window, and the window opened, and the creature came in; and it came across the room, and her terror was so great that she could not scream, and it came up to the bed, and it twisted its long, bony fingers into her hair, and it dragged her head over the side of the bed, and—it bit her violently in the throat.

'As it bit her, her voice was released, and she screamed with all her might and main. Her brothers rushed out of their rooms, but the door was locked on the inside. A moment was lost while they got a poker and broke it open. Then the creature had already escaped through the window, and the sister, bleeding violently from a wound in the throat, was lying unconscious over the side of the bed. One brother pursued the creature, which fled before him through the moonlight with gigantic strides, and eventually seemed to disappear over the wall into the churchyard. Then he rejoined his brother by the sister's bedside. She was dreadfully hurt, and her wound was a very definite one, but she was of strong disposition, not even given to romance or superstition, and when she came to herself she said, "What has happened is most extraordinary and I am very much hurt. It seems inexplicable, but of course there *is* an explanation, and we must wait for it. It will turn out that a lunatic has escaped from some asylum and found his way here." The wound healed, and she appeared to get well, but the doctor who was sent for would not believe that she could bear so terrible a shock so easily, and insisted that she must have change, mental and physical; so her brothers took her to Switzerland.

'Being a sensible girl, when she went abroad she threw herself at once into the interests of the country she was in. She dried plants, she made sketches, she went up mountains, and, as autumn came on, she was the person who urged that they should return to Croglin Grange. "We have taken it," she said, "for seven years, and we have only been there one; and we shall always find it difficult to let a house which is only one storey high, so we had better return there; lunatics do not escape every day." As she urged it, her brothers wished nothing better, and the family returned to Cumberland. From there being no upstairs in the house it was impossible to make any great change in their arrangements. The sister occupied the same room, but it is unnecessary to say she always closed the shutters, which, however, as in many old houses, always left one top pane of the window uncovered. The brothers moved, and occupied a room together, exactly opposite that of their sister, and they always kept loaded pistols in their room.

'The winter passed most peacefully and happily. In the following March, the sister was suddenly awakened by a sound she remembered only too well—scratch, scratch, scratch upon the window, and, looking up, she saw, climbed up to the topmost pane of the window, the same hideous brown shrivelled face, with glaring eyes, looking in at her. This time she screamed as loud as she could. Her brothers rushed out of their room with pistols, and out of the front door. The creature was already scudding away across the lawn. One of the brothers fired and hit it in the leg, but still with the other leg it continued to make way, scrambled over the wall into the churchyard, and seemed to disappear into a vault which belonged to a family long extinct.

'The next day the brothers summoned all the tenants of Croglin Grange, and in their presence the vault was opened. A horrible scene revealed itself. The vault was full of coffins; they had been broken open, and their contents, horribly mangled and distorted, were scattered over the floor. One coffin alone remained intact. Of that the lid had been lifted, but still lay loose upon the coffin. They raised it, and there, brown, withered, shrivelled, mummified, but quite entire, was the same hideous figure which had looked in at the windows of Croglin Grange, with the marks of a recent pistol-shot in the leg: and they did the only thing that can lay a vampire—they burnt it.'

Death certification was undoubtedly careless and some English vampire belief may have grown up because of premature burial.

There was the case, for instance, of John Macintire who was completely paralysed after a lingering illness in 1824. He was certified dead but declared that, at the time, he could hear and feel perfectly although the power of speech and movement had gone. Luckily Macintire was exhumed—by the Resurrection Men. He got as far as the dissecting table but awoke when the demonstrator pierced his chest with a knife.

Fear of premature burial caused some people to leave instructions in their wills for a system of electric wiring to be arranged down the side of their graves, concluding with a bell-push on the inside of the coffin and an alarm bell at the other end. One man made sure that his executors should arrange for at least three doctors to give their certificate of death after very careful examination. A fourth doctor was then, after a period of four hours, to sever his arteries at four-hourly intervals. Here was a man determined not to wake in his tomb—and become one of the undead.

Irish Vampire Practice and Protection

The old Irish, like the Gauls, drank their friends' blood. When the so-called Irish traitor Murrogh O'Brien was executed at Limerick his foster-mother drank the blood that ran from the severed head, claiming that the earth was not worthy to drink it.

In old Ireland there was a traditionally-motivated vampire named the *Dearg-due*, which means the red blood-sucker. The only way to keep the *Dearg-due* in its grave was to build a cairn of stones over the top. Another legend claims that there is a female vampire lurking near Waterford. The actual spot is under a ruined church near Strongbow's tree, and it is to this sinister place that the vampire lures, by her fatal beauty, men with good red blood running in their veins.

A more recent case is reported by R. S. Breene in *The Occult Review*, October 1925.

> The incident happened in a county in Ireland where the vast majority of the inhabitants have always been ardent Roman Catholics. People of this sort would never dream of inventing such a story about an ecclesiastic. So strong is their veneration of the priesthood, and their belief in the sanctity of their parish

clergy, that it is almost impossible to understand how such circumstances as I here narrate could be associated in the popular mind with the name and memory of one who had received Holy Orders. Yet it was from Roman Catholics who described themselves as eye-witnesses that the information was derived...

A member of the family of M—, a farming connexion, had been ordained to the priesthood, and eventually was put in charge of a little hill parish by the local Bishop. He is reputed to have been a quiet, inoffensive man, not given much to the companionship of his flock, and rather addicted to reading and study. His parishioners listened with edification to his sermons, brought their children to him for the rite of baptism, made their confession to him at intervals, and took the sacred bread of the Holy Communion from his hands on Sundays and the greater festivals of the Church...He was hospitable to strangers, and had frequently placed beds in his little parochial house at the disposal of belated travellers and even tramps. Yet no one in his immediate neighbourhood would have thought of going to see him socially. They went to him on the Church's business, or they did not go at all. He was, in a word, respected, though not greatly liked.

When he had little more than passed his fiftieth birthday he suddenly fell ill and died, after a brief confinement to his chamber. He was buried with all the simple pomp that surrounds the obsequies of an Irish country priest. His body, I should have said, was removed before the funeral to his mother's house, which was several miles distant from his parish. It was from there that the funeral took place. It was a sad picture when the body came home to the aged mother, whose chief pride in her later years had been her 'boy in the Church', the priest; and it was sadder still when the coffin set out once more from the whitewashed farmhouse, to carry its occupant upon his last journey to the rocky graveyard in the hills where all his kin had laid their bones for generations. According to custom, all the male and female members of the connexion accompanied the corpse. The bereaved mother was left to her thoughts for the rest of the day in the house of death...

Meanwhile the funeral cortège wended its slow way (a long procession of traps, jaunting-cars and spring-carts) towards its destination in the mountains. They did not waste much time in getting their sad task over and done, but they had a long road to traverse, and the sun was already declining in the heavens as they climbed the last succession of hills on the way to the homestead they had left in the morning ... They were all sober, but many of them, particularly the womenfolk, had fallen asleep. Night was already in the air. The shadows were lengthening below the hill-crests, but upon the white limestone highway everything was still in broad daylight. At the foot of a slope the mourners in the first cars suddenly became aware of a solitary figure coming down towards them walking rapidly. As the distance between them and the pedestrian lessened they were surprised to see that he was a priest. They knew of no priest who could be there at such a time. Those who had taken part in the ceremonies at the grave had not come so far with them on the return journey. They began to speculate as to who the man could be. Remarks were exchanged, and meanwhile the newcomer had met the foremost car. Two men were awake in it. There could be no mistake. *They saw at once, and quite clearly, that they were face to face with the man whom they had laid in his grave two or three hours before.* He passed them with his head slightly averted, but not sufficiently to prevent them from making absolutely certain of his identity, or from noting the intense, livid pallor of his skin, the hard glitter of his wide-open eyes, and the extraordinary length of his strong, white teeth, from which the full red lips seemed to be writhed back till the gums showed themselves. He was wearing, not the grave-clothes in which he had been attired for his burial, but the decent black frock-coat and garments to match in which they had last seen him alive. He passed down the long line of vehicles, and finally disappeared round the turn in the road. Someone in every loaded trap or car had seen him; in short, most of those who had been awake and on that side. A thrill of terror passed through the whole party. With hushed voices and blanched cheeks they pushed on quickly, now only anxious to get under some sheltering roof and round some blazing hearth before dread night should fall upon them.

Their first call was at the M— farmhouse. In the front was a little porch built round the door, with a small narrow window on either side. About this they gathered, and hurriedly decided to say no word of what had happened to the bereaved mother. Then someone knocked, but received no answer. They knocked again, and still being denied admittance, they began to be uneasy. At last someone thought of peeping in through one of the little side-windows, when he saw old Mrs M— lying face downward on the floor. They hesitated no longer, but literally broke in, and it was some little time before they were able to bring her round again to consciousness. This, briefly, is what she told them.

About half an hour earlier, she had heard footsteps on the flags outside, followed by a loud challenging knock. She was surprised that they should have returned so soon, and, besides, she had been expecting the sound of the cars approaching. She decided that it could not be any of the family, and so, before opening, she looked out at the side. There, to her horror, she saw her dead son standing in the broad daylight much as she had last seen him alive. He was not looking directly at her. But she, too, noted the extraordinary length of his teeth, the cold blaze of his eyes, I might say the wolfishness of his whole bearing, and the deathly pallor of his skin. Her first instinctive movement was to open the door. Then fear swept over her, swamping even her mother-love. She felt her limbs giving way under her, and quickly sank into the oblivion in which she lay until they found her.

Vampire Practice in Scotland and Wales

In *Scotland* the common people believed that the formidable ancient castles were built by the Picts, who appeased the spirit of the soil by washing the foundation stone in the blood of a human victim. The Gauls went one further by burying alive within the walls of their newly-constructed edifice some man or woman as a human sacrifice. In fact St Columba was said to have walled up St Ora to placate the unruly spirits who each night tore down the structure reared around them during the day.

One legendary Scottish vampire was the *baobhan sith* who took the form of groups of beautiful girls, dressed in green clothes, with long golden hair. The following fearsome anecdote appears in K. M. Briggs' examination of fairy belief, *The Anatomy of Puck*.*

Four men were hunting in the wilds of Ross-shire, and took refuge for the night in a deserted shieling. To keep themselves warm they began to dance. Three of them danced, and one supplied the mouth music. As they danced one of them wished that their sweethearts were with them. At once four beautiful girls came into the building, in green clothes, with long golden hair. Three of them danced, and one sat by the singer. Presently the

* Published by Routledge & Kegan Paul, 1959.

> singer noticed drops of blood falling from his friends. He started up, and his partner flew at him. He escaped from her, and took refuge among the horses, where he was safe until daybreak. In the morning he went back to the shieling, and found the bloodless bodies of his companions, sucked to death by the dreadful *baobhan sith.*

Another evil spirit was the Redcap, who is detailed in W. Henderson's *Folklore of the Northern Counties of England and the Borders* (1879) as

> a malignant spirit who haunts old pele-towers and places where deeds of violence have been done. He is like a squat old man, with grim, long-nailed hands and a red cap, dyed in blood. It is dangerous to try to sleep in any ruined castle that he haunts, for if he can he will re-dip his cap in human blood. He can be driven off by words from Scripture or the sight of a cross-handled sword. In other places he is less sinister. There is, for instance, a redcap who haunts Grandtully Castle in Perthshire, who is rather lucky than unlucky.

Wales has some traditionally vampiristic folk-legends, the most original of which is the strange story of the Vampire Chair. A dissenting minister visited a farmhouse which had been converted from an old Dower House. After sitting in an old armchair and sleeping in a beautiful bed the minister awoke to find teeth-marks in his hands and sides. He later found similar marks on his horse. Rising to the occasion, the minister calmly explained to his hosts that the dead owner of the furniture had returned as a vampire. With equal calm the man of the house replied: 'It has happened to two ministers before—but not to ministers' nags!'

Vampire Practice and Protection in Scandinavia

As has already been mentioned, in Scandinavia it was believed that the dead were alive in their barrows. This legend was translated to Britain with the coming of the Norsemen. The *Grettus Saga* states that the living dead in these barrows might turn into the monsters of vampiredom.

K. M. Briggs' *Anatomy of Puck* has this to say:

> The Scandinavian ghosts ... were tangible and physically dangerous, vampires rather than apparitions. They aroused a primitive type of ghost-fear; and this ravening spirit comes in some ways near to the original Senecan ghost. The Jacobeans were familiar with a typical and interesting example in Saxo Grammaticus, the story of Asmund's conflict with the vampire spirit of Aswid.* It is interesting because the ghost had completely changed in affections and character after death. The compact by which the survivor of the two friends should be walled up in the other's tomb arose out of their heartfelt affection; but death cancelled that. Every night the dead man came to life again, a ravenous ghoul; and when he had devoured his horse and dog he attacked his friend, who only escaped by chance from the tomb, wounded and mortally exhausted. Nothing quite like that distortion of character appears in the Elizabethan drama. Andrugio's ghost shows an inhuman cruelty; but in the overstrained temper of the play it is impossible to say whether this is an intentional effect. The rawhead-and-bloody-bones so often mentioned by the Elizabethans was probably a native ghost of the ghoulish Scandinavian type; and many other ghoulish spirits existed in British folk-lore.

In *Denmark*, the *Mara* was a fiendish female vampire who went around during the day in human form. It was fatal to fall in love with her, for one would experience feelings of suffocation and strangulation—as if the hands of some primeval force were around one's neck. The only way to see the human form of the spectral *Mara* was to lie flat on one's back, holding a knife on one's chest, with the blade pointing upwards. When the spectre then adopted human form the point of the knife would prick the *Mara* and she would be frightened away.

In *Iceland* the *Eyrbyggia Saga* relates the story of the vampires in the year 1000 who slew eighteen servants in a household. In *Finland* the Cereanis imagined that the spirits that cause illness (especially fever and ague) were recruited on the death of murderers, those who died due to a violent death, and old maids.

Gipsy Vampire Practice and Protection

The gipsy vampire is a compound of Eastern European traditions,

* Usually known as Assueit.

yet in many ways gipsy lore has embellished or refined the more domestic legends. The name of the gipsy vampire is *Mulo* (plural *Mulé*) which means, quite simply, 'one who is dead'. This particular vampire is the soul of a dead person and all gipsies become *Mulé* after death. So clannish is the tribal spirit amongst gipsies that no gipsy ghosts or *revenants* are ever feared.

The *Mulé* only live at night, and at exactly midday when the sun is passing from east to west. During this period the landscape, the road, even the smallest domestic objects belong to the *Mulé*. In J-P. Clébert's book *The Gipsies* (Vista, 1963) it is said that

> the *Mulo*'s 'headquarters' or point of attachment is the body of a dead man. His dwelling-place is the grave or tomb of the deceased. But he is not firmly attached to the body. Death has liberated him, and he can wander, travel, go to and from this base. He is not the corpse; he is the man himself in the form of his double.

At cockcrow the *Mulo* returns to his grave. However, his habits are far more civilised than those of his Eastern European cousin, for the *Mulé* are not blood-suckers in any way. Nevertheless they are still extremely menacing. Amongst some groups of gipsies the *Mulo* would reappear in the evening at the camp, ask for his wife, and spend the night with her. According to Clébert

> The *Mulo* is a vampire-like figure. The child born dead becomes *Mulo* and grows until he attains eight years of age; only then does he enter the country of the dead. There is not a bone in his body, and his hands are without the middle finger, which he must leave in the grave. Once a year, on the anniversary of his birth, his companions boil him so that he shall regain his strength. On New Year's night the *Mulé* kidnap women, whom they boil in big cauldrons so that they may shed their bones and become boneless women *Mulé*.

Throughout Central Europe great importance was inevitably attached to the vampire myth and this obviously affected the various bands of gipsy tribes. Traces of belief in metempsychosis have been recorded amongst Carpathian gipsies and, as Jean-Paul Clébert remarked in his book *The Gipsies*, 'it is in the sense of the Latin *spiritus* and the Greek *pneuma* that the significance of the *Mulo* must be sought.'

Professor T. P. Vukanovič collected together in his book *Gipsy World* some fascinating information about the belief and customs of Yugoslavian gipsies in connection with vampirism:

> Both among the Orthodox and Moslem Gypsies in these parts it is believed that a vampire has a great desire for the female sex. Thus in Podrima they think that immediately he rises from the grave he goes, if a married man, to his former wife to spend the night with her in love intercourse. If he was an adult but unmarried man he would visit any young and pretty woman, usually a country widow or divorcée, for this purpose.
>
> In the village and town settlements, however, the Moslem Gypsies think that a vampire goes for love intercourse to that woman for whom he had a fancy when alive, be she widow, divorcée or a married woman living with her husband. She must not speak of this affair to anyone, but only scream aloud when the vampire is with her while the rest of the family sit in silence.
>
> In Novopazarski Sandžak these Gypsies believe that a vampire can come to his wife at night and procreate a 'child', known as a '*Vampijerović*'. In Kosovo-Metohija the Orthodox Gypsies call such a child, supposed to be born of a Gypsy mother and vampire father through their intercourse after the husband's death, *Vampirić* ('little vampire'), the child born posthumously. If it is a boy he is named *Vampir*, if a girl *Vampirera*; and by the Moslem priest's family. In Stari Ras and Novopazarski Sandžak in Vokš they consider that a vampire can only beget a son and not a daughter, and that it cannot spring from an Orthodox or Moslem priest's family. In Stari Ras and Novopazarski Sandžak this child goes by the name of *Lampijerović*, and in the latter district there is a whole village of *Lampijerović*-es, so-called from a vampire of whom they are the direct descendants. Among all Balkan peoples it is thought that these children have the power to see and kill vampires. But there is also a belief that the vampire helps his wife in her housework, winds the thread while she is weaving, threads the cotton through the eye of a needle as she sews, talks with her, and eats the sweets she has prepared for him.
>
> According to the Orthodox Gypsies in Stari Ras a vampire pursues his wife by day also, finding out where she will spend

the night so that he may come to her. The child born as a result of this sexual intercourse is supposed to be slippery like jelly, and cannot live.

Since the Moslem Gypsies in Novopazarski Sandžak are convinced that a vampire issues from its grave chiefly to make love to its wife, it is she who is 'most harassed'. On the third night after burial it visits her for the first time, and she 'feels' it but cannot protect herself from these assaults. The vampire disturbs her from early dawn till cock-crow, and she 'looks like a corpse, as if she were enchanted; you can spot her instantly. She is terrified; she neither eats nor drinks, becomes emaciated; one night seems to her as long as a year.' She says that when the vampire came to her it 'forced her down immediately'; and she dares not go anywhere alone. There may be people near her who yet do not know how much she suffers from this evil thing. Often a vampire may compel his wife to bring him something to eat and not like it, and then complain all night long saying: 'Bring me something else, this food is not good.'

In Prizren the Moslem Gypsies firmly believe that these love meetings between a vampire and its former wife are the most important of its occult actions.

The Occult Acts of a Vampire

Among both the Gypsies and the many Balkan races in these regions the number of occult acts attributed to a vampire, though neither large nor varied, are none the less very characteristic. On the one hand the vampire disturbs peaceful family life by entering a house or other buildings and breaking the night's rest of the members of the household, and on the other it does harm to cattle, horses and the like, and damages agriculture which, besides cattle-breeding and selling, is one of the main occupations of the rural Gypsies.

Above all it must be noted that, among the Moslem and Orthodox Gypsies in every part of Kosovo-Metohija, the belief is widespread that a vampire appears about six weeks after death, wanders about houses where it damages roofs, breaks tiles, pots, mugs, bottles and all other crockery, rides horses in the stables and stalks up and down in the attics. In the villages of Pirani and Upper Srbica Moslem Gypsies think that a vampire is very strong, and harms the cattle by riding them at night; and in Upper Morava that it likes to visit the house of its living relatives and then smash up their furniture and other possessions:

while in Vokš they believe on such visits it clears things up but does not eat anything.

In Novopazarski Sandžak the Orthodox Gypsies go further, and say that a vampire can wipe out the whole house of his live family. Thus there is a story of a certain Afis Adem Ranoševać who, as a vampire, came to the house of his relations, 'hurled things about the room and would not allow anyone to light a lamp'. On the contrary, Orthodox Gypsies in Stari Ras do not think a vampire does much harm: 'only clatters about with the dishes in a house and knocks a few of them down'.

By the Orthodox Gypsies of Kosovo-Metohija it is believed that, when a woman becomes a vampire, she rises from the grave as soon as she is buried and catches people and cattle by the legs and injures them. She also stalks about in the attics, across the roofs, and wanders around the various settlements. But they think too that there are some vampires who, when they come into their relatives' homes, bring with them little wax candles nearly burned out. Such a one brings washing-soap (several blocks of it) and leaves it in the cupboard where the flour is kept, knocks on the chimney and tidies up things. This vampire does no harm to its relations.

The most significant fact is that, according to the belief of both the Gypsy and Balkan peoples, a vampire slaughters and chokes tame animals. In Prizrenski Podgor and Podrima it is supposed by the Moslem Gypsies to 'let the sheep out of their pens and folds, chase them to their pasture, watch them while they graze and, when necessary, whistle through its lips like a live man'. They think the vampire always kills the best cattle, but they will not eat the meat themselves, only sell it to others. Among the Balkan people, too, as well as the Gypsies in these regions, it is not considered good to eat the flesh of any animal killed by a vampire. It is said that such meat is very red and it is thrown away. This interesting taboo is all the more surprising when we bear in mind that it has been scientifically recorded that Gypsies often eat carrion and do not find the flesh of dead animals abhorrent.

In the little town of Uroševac (Lugovi district) Moslem Gypsies believe that any cattle that have died have been killed by a vampire.

To prove how deeply rooted is the belief of these Gypsies in the malevolent influence of the vampire as a supreme occult being, the best evidence is offered by a story current in Lugovi that one of them destroyed forty head of cattle during the summer of 1946.

Who can see a Vampire and How

Concerning the question to whom and in what manner a vampire appears I have been able to collect the following data. In the village of Caparci (Podrima) the Moslem Gypsies believe that anyone at all could see a vampire: all he would have to do is to look under his own muscles, with his arms akimbo, but should he do so he would fall seriously ill immediately afterwards. In the same region, in the villages of Upper and Lower Srbica, they think that a vampire is only visible to his son *Dhampir*, to a magician or sorcerer, and to nobody else; but, according to the Gypsies in Lešani, any man could see a vampire providing that a *Dhampir* handed him his shirt, having taken it off in the place where he is hunting a vampire, and that the curious fellow looked through its sleeve. The same result would be achieved by looking under the arm of a sorcerer (or through the sleeve of his shirt), when he is performing some of the preliminary acts of magic for the destruction of a vampire; but as a consequence, if the man did see the creature, he would suffer from malaria for three years afterwards and ultimately die. However, if the magician had allowed somebody to take a look, and that person died of fright afterwards, he would be obliged to pay compensation to the man's family. So both the Gypsies and their Balkan neighbours say that the magician always warns those who are curious to see for themselves what a vampire looks like, of the consequences of such rashness.

Among the Moslem Gypsies in Lugovi and Uroševać (Kosovo), there is a belief that a vampire can be seen by a twin brother and sister born on a Saturday who wear their drawers and shirts inside out. Here too they think that a vampire is visible to any person to whom a magician gives a certain kind of plant when he is in the act of destroying the creature. There is a story told by these Gypsies of a man who asked the magician to give to him this plant, but his request was at first refused and only granted in the end. Then the cowherds came with the cattle, and in the midst of the cattle was the vampire. The man who had the magic plant beheld it instantly, but then grew sick with fright, so that he had to lie in bed for six weeks afterwards.

In Novopazarski Sandžak the Moslem Gypsies believe that a vampire can always be seen by its wife when it visits her for sexual intercourse, though all the other persons present can only hear it stumping about the house, but in Loćani, in the district of Vokš, they think that if any member of the family wishes to see a vampire he ought to stand behind the magician who is destroying it and look through his arm.

The Moslem Gypsies in Upper Morava hold the strange belief that a stallion can also see a vampire.

Preventive and Defensive Measures against the Appearance of a Vampire

Among the Gypsies I have been studying, several protective measures are in use against the appearance of a vampire. Thus in Podrima, Drenica, Metohiski Podgor and Lab (Kosovo-Metohija) the Moslem Gypsies consider it good to keep a piece of juniper wood in the house, as that would prevent a vampire from coming into it, or, even if it did come, from doing any harm.

In the region of Lugovi and Uroševać they believe that a settlement can be protected from a vampire by finding a twin brother and sister born on a Saturday and making them wear their shirts and drawers inside out (*cf* previous section). This pair could see a vampire out of doors at night, but immediately it saw them it would have to flee, head over heels.

In Upper Morava the Moslem Gypsies leave a hen's egg in the place where a vampire is supposed to appear, hide themselves and watch. As soon as they no longer see the egg where they put it, they think that the vampire has made its appearance, and one of the peasants fires a gun from an ambush and kills it.

According to the Orthodox Gypsies in Stari Ras, if anyone is afraid of a vampire he ought to place some thorns (the best are hawthorn and acacia thorns) in the windows. The vampire then can neither enter the house nor harm it. They also have a custom of putting thorns into a hole in the grave from which it is thought the vampire emerges, so that it pricks itself when it arises, and dies.

In Mamuša the Moslem Gypsies believe that no vampire can come to a village which was first ploughed by two orphans and two heads of cattle, twins born of the same cow, regardless of their sex.

The custom of these Gypsies in Podrima and Prizenski Podgor, when a vampire re-appears in a village, is to go to the Moslem priest, get a fetish from him, and stick it over the front door.

Part Three

The Pagan Vampire

The Blood Taboo

The horrors of cannibalism, of sacrifice and ancestor-worship have already been described in Part One, as has the importance of blood in the vampire myth. Here are some examples of the strength of the blood taboo and the conflicting attitudes that different races and religions have had towards it.

In the *Odyssey* Ulysses, anxious to converse with the dead, poured into a ditch the thick, black blood of two recently slaughtered rams. The dark host then slowly drank the liquid and as they drank the power of speech was returned to them, and they took on a positive, if alarming, form.

In *Leviticus* XVII, 10-14, the tribes of Israel are commanded:

If any man whosoever of the house of Israel, and of the strangers that sojourn amongst them, eat blood I will set my face against his soul, and will cut him off from amongst his people: because the life of the flesh is in the blood; and I have given it to you, that you may make atonement with it upon the altar for your souls, and the blood may be an expiation for the soul. Therefore I have said to the children of Israel:

No soul of you, nor of the strangers that sojourn among you, shall eat blood. Any man whatsoever of the children of Israel, and of the strangers that sojourn among you, if by hunting or by fowling, he takes a wild beast or a bird, which is lawful to eat, let him pour out its blood, and cover it with earth. For the life of all flesh is in the blood: therefore I said to the children of Israel: You shall not eat the blood of any flesh at all, because the life of the flesh is in the blood, and whosoever eateth it, shall be cut off.

In *The Vampire: Its Kith and Kin,* Montague Summers points out that amongst African tribes, Australian Aborigines and the Polynesians

...mourning for the dead is always accompanied by the laceration of the body until blood freely flows, and it is even not unknown for relatives of the deceased to inflict terrible mutilations upon themselves, and he who is most pitiless and most barbarous is esteemed to show the greater honour and respect to the departed. The important point lies in the fact that blood must be shed, and this appears to constitute some covenant with the dead, so that by freely bestowing what he requires they prevent him from returning to deprive them of it forcibly and in the most terrifying circumstances. If they are not willing to feed him with their blood he will come back and take it from them, so naturally it is believed to be far better to give without demur and gain the protection of the ghost, rather than to refuse what the phantom will inevitably seize upon in vengeance and in wrath.

The Aborigines thought of blood as an antidote for the sick or the weak—forming a primitive basis for 'leeching' and later blood transfusing. In New South Wales the strong were bled and their blood was fed to the weak. Most of the Aborigines believed in the existence of the soul after death, and took for granted that blood was the strength in life. Therefore incisions were made in the living to shed blood for the dead—i.e. for the nourishment of the soul.

Many primitive peoples believed that the soul was contained in the blood and it is therefore not difficult to see why they then considered the divine spirit to be the blood of a god. So that man could attain divine status the gods were symbolically sacrificed. The sacrificial symbol was generally a young man at the height of his physical and mental powers which would ensure that the sacrifices could absorb the full pride of their slaughtered god. Aztec history holds a comparable and extraordinarily vicious account of this practice. The ceremony involved the slaughter but eventual resuscitation of the maize-goddess Chicomecohuatl. Volta states that 'on the day of the autumn equinox the priest celebrated the sanguinary marriage of a virgin with Nature, the latter and not the virgin being the one fecundated'. The horrific ritual went as follows:

The victim, dressed as a bride, and covered in extravagant jewellery, danced through the streets in front of a dizzy, weary and hungry crowd—a crowd who had rigorously fasted for a week. Having arrived in Chicomecohuatl's temple the frenetic bride danced throughout the night to the music of horns, flutes and trumpets and amidst the hysterical prayers of the crowd. The scene was macabre in the extreme with an atmosphere charged with incense, and great mounds of sugar-cane, seeds, and flowers stacked around the temple floor.

At dawn the crowd fell on its knees and by making incisions in their ears, caused their own blood to splash into a dish. At this point the music stopped—and the blood was offered to the bride. Then she was sprung upon by the priest, thrown upon the ground—and her head was severed from her body. The blood that streamed from the stump and the head was caught in bowls and taken away to fertilize the earth. The priest, meanwhile, skinned the bride and wore the skin as a costume. The appalling ritual having been concluded, the priest then joined the crowd in a dance of joy.

Other Aztec rituals involved 'the elemental concept of the transfer of "soul-stuff" by close contact with the flesh and the blood'. Children were continuously sacrificed to the gods and their blood was collected by the priests to knead into an image of the god Vitzilopochblc, which was made of maize dough, and part of which was given to the reigning Aztec monarch to eat. The moon god, Totec, also had to be continuously appeased, particularly during the period that preceded the first sowing of seed. To achieve this a prisoner was tied to a timber frame and executed by bowmen. As the arrows scored the prisoner's body so the blood ran down, sacramentally fertilizing the soil and appeasing Totec.

Hogg, in his complex work on cannibalism, states that:

> Perhaps the most fundamental, as well as the most universal of these religio-magical beliefs is that a man who eats part of another man's body will immediately come to possess some of the qualities that belonged to him when he was still alive. This was the transference of the 'soul-stuff', or 'life-principle' (there are many other words and phrases to describe this essential ingredient that could, so primitive man thought, be transferred thus from the dead to the living). For a man to eat the heart of a man he had slain in battle meant that he acquired that amount of extra courage; it was all the better if he had been fortunate enough to slay a doughty warrior. The child of an Australian tribesman might be encouraged to eat some part of his dead father's flesh, so that when he grew up he would resemble his father in his courage, or skill as a tracker, or powers of leadership.
>
> There were many variants of this method of transferring the 'soul-stuff' from the dead man to the living man. Sometimes the blood of the dead man would be swallowed, preferably while it was yet warm. Less primitive, or more highly developed, tribes contented themselves with licking the blood off the spear that had killed the enemy; or even, as an ultimate refinement, eating the first meal after the battle without first cleansing the hands of any blood that had been splashed on to them.

Deliberate offerings of blood were therefore made both to the dead and to the gods, and the gods were symbolically slaughtered so that Man could achieve godhead. The key word throughout is blood—blood the life, the soul, the fountainhead. A much prized and much desired fluid. But those who desired could not always obtain it and those who were left out could be termed the underprivileged dead—the demons, spirits and ghosts who were forever searching for a drop or two of soul-replenishment. These unfavoured dark forces were much feared and their only catalysts were sorcerers or witches who wanted to use them for their own nefarious purposes. Most demons, spirits or ghosts, all of whom were forerunners of the vampire, would do anything for a pint of blood—for by having this they would temporarily assume both form and tissue.

In West Africa the Caffres believed that a few drops of blood would rejuvenate their *revenants*—ghosts of evil men who would return after death on murder bent. If a drop of blood was spilt on the ground it must immediately be covered with earth. If it fell on the body then an instant purification ceremony must begin. They were also guarding against the sorcerers who would take advantage of the spillage and use the blood for black magic purposes. The same fears existed in New Guinea where wounded natives would cast their bloodied bandages far out into the sea just in case a thirsty ghost or avaricious sorcerer managed to get spectral or horny hands upon the life-stuff.

There is a strong connection between sexual passion and blood, and as Summers puts it

> a vast number of cases have been recorded in which persons who are normal, find intense pleasure in the thought of blood during the sexual relations, although perhaps if blood was actually flowing they might feel repulsion.

In her book *The Vampire* Ornella Volta quotes examples of blood actually used as an aphrodisiac. The first is an extract from the Marquis de Sade's *Justine*:

> 'Countess, your arms!'
>
> He seized her with ferocity, and treated her exactly as he had treated me: hanging her from the ceiling by her wrists with two black ribbons; he charged me to see to the bandaging, which he then personally supervised: they did not appear tight enough to him and he pulled them as hard as possible so that the blood—said he—would burst forth; he then fingered the veins and almost simultaneously transfixed them both. The blood gushed out in a long jet. The count was delighted...

Secondly, she takes an extract from Georges Bataille's *Le Bleu Du Ciel*:

> I pierced her thigh through her clothes with the points of a fork without a moment's hesitation. She began to shriek and in the disordered movement she made to escape from me, two glasses of red wine were spilt on the table. I threw my head back and lifted up her skirts to observe the wound. The underwear was of good quality, and her naked thigh pleased me: one of the points of the fork, sharper than the other, had torn her skin and blood was seeping out but it was only a scratch of no importance. I threw myself at her and there was no time to prevent me from pressing my lips to her thigh in order to suck the tiny quantity of blood running from it, due to my own work... the other guests came to watch me, rather surprised, with an embarrassed little laugh ... I then refilled the glass with red wine and made her drink it.

Finally, to illustrate the role of blood in witchcraft here is how Eliphas Levi in *The History of Magic* saw a fifteenth-century magician named Bombast:

> He healed wounds by applying powerful reactives to the spilt blood, thus sending back its physical soul and purified sap to the body. To cure a diseased limb he made a limb of wax and, by will-power, transferred thereto the magnetism of the diseased limb. Then he treated the wax with vitriol, iron and fire, thus reacting by imagination and magnetic correspondence on the sick person himself, to whom the limb of wax had become an appendix and supplement. Paracelsus knew the mysteries of blood; he knew why the priests of Baal made incisions with knives in their flesh, and then brought down fire from heaven; he knew why orientals poured out their blood before a woman to inspire her with physical love; he knew how spilt blood cries for vengeance or mercy and fills the air with angels or demons. Blood is the instrument of dreams and multiplies images in the brain during sleep, because it is full of the Astral Light. Its globules are bisexual, magnetised and metalled, sympathetic and repelling. All forms and images in the world can be evoked from the physical soul of blood.

Roots of Witchcraft and Demonry

The vampire myth is strongly interlinked with witchcraft and demonry. As has been described in Part One, a witch or a sorcerer is very likely to return from the grave as a vampire, sucking the blood of the corpse to keep his or her body from decaying. The vampire himself practises black magic and there are strong links between vampirism and witchcraft.

In some countries it was thought that the vampire was the offspring of a union between a witch and the Devil. Demonologist Ludovic Maria Sinistrari, in his *De Demonialitate*, translated by Summers in 1927, says:

> It is undoubted by theologians and philosophers that carnal intercourse between Mankind and the Demon sometimes gives birth to human beings; and that is how Antichrist is to be born, according to some doctors, for example, Bellarmine, Suarez and Thomas Malvenda. They further observe that, from a natural course, the children thus begotten by Incubi are tall, very hardy and bloodily bold, arrogant beyond words, and desperately wicked.

There are two separate theories in sorcery about the origin of vampires. The first is that the soul of a living man (sometimes a living sorcerer) left its corporate body in sleep and went out into the outside world. Its shape could be something as slight as a piece of straw or fluff or down. In this way the antagonistic soul could slip through keyholes and attack its sleeping victim. The sleeper could only protect himself by waking and resisting the attentions of the blood-thirsty soul. If he did this successfully, and harmed the minute soul-embodiment, then its bodily owner would be harmed or—at best—destroyed. The second theory was that the soul of a dead man roved abroad, sucking at the blood of living men. Vampires could appear in the character of a poltergeist and cause poltergeist disturbances. There was a reported incident involving this on the island of Mycore in 1700 when a poltergeist vampire was supposed to have entered houses after being buried for two days. Furniture was upset, lamps were put out and the local peasantry panicked.

Witchcraft itself has a long and complex history. As a practice it was not considered to be really dangerous or even particularly evil until the fifteenth century. Before this date both witches and sorcerers were merely regarded as a nuisance. Punishment was very light and if caught at her craft, a witch would only receive some minor penalty—such as a forty-day penance during which time she was meant to meditate upon her malpractices. The Church was particularly unworried and was in the wholesome state of disbelieving in magic. All practitioners of black magic were looked upon as lost souls in need of Godly repatriation, rather than any kind of threat to ecclesiastical control.

To the peasants (and indeed the aristocracy) witches were a psychological uplift. They were quite prepared to brew up love-potions (for a price) and were proverbial curers of warts, skin conditions and imagined maladies. The witch could equally well prepare potions against an enemy and his cattle or prepare a potion to cure the sickness of her employer's cattle. She was a versatile, well-ordered and necessary cog in the feudal system and had it not been for her sudden recognition as a figure of evil by the Church then all would have been well with her for a good many more centuries.

Bernhardt J. Hurwood, the American occult writer, says in *Monsters Galore* (1965):

> Unfortunately from the Church point of view, Witchcraft and Satanism began to gain converts. Under the feudal system the greater masses of people were poverty-stricken and little more than slaves to the powerful lords and barons. Since the Church had to rely on the rich for support, its obvious alliance was with the ruling classes. The poor, living in squalor with no hope of improving their lot during their lives, could hardly fill their growling stomachs, or clothe their naked children with shining promises of paradise in the hereafter. There began to grow among the people the earliest rumblings of a desire for freedom, for individual dignity, for hope of a better life on earth. They felt that God was letting them down and they turned to Satan. Satan promised them riches, power; tangible things while they lived. Thus witchcraft began to flourish.

As the Church began to pronounce heavily against witchcraft, the Satanists began to organise themselves into a rival body. Their rites, modelled on those of the established Church, took the shape of, say, an inverted mass at the Sabbath and a reversal of the Christian Mass at the Black Mass. In these ceremonies total self-indulgence was enjoyed, orgies were held and centuries of inhibition and privation were exorcised. The Cross was turned upside-down, God renounced, the Bible spat upon, the Lord's Prayer repeated backwards.

In 1484 Innocent VIII issued the Papal Bull against Witchcraft. Part of it read as follows:

> It has indeed lately come to Our ears, not without afflicting Us with bitter sorrow, that in some parts of Northern Germany, as well as in the provinces, townships, territories, districts, and dioceses of Mainz, Cologne, Trèves, Salzburg, and Bremen, many persons of both sexes, unmindful of their own salvation and straying from the Catholic Faith, have abandoned themselves to devils, incubi and succubi, and by their incantations, spells, conjurations, and other accursed charms and crafts, enormities and horrid offences, have slain infants yet in the mother's womb, as also the offspring of cattle, have blasted the produce of the earth, the grapes of the vine, the fruits of trees, nay, men and women, beasts of burthen, herd-beasts, as well as animals of other kinds, vineyards, orchards, meadows, pastureland, corn, wheat, and all other cereals; these wretches furthermore afflict and torment men and women, beasts of burthen, herd-beasts, as well as animals of other kinds, with terrible and piteous pains and sore diseases, both internal and external; they hinder men from performing the sexual act and women from conceiving, whence husbands cannot know their wives nor wives receive their husbands; over and above this, they blasphemously renounce that Faith which is theirs by the Sacrament of Baptism, and at the instigation of the Enemy of Mankind they do not shrink from committing and perpetrating the foulest abominations and filthiest excesses to the deadly peril of their own souls, whereby they outrage the Divine Majesty and are a cause of scandal and danger to very many. And although Our dear sons Henry Kramer and James Sprenger, Professors of Theology of the Order of Friars Preachers, have been by Letters Apostolic delegated as Inquisitors, the first in the aforesaid parts of Northern Germany ... and the second in certain territories which lie along the borders of the Rhine, nevertheless not a few clerics and lay folk of those coun-

> tries, seeking too curiously to know more than concerns them ... are not ashamed to contend with the most unblushing effrontery that these enormities are not practised in those provinces, and consequently the aforesaid Inquisitors have no legal right to exercise their powers of inquisition in the provinces, townships, dioceses, districts, and territories, which have been rehearsed, and that the Inquisitors may not proceed to punish, imprison, and penalise criminals convicted of the heinous offences and many wickednesses which have been set forth. Accordingly in the aforesaid provinces, townships, dioceses, and districts, the abominations and enormities in question remain unpunished not without open danger to the souls of many and peril of eternal damnation.

Now the Catholic Church had declared direct war on the Satanists and it was to be a fight to the death— the death of thousands of innocent people who, wrongly suspected of witchcraft, were ducked, drowned or torn apart by the Church and its ministering purists. The book *Malleus Maleficarum,* following hot on the heels of the Papal Bull, led to an inglorious and dangerous Inquisition. The investigators, Sprenger and Kramer, accused witches of being able to cooperate with the Devil, to copulate with the Devil, to sway the minds of men to love or hate, to remove the male organ at will, to obstruct the sexual act, to influence generation, to change men into beasts, to kill the child in the womb, and to procure abortion. Both inquisitors (who were also Dominican Friars) held women primarily responsible for the evils of witchcraft.

In England witches were hung but elsewhere they were invariably burnt or drowned. Hanging was considered a doubtful retribution for, as in the case of the vampire, it was thought vital to utterly consume the body in case it was able to rise from even a small remaining particle of flesh or bone. A case in point was the unfortunate Lady Pittadro who was suspected of practising witchcraft in 1649 in Scotland. But she died before her trial and her body was buried. A row immediately broke out and feelings ran high. The Scottish General Assembly were amongst the noisiest complainers, insisting that the body should be burnt. Their records on the matter state:

> Concerning the matter of the buriall of the Lady Pittadro, who, being under a great scandall of witchcraft, and being incarcerat in the Tolbuith of this burgh during her triall before the Justice, died in prison. The Commission of the General Assembly, having considered the report of the Committee appointed for that purpose, doe give their advyse to the Presbyterie of Dumferling to show their dislike of that fact of the buriall of the Lady Pittadro, in respect of the manner and place, and that the said Presbyterie may labour to make the persons who hes buried her sensible of their offence in so doeing; and some of the persons who buried hir, being personallie present, are desired by the Commission to show themselvis to the Presbyterie sensible of their miscarriage therein.

Records of a case in Maidstone (1652) read as follows:

> Anne Ashby, alias Cobler, Anne Martyn, Mary Browne, Anne Wilson and Mildred Wright of Cranbrooke and Mary Read, of Lenham, being legally convicted, were according to the laws of the Nation, adjudged to be hanged, at the common place of Execution. Some there were that wished rather they might be burnt to Ashes; alledging that it was a received opinion among many, that the body of a witch being burnt, her blood is prevented thereby from becoming hereditary to her Progeny in the same evill.

Demonry was a rather more complex business, as in the sixteenth century the air was reputed to be inhabited by some 7,405,926 demons, all able to change both shape and form. They were mainly in evidence at night, could easily be swallowed and were anxious to possess any likely human being. The exorcism of demons, like witches and vampires, was mostly effected by burning.

Some Interesting Phobias

To fully appreciate the ease with which vampire fear spread it is important to look at some of the customs or phobias of the time. Here are three typical examples of primitive neurosis:

1. *Sin-eating and Soul Cakes*

In remote East Anglian villages the parents of a sinful offspring who had died unredeemed would lure a stranger into their midst. They would then persuade the stranger to share in the wake. This would involve sitting around the corpse and partaking of drink and food in the traditional manner. The parents of the sinner, carefully refraining from eating, would ask their unwilling mourner to eat a series of small, dry cakes. By doing this he was apparently supposed to partake of their child's sin—and take that sin as his own.

Soul cakes are a slightly different version of the same tradition. They are most prevalent in Belgium where 'soul-cakes' or 'soul bread' are baked on November 1st to be eaten on the following day. Presumably they were intended to fortify the dead. In varying forms the custom is perpetuated in many different areas. At Dixmude, for instance, it is believed that a soul is released from hell for every cake eaten. In Germany and Austria cakes are offered to the dead by the living. Here these cakes are known as souls, and are composed in a specific way. Montague Summers relates that the season of the dead was observed with tremendous honour. 'In the villages they believed that as the curfew rings the departed will come back to their old accustomed places round the hearth and two or three chairs are always left vacant in the circle.'

2. *Funeral Feasting*

Banquets were often taken to the tomb in Greece—and still are. In 1928 in England the *Daily Express* reported:

> The objection of a local council to the placing of food on a grave, a practice which is alleged to be causing scandal, has led to a curious action which is entered on the cause list for today. The action comes before Mr. Justice Eve in the Chancery Division.
>
> The plaintiff in this action is Miss Hoskyns-Abrahall, who is seeking an order from the court to prevent the Paignton Urban District Council from obstructing her in this practice.
>
> Officials of the Council were in London yesterday waiting for the case to come on. One of them stated in an interview that the grave in question in Paignton Cemetery was that of Mr. Hos-

kyns-Abrahall, a former Church of England clergyman, who died about ten years ago, and his wife. Miss Hoskyns-Abrahall, a relative of the clergyman, had been in the habit of visiting the grave and descending into the vault. There she spent many hours. At every visit she brought provisions—chickens, pigeon-pies, fruit, bread, wine, and various dainties—which she left behind on the grave.

These had a habit of disappearing, and the position was such that the council had to take action to prevent provisions being left on the grave.

It is understood that Miss Hoskyns-Abrahall maintains that she is carrying out an ancient rite of the Greek Church.

An official of the Greek Legation explained yesterday that the custom of placing bread on a grave, a survival from ancient Greek pagan worship, still persists in Greek villages.

'The bread is placed in water on a large plate and left with the body. The idea,' he said, 'is that it is thought the soul needs some nourishment, and that it can only find it in the place which the body once inhabited.' (*Daily Express*)

The population of many countries, in both pagan and Christian times, have carried food to the dead in their tombs. The tradition appears to be a hangover from the process of sacrifice—and the need to appease the hungry and possibly vengeful dead.

3. *Need-Fires*

Need-fires, perhaps one of the most romantic symbols of pagan times, are a much-practised form of purification. A need-fire cannot be started by a match, nor can it be started by flint or steel. Prolonged friction is the only way, firstly lighting a piece of cloth and secondly, via the cloth, lighting a bonfire. The ceremony must be carried out at night, without a single speck of artificial light. Should any man-made light appear the old magic will die and the need-fire will not perform its ceremony of purification. At one stage the need-fire was kindled as a preventive measure but it is more usual to begin the fires at a time of catastrophe. Plague was a favourite catalyst of the need-fire—and other bonfires were begun from a brand plucked from the original. Another reason for the lighting of these fires was cattle disease—and often cattle were driven through the smoke of this cleansing operation. The practice was mainly centred in Germany, in Switzerland and in Scandinavia. In Yorkshire and Northumberland also, however, these bonfires were kindled in the traditional manner, right up until the beginning of the century.

Need-fires in Russia and Central Europe performed a slightly different function in that it was believed that all cattle disease sprang from vampirism—i.e. that the cattle were being slowly wasted by this predatory blood-sucker. The fire was lit surrounding the diseased cattle—and as a vampire finds passing through fire impossible, it was assumed that the health of the herd would be restored. St Roch, a Polish saint, was the principal human being responsible for the kindling of need-fires. During the course of his life, he had continually cared for both men and animals brought down by the plague. As a result he was considered to possess a charm against plague and after his death, public prayers were held in his honour—in order to diminish the threat or the current crisis. As vampires are reckoned to be plague-spreaders in Poland, St Roch is thought of as the protection against them.

A particular example of the superstition surrounding the need-fire occurred in 1598 at Neustaat near Marburg, where cattle disease was particularly rife. In desperation the town councillors turned towards magic and the order was given out that all man-made fires should be extinguished. Sparks were then produced by friction and the diseased cattle were driven through the smoke of a massive bonfire. Unfortunately it is recorded that this magic rite had absolutely no effect and the disease was as rife as ever. The chief organiser of the kindling, a so-called magician named Kohler, was executed as a result of his inefficiency.

Sir James Frazer in *The Golden Bough** has this to say about the ceremony:

> When the need-fire was at last kindled, the bonfire was lit from it, and as soon as the blaze was somewhat died down, the sick animals were driven over the glowing embers, sometimes in a regular order of precedence, first the pigs, next the cows, and last of all the horses. Sometimes they were driven twice or

* Macmillan, 1925.

thrice through the smoke and flames, so that occasionally some of them were scorched to death. As soon as all the beasts were through, the young folk would rush wildly at the ashes and cinders, sprinkling and blackening each other with them; those who were most blackened would march in triumph behind the cattle into the village and would not wash themselves for a long time. From the bonfire people carried live embers home and used them to rekindle the fires in their houses. These brands, after being extinguished in water, they sometimes put in the mangers at which the cattle fed, and kept them there for a while. Ashes from the need-fire were also strewed on the fields to protect the crops against vermin; sometimes they were taken home to be employed as remedies in sickness, being sprinkled on the ailing part or mixed in water and drunk by the patient.

He goes on to describe protection against vampirism by need-fires:

> Among Slavonic peoples it appears that the foes whom the need-fire is designed to combat are not so much living witches as vampyres and other evil spirits, and the ceremony aims rather at repelling these baleful beings than at actually consuming them in the flames. But for our present purpose these distinctions are immaterial. The important thing to observe is that amongst the Slavs the need-fire, which is probably the original of all the ceremonial fires now under consideration, is not a sun-charm, but clearly and unmistakably nothing but a means of protecting man and beast against the attacks of maleficent creatures, whom the peasant thinks to burn or scare by the heat of the fire, just as he might burn or scare wild animals.
>
> Again, the bonfires are often supposed to protect the fields against hail and the homestead against thunder and lightning. But both hail and thunderstorms are frequently thought to be caused by witches; hence the fire which bans the witches necessarily serves at the same time as a talisman against hail, thunder, and lightning. Further, brands taken from the bonfires are commonly kept in the houses to guard them against conflagration; and though this may perhaps be done on the principle of homeopathic magic, one fire being thought to act as a preventative of another, it is also possible that the intention may be to keep witch-incendiaries at bay. Again, people leap over the bonfires as a preventative of colic, and look at the flames steadily in order to preserve their eyes in good health; and both colic and sore

eyes are in Germany, and probably elsewhere, set down to the machinations of witches. Once more, to leap over the midsummer fires or to circumambulate them is thought to prevent a person from feeling pains in his back at reaping; and in Germany such pains are called 'witch-shots' and ascribed to witchcraft.

Crossroads and the Mandrake

The Mandrake, a hardy little plant, was reputed to be nurtured by rotting flesh. In Wales witches apparently slept during the day at the crossroads, concealed by boulders. At night they pursued children and, on catching them, consumed their flesh. The crossroads were also famous for their gallows, from which criminals hung until their bodies decomposed. Underneath this carrion the mandrake grew and thrived. As a result the plant received the reputation of being a plant of magical power and of fertility.

In Germany the mandrake was called the Little Gallows Man and was reputed to thrive on the semen or urine that fell from the corpse on the gallows. Folk-lore forbade the uprooting of the mandrake, for if its roots were torn from the ground, the plant would scream and its persecutor would soon die, with the screams of the mandrake ringing in his ears. The only way the plant can be dug up is recounted by Montague Summers:

> A dog is taken and round his tail is tied a string, one end of which is attached to the plant. A man whose ears are stopped fast with wax and wool tempts the dog away with some dainty. As the animal tugs at the cord the mandrake will be pulled from the ground, but the poor beast will fall dead at the scream it gives.

Crossroads themselves have always played an important role in mythology. In Russia it was said that corpses lurked at crossroads, ready to ensnare the unwary traveller. In Ceylon a creature known as the Black She Devil lurks about crossroads with evil intent, as does the devil Maha Sohom (devil of the tombs) who quaffs elephants' blood there.

The Pagan Vampire

Ancient Greece, Assyria, Babylon, India and Israel all have traces of the vampire legend. The legends are romantic yet extraordinarily primitive.

1. *Ancient Greece*

Greek tragedy is full of the most appalling blood-letting. But the nearest one gets to a vampire in ancient Greece is the Empusa, or Lamia, a demon that had a tangible body—but not one composed of human flesh and blood. Keats based his poem *Lamia* on the following legend, recounted in the *Life of Apollonius of Tyana* by Philostratus. Philostratus is discussing one of Apollonius's pupils:

> Among the latter was Menippus, a Lycian of twenty-five years of age, well endowed with good judgment, and of a physique so beautifully proportioned that in mien he resembled a fine and gentlemanly athlete. Now this Menippus was supposed by most people to be loved by a foreign woman, who was good-looking and extremely dainty, and said that she was rich; although she was really, as it turned out, none of these things, but was only so in semblance. For as he was walking all alone along the road towards Cenchreae, he met with an apparition, and it was a woman who clasped his hand and declared that she had been long in love with him, and that she was a Phoenician woman and lived in a suburb of Corinth, and she mentioned the name of the particular suburb, and said: 'When you reach the place this evening, you will hear my voice as I sing to you, and you shall have wine such as you never before drank, and there will be no rival to disturb you; and we two beautiful beings will live together.' The youth consented to this, for although he was in general a strenuous philosopher, he was nevertheless susceptible to the tender passion; and he visited her in the evening, and for the future constantly sought her company as his darling, for he did not yet realise that she was a mere apparition.
>
> Then Apollonius looked over Menippus as a sculptor might do and he sketched an outline of the youth and examined him, and having observed his foibles, he said: 'You are a fine youth and are hunted by fine women, but in this case you are cherish-

ing a serpent, and a serpent cherishes you.' And when Menippus expressed his surprise he added: 'For this lady is of a kind you cannot marry. Why should you? Do you think that she loves you?' 'Indeed I do,' said the youth, 'since she behaves to me as if she loves me.' 'And would you then marry her?' said Apollonius. 'Why, yes, for it would be delightful to marry a woman who loves you.' Thereupon Apollonius asked when the wedding was to be. 'Perhaps tomorrow,' said the other, 'for it brooks no delay.' Apollonius therefore waited for the occasion of the wedding breakfast, and then, presenting himself before the guests who had just arrived, he said: 'Where is the dainty lady at whose instance ye are come?' 'Here she is,' replied Menippus, and at the same moment he rose slightly from his seat, blushing. 'And to which of you belong the silver and gold and all the rest of the decorations of the banqueting hall?' 'To the lady,' replied the youth, 'for this is all I have of my own,' pointing to the philosopher's cloak which he wore.

And Apollonius said: 'Have you heard of the gardens of Tantalus, how they exist and yet do not exist?' 'Yes,' they answered, 'in the poems of Homer, for we certainly never went down to Hades.' 'As such,' replied Apollonius, 'you must regard this adornment, for it is not reality but the semblance of reality. And that you may realise the truth of what I say, this fine bride is one of the vampires, that is to say of those beings whom the many regard as lamias and hob-goblins. These beings fall in love, and they are devoted to the delights of Aphrodite, but especially to the flesh of human beings, and they decoy with such delights those whom they mean to devour in their feasts.' And the lady said: 'Cease your ill-omened talk and be gone'; and she pretended to be disgusted at what she heard, and no doubt she was inclined to rail at philosophers and say that they always talked nonsense. When, however, the goblets of gold and the show of silver were proved as light as air and all fluttered away out of their sight, while the wine-bearers and the cooks and all the retinue of servants vanished before the rebukes of Apollonius, the phantom pretended to weep, and prayed him not to torture her nor to compel her to confess what she really was. But Apollonius insisted and would not let her off, and then she admitted she was a vampire, and was fattening up Menippus with pleasures before devouring his body, for it was her habit to feed upon young and beautiful bodies, because their blood is pure and strong. I have related at length, because it was necessary to do so, this the best-known story of Apollonius; for many

> people are aware of it and know that the incident occurred in the centre of Hellas; but they have only heard in a general and vague manner that he once caught and overcame a lamia in Corinth but they have never learned what she was about, nor that he did it to save Menippus, but I owe my own account to Damis and to the work which he wrote.

Other ancient Greek demons and vampires include the Maniae (horribly deformed people), the Larvae (spirits that persecute children), the Mormo (a hideous female spirit), the Gilo (night-wandering phantoms), and the Striges (in one form the Striges appear as beautiful vampires and in another as blood-sucking, cradle-snatching birds).

Revenants in ancient Greece were the forerunners of the docile *revenant* discussed earlier. Far from being villainous or sinful these *revenants* were the Heroes, whose virility was strong enough to overcome death. However, they still needed blood in variable quantities to sustain them temporarily.

2. *Ancient Assyria and Babylon*

The vampire figure in this area was known as the Ekimmu; it was also cannibalistic and an occupier of the soul. The Ekimmu was a corpse who could find no rest. The reasons behind this restlessness were many and varied, for life was surrounded by taboo—and to break even the most minor taboo immediately made the miscreant liable to become an Ekimmu. Taboos included death as a result of murder, battle, prison, starvation, certain forms of illness, pregnancy, drowning, and attack by wild animals. Therefore the Ekimmu population was almost as big as the Assyrian population. R. Campbell Thompson, in his book *Devils and Evil Spirits of Babylonia* (1903), confirms that the Ekimmu was the soul of a dead person unable to rest, who wandered as a spectre over the earth. He goes on to say: 'If it found a luckless man who had wandered far from his fellows into haunted places, it fastened upon him, plagueing and tormenting him until such time as a priest should drive it away with exorcisms.'

Exorcism of the Ekimmu was through incantation:

Of giant strength and giant tread,
Demons (like) raging bulls, great ghosts,
Ghosts that break through all houses,
Demons that have no shame,
Seven are they!
Knowing no care,
They grind the land like corn;
Knowing no mercy,
They rage against mankind:
They spill their blood like rain,
Devouring their flesh (and) sucking their veins.
Where the images of the gods are, there they quake
In the temple of Nabu, who fertiliseth the shoots of wheat.
They are demons full of violence
Ceaselessly devouring blood.
Invoke the ban against them,
That they no more return to their neighbourhood.
By Heaven be ye exorcised! By Earth be ye exorcised!

3. *Israel*

The Lilith was a female demon, one of the seven Babylonian spirits of evil borrowed by the Hebrews. Talmudists considered the Lilith to be Eve, Adam's erring wife from the Garden of Eden. Soured by her rejection she took to the air, and became a blood-sucking demon who mainly preyed on children. The Lilith mischievously filled the minds of sleeping men with erotic dreams, thus causing them to excrete semen. The Lilith is recorded in the Bible as follows:

A) Authorised Version, Isaiah xxxiv, 14. 'The wild beasts of the desert shall also meet with the wild beasts of the island, and the satyr shall cry to his fellow; the screech-owl also shall rest there, and find for herself a place of rest.' With reference to 'screech-owl' there is a note saying 'or, night monster'.

B) Revised Version, Isaiah xxxiv, 14. 'And the wild beasts of the desert shall meet with the wolves, and the satyr shall cry to his fellow; yea, the night-monster shall settle there, and shall find her a place of rest.' Here the marginal notes include a reference to night monster, '*Heb.* Lilith'.

The Lilith, like the Greek Striges and Lamiae, were sorcerers and magicians whose main aim in life was to kill new-born children. The early Christians, however, considered the Lilith to be Queen of the Succubi—the female demons who had sexual intercourse with men whilst they slept.

4. *Ancient India*

The ancient Indian vampire, the Vetala, was not as vicious nor as demented as the Rákshasas—these were cannibalistic, animated dead bodies and interfered with religious ceremonies. They were peculiarly hideous to look at, for they were usually deformed, strangely coloured and had eyes that were simply long, sinister slits. Their nails were poisoned and were extremely dangerous to the touch. Their appetites extended beyond human flesh to horse-flesh and the Rákshasas were also deemed to be extraordinarily wealthy—wealth that they would distribute at whim to those mothers who had won their favour.

The goddess Kali was a very positive vampire. Her rôle as Goddess included destruction, plague and violent death. Her physical features include dark flowing hair and the useful addition of four arms. She was pictorially represented as beckoning to her worshippers with two arms whilst the third arm held a sword and the fourth a severed head. The head belonged to the King of the Demons who was called Raktaviya and was severed by the idiot-grinning, tongue-lolling, red-eyed Kali during a furious battle which she won by drinking Raktaviya's blood.

The Thugs, the worshippers of Kali, practised thuggee (garrotting, strangling and robbing their victims) until the nineteenth century, when the practice was outlawed by the British. The word 'thug' comes from the Hindu and means 'deceiver', and this group were eventually held responsible for over thirty thousand ritual murders.

Part Four

The Vampire in Christianity

Power and the Church

The wind doth blow today, my love,
And a few small drops of rain;
I never had but one true-love,
In cold grave she was lain.

I'll do as much for my true-love
As any young man may;
I'll sit and mourn all at her grave
For a twelvemonth and a day.

The twelvemonth and a day being up,
The dead began to speak:
'Oh who sits weeping on my grave,
And will not let me sleep?'

'Tis I, my love, sits on your grave,
  And will not let you sleep;
For I crave one kiss of your clay-cold lips,
  And that is all I seek.

You crave one kiss of my clay-cold lips;
  But my breath smells earthy strong;
If you have one kiss of my clay-cold lips,
  Your time will not be long.

'Tis down in yonder garden green,
  Love, where we used to walk,
The finest flower that ere was seen
  Is withered to a stalk.

The stalk is withered dry, my love,
  So will our hearts decay;
So make yourself content, my love,
  Till God calls you away.

The Unquiet Grave, traditional folk-song

Christianity not only perpetuated some of the established pagan taboos but also created some of its own. For instance, two of the main candidates for vampirism were the suicide and the excommunicant—both of whom had been outlawed by the Church. The doctrine of transubstantiation itself, symbolic and spiritual as it is, bears considerable resemblance to sacrifice, cannibalism and ancestor worship and led to misunderstandings amongst primitive converts to Christianity (see Part One).

The infamous *Malleus Maleficarum* also did much to spread belief in vampires:

> It is the height of folly to attempt to deny that such bodies are not infrequently found in their graves incorrupt and that by use of them the Devil, if God permits him, devises most horrible complots and schemes to the hurt and harm of mankind.

Leo Allatius, in his *De Graecorum hodie quorundam opinionatibus*, which was published at Cologne in 1645, describes an ordinance from the Greek Church instructing the faithful in the act of vampire-bashing.

> Concerning a dead man, if he be found whole, the which they call *vrykolakas*.

It is impossible that a dead man should become a *vrykolakas*, unless it be by the power of the Devil who, wishing to mock and delude some that they may incur the wrath of Heaven, causeth these dark wonders, and so very often at night he casteth a glamour whereby men imagine that the dead man whom they knew formerly, appears and holds converse with them, and in their dreams too they see strange visions. At other times they may behold him in the road, yea, even in the highway walking to and fro or standing still, and what is more than this he is even said to have strangled men and to have slain them.

Immediately there is sad trouble, and the whole village is in a riot and a racket, so that they hasten to the grave and they unbury the body of the man ... and the dead man—one who has long been dead and buried—appears to them to have flesh and blood ... so they collect together a mighty pile of dry wood and set fire to this and lay the body upon it so that they burn it and they destroy it altogether.

Oddly enough, unlike Allatius, the ordinance tends to treat the myth as merely a slice of pagan superstition—until the last few lines when the real crunch comes.

Be it known unto you, however, that when such an incorrupt body shall be discovered, the which, as we have said is the work of the Devil, ye must without delay summon the priests to chant an invocation to the All Holy Mother of God ... and solemnly to perform memorial services for the dead with funeral meats.

Another inflammatory theologian was Father François Richard, who claimed that three necessary components of witchcraft were the Devil, a witch and the permission of God. Good Father Richard wrote:

The Devil revitalizes and energizes these dead bodies which he preserves for a long time in their entirety; he appears with the actual face and in the likeness of the dead, stalking abroad up and down the streets, and presently he will parade the country roads and the fields; he bursts his way into men's houses, filling many with awful fear, leaving others dumb with horror, whilst others are even killed; he proceeds to acts of violence and blood, and strikes terror into every heart.

The basic confrontation between Christianity and paganism was over the sanctity of death. Man has always found it difficult to stand the final parting, and in pagan times it had been believed that the dead were only minutes away and that their parting with the living was purely a temporary manoeuvre. The Christian belief was of course more spiritual, but the grave of the Christian dead and the burial mound of the pagan dead are interlinked in that in both cases a final home or dwelling-place is provided.

Apart from suicide and excommunication, there were other Christian reasons for the walking of the dead. These included:

1. Those buried with mutilated rites
2. Those buried unbaptised
3. Those buried apostate.

These and other taboos were used as a direct threat by the Church to its congregation. The only defence, to a primitive society, against the powers of darkness and the devil is the benediction and exorcism of the Church. But if the Church, seeking ultimate power, *creates* the powers of darkness and the devil, then its faithful are caught in a vicious circle.

Dom Augustine Calmet, however, writing about the history of Hungarian vampirism from the fourteenth to the seventeenth century, was refreshingly sane about the whole business:

> For my part I think the whole history vain and utterly without foundation, and the more absurd and contradictory are the various tales which were told, the more strongly am I confirmed in the opinion which I have formed.
>
> Supposing, indeed, there were any truth in the accounts of these appearances of Vampires, are they to be attributed to the power of God, to the Angels, to the souls of those who return in this way, or to the Devil? If we adopt the last hypothesis it follows that the Devil can endue these corpses with subtlety and bestow upon them the power of passing through the earth without any disturbances of the ground, of gliding through the cracks and joints of a door, of slipping through a keyhole, of increasing, of diminishing, of becoming rarefied as air or water to penetrate the earth; in fine of enjoying the same properties as we believe will be possessed by the Blessed after the Resurrection, and which distinguished the human Body of our Lord after the first Easter

> Day, inasmuch as He appeared to those to whom He would show Himself for 'Jesus cometh, the doors being shut, and stood in the midst, and said: Peace be to you.'
>
> Yet even if it be allowed that the Devil can re-energize dead bodies and give them movement for a certain time, can he also bestow these powers of increasing, diminishing, becoming rarefied, and so subtle that they can penetrate the earth, doors, windows? We are not told that God allows him the exercise of any such power, and it is hard to believe that a material body, gross and substantial, can be endowed with this subtlety and spirituality without some destruction or alteration of the general structure and without damage to the configuration of the body. But this would not be in accord with the intention of the Devil, for such a change would prevent this body from appearing, from manifesting itself, from motion and speech, ay, indeed from being eventually cut to pieces and burned as so often happens in the case of Vampires in Moravia, Poland, and Silesia.

However, Calmet was a rare figure. Most theologians believed in the work of the Devil; St Thomas Aquinas stated that the Devil could form a body out of the air and give it any desired shape or form. Thus vampirism became credible.

In 1679 Philip Rohr, scholar and investigator of the occult at Leipzig University, published his *Dissertatio De Masticatione Mortuorum*, loosely translated as 'A Thesis on The Masticating Dead'. This document was entirely based on a current scare that the dead were gnawing at their shrouds and at their limbs, and whilst doing this emitting 'a grunting noise like the sound of porters chawring and rooting with their groyns'. This charming picture was the subject of a heavily-documented testimony by Rohr which was interesting in its rejection of current religious belief in the motivation of the undead. Rohr claimed that the Devil had no power to raise the dead; but he did not deny that the dead could emerge from their graves by Divine permission, with the help of some devilish agency. He goes on to try and prove that the dead had been known to eat in their tombs, sometimes masticating their own limbs. But Rohr also fully accepts catalepsy or suspended animation as a reason for waking in the tomb. Yet, curiously, he does not fully connect the emergence from catalepsy and the shroud- and limb-gnawing which is surely merely the hunger of the starving.

Rohr concludes his dissertation by accepting the activity of the dead or the 'undead' as the work of a Devil with limited powers, assisted by the magical properties of witchcraft and its practitioners. He points out that remedies against the Devil's mischief in the grave must be confined to the following Christian observances:

1) Mass should be regularly attended.
2) Communicants must be totally devout.
3) The adorable Prisoner of the Tabernacle must be continuously visited.
4) The Sacrament must be fervently worshipped.
5) The Holy Relics are the only safeguard against evil spirits and must be used, at all times, to drive them away.

Rohr adds that such pious practices as the 'carrying upon one's person the first fourteen verses of the Gospel according to St John, engraved or written out in a fair hand', the wearing of holy medals, and mortifications should be practised and a skilled director in mystic theology should be employed. Finally he concludes with the following prayer:

> Let us therefore most humbly pray to Almighty God that He would avert from this province and especially from this home and nursery of all liberal arts and sciences every ill, and that He may be pleased to shield us from the innumerable crafts of Satan! From the snares of the devil, and from all pestilence, Good Lord deliver us.

Suicide

Although a more liberal approach has been taken this century to the suicide, traditional Christian teaching dictated that it was against the will of God to take one's own life, and therefore a suicide was a serious miscreant. Divine domination must reign and man must submit to the grim reaper and not to his own hand.

During the decadent periods of both Greece and Rome, however, suicide was much applauded whilst the Goths and the Norsemen regularly used to indulge in it as a form of nobility. Summers quotes from the Greek writer Athenaeus:

> And Seleucus says, 'that some of the Thracians at their drinking parties play the games of hanging; and fix a round noose to some high place, exactly beneath which they place a stone which is easily turned round when anyone stands upon it; and then they cast lots, and he who draws the lot, holding a sickle in his hand, stands upon the stone, and puts his neck into the halter; and then another person comes and raises the stone, and the man who is suspended, when the stone moves from under him, if he is not quick enough in cutting the rope with his sickle, is killed; and the rest laugh, thinking his death good sport.'

Athenaeus goes on to say:

> But Posidonius, in the third, and also in the twentieth book of his Histories, says 'The Celtae sometimes have single combats at their entertainments. For being collected in arms, they go through the exercise, and make feints at, and sometimes they even go so far as to wound one another. And being irritated by this, if the bystanders do not stop them, they will proceed even to kill one another. But in olden times,' he continues, 'there was a custom that a hind-quarter of pork was put on the table, and the bravest man took it; and if anyone else laid claim to it, then the two rose up to fight till one of them was slain. And other men in the theatre having received some silver or gold money, and some even for a number of earthen vessels full of wine, having taken pledges that the gifts promised shall really be given, and having distributed them among their nearest connexions, have laid themselves down on doors with their faces upwards, and then allowed some bystander to cut their throats with a sword.'

In more recent times various notable epidemics of suicide have raged. Russia had a particularly bad outbreak in the seventeenth century, which was repeated several times between then and our own day. Many of these bouts were caused by some prophesy of doom or other, so when a Russian visionary pointed out that the end of the world was due to take place in 1666 mass panic broke out. Occupations ceased, the barricades were put up, hundreds committed suicide and others, lacking the guts to kill themselves, asked others to do it for them. Wholesale murder broke out as a result. Large communities, hysterically bent on martyrdom, committed mass suicide in an attempt to avoid the suspected mass destruction. In Vetlovga a doorless and windowless tower was built into which would-be martyrs were lowered through a hatch in the roof. There they would starve to death with great dignity. Unfortunately hunger pangs put a stop to all that, and a few hours later there was a massive clamour to get out. No-one, however, had thought of that as the man who lowered the martyrs in had joined them by sliding down the rope and unhooking it from the hatch. Great was the lamentation—and the sudden desire for life. Gallingly, the suspected holocaust came and went and nothing happened—except that a large number of people, trapped in a doorless and windowless tower, died of starvation.

Immolation by fire was another answer to impending doom. The zealot would calmly point out that, as Elias ascended to heaven in a blazing chariot, then those choosing suicide by fire would ascend in the same triumphant way. Thousands began to adopt the technique. Montague Summers describes the terrible pyres:

> These immolations generally took place during the dark winter season and from midnight until the faint streaks of dawn the red glow of these horrid furnaces could be seen in every direction. For hundreds of verstas the land became a veritable Tophet. As the morning broke, hordes of wolves attracted by the stench of roasting flesh assembled to pull trunks and limbs from the embers; a dark cloud of suffocating smoke, greasy with human fat that fouled both ground and houses, hung low in the sky, and ere many days were past the plague was stalking abroad with fatal voracity.

All kinds of taboos surrounded the burial of suicides—including the fact that they would, unless proper precautions were taken, immediately become vampires after death. In England, until the time of George IV, suicides were buried at crossroads with a stake driven through their bodies. In 1823 a degree of liberalisation crept in and suicides were buried privately, between the hours of nine and twelve p.m. without religious ceremony. In 1882 it was decided that the burial of a suicide was at the discretion of the priest and the mourners—they should decide the appropriate degree of religious rite.

The suicide, totally frustrated and unhallowed in death, had the reputation of being a wanderer abroad, so it was considered essential that he should be buried at the crossroads. He would then have some difficulty in deciding which path to choose and his activities would be considerably delayed.

Excommunication

Here was the Church's ultimate weapon—a withdrawal of all spiritual privileges and lasting damnation beyond the grave. No wonder those who were excommunicated were considered to lie uneasy in their graves—and to return as hell-bent vampires. Naturally excommunication could be withdrawn but obviously it was essential to do it before death—although an exorcism could be performed after death with some successful results.

The Catholic Church accepted the fact that as the Bishops were the successors of the Apostles then it was the Bishops who had the prime right to excommunicate—and of course to re-communicate. The Greek Orthodox Church went a stage further by saying that the excommunicant would not decompose in his unhallowed grave. G. F. Abbott, in his *Macedonian Folk-Lore* (1903), relates an irreverent story of the complications one excommunication caused:

> How great is the dread of an ecclesiastic's wrath can be realized from the following anecdote related to the writer as a 'true story' by a person who entertained no doubts as to its authenticity. Many years ago there was an Archbishop of Salonica who once in a moment of anger cursed a man of his diocese: 'May the earth refuse to receive thee.' Years went by, and the Archbishop embraced Islam. Owing to his erudition and general ability, he was raised by the Mohammedans to the office of head Mullah. Meanwhile, the individual who had incurred the prelate's wrath died, and was buried in the usual fashion. Now it came to pass that when, at the expiration of three years, the tomb was opened, the inmate was found intact, just as if he had been buried the day before. Neither prayers nor offerings availed to bring about

the desired dissolution. He was inhumed once more; but three years later he was still found in the same condition. It was then recalled to mind by the widow that her late husband had been anathematized by the apostate Archbishop. She forthwith went to the ex-prelate and implored him to revoke the sentence. This dignitary promised to exert his influence, which it appears had not been diminished a whit by his apostasy; for once a bishop always a bishop. Having obtained the Pasha's permission, he repaired to the open tomb, knelt beside it, lifted up his hands and prayed for a few minutes. He had hardly risen to his feet when, wondrous to relate, the flesh of the corpse crumbled away from the bones, and the skeleton remained bare and clean as if it had never known pollution.

Finally, in this survey of excommunication in different faiths here is an extract from Ricaut's *The Present State of the Greek and Armenian Churches* which was published in 1679. I quote from the chapter dealing with 'The Power of Excommunication, and upon what frivolous occasions it is made use of':

They believe that the Bodies of the Excommunicated are possessed in the Grave by some evil spirit, which actuates and preserves them from Corruption, in the same manner as the Soul informs and animates the living body; and that they feed in the night, walk, digest, and are nourished, and have been found ruddy in Complexion, and their Veins, after forty days' Burial, extended with Blood, which, being opened with a Lancet, have yielded a gore as plentiful, fresh, and quick, as that which issues from the Vessels of young and sanguine persons. This is so generally believed and discoursed of amongst the *Greeks*, that there is scarce one of their Country Villages, but what can witness and recount several instances of this nature, both by the relation of their Parents, and Nurses, as well as of their own knowledge, which they tell with as much variety as we do the Tales of Witches and Enchantments, of which it is observed in Conversation, that scarce one story is ended before another begins of like wonder.

The invaluable Ricaut was told the following story by a Greek priest who insisted that the account was completely true and that he had witnesses to prove it.

'I knew' (said he) 'a certain person, who for some misdemeanours committed in the *Morea*, fled to the Isle of *Milo*, where though he avoided the hand of Justice, yet could not avoid the Sentence of Excommunication, from which he could no more fly, than from the conviction of his own Conscience, or the guilt which ever attended him; for the fatal hour of his death being come, and the Sentence of the Church not being revoked, the Body was carelessly and without Solemnity interred in some retired and unfrequented place. In the meantime the Relations of the deceased were much afflicted, and anxious for the sad estate of their dead Friend, whilst the *Paisants* and *Islanders* were every night affrightened and disturbed with strange and unusual apparitions, which they immediately concluded arose from the Grave of the accursed Excommunicant, which, according to their Custom, they immediately opened, and therein found the Body uncorrupted, ruddy, and the Veins replete with Blood: The Coffin was furnished with Grapes, Apples, and Nuts, and such fruit as the season afforded: Whereupon Consultation being made, the *Kaloires* resolved to make use of the common remedy in those cases, which was to cut and dismember the Body into several parts, and to boyl it in Wine, as the approved means to dislodge the evil Spirit, and dispose the body to a dissolution: But the friends of the deceased, being willing and desirous that the Corps should rest in peace, and some ease given to the departed Soul, obtained a reprieve from the Clergy, and hopes, that for a sum of Money (they being Persons of a competent Estate) a Release might be purchased from the Excommunication under the hand of the Patriarch: In this manner the Corps were for a while freed from dissection, and Letters thereupon sent to *Constantinople*, with this direction, that in case the Patriarch should condescend to take off the Excommunication, that the day, hour and minute that he signed the Remission should be inserted in the Date. And now the Corps was taken into the Church (the Countrypeople not being willing it should remain in the Field) and Prayers and Masses daily said for its dissolution, and pardon of the Offender: When one day after many Prayers, Supplications and Offerings (as this *Sofronio* attested to me with many protestations) and whilst he himself was performing Divine Service, of a sudden was heard a rumbling noise in the Coffin of the dead party, to the fear and astonishment of all persons then present; which when they had opened, they found the Body consumed and dissolved as far into its first Principles of Earth, as if it had been seven years interred. The hour and minute of this dissolution was immediately noted and precisely observed, which being compared with the Date of the Patriarch's release, when it was signed at *Constantinople*, it was found exactly to agree with that moment in which the Body returned to its Ashes.

The embarrassing thing was that in the Orthodox, Roman and Greek Churches the incorruption of a body was said to be proof of sanctity (see Part One). So a very positive line had to be drawn between the preserved saint and the preserved sinner. The Greek Church decreed that in the case of a saint the body preserved its natural colour and gave off an agreeable odour, but in the case of the sinner turned black, swelled up like a drum and gave off a revolting smell. Suspected vampires, exhumed from their graves, were of an unfortunately ruddy colour and had healthy-looking, blood-distended veins.

'Whatever You Shall Bind on Earth, Shall Be Bound Also in Heaven' was the text on which the Greek Church based its power. Not only excommunicants, of course, needed to be released by the Church—there were others such as murderers, suicides, unexcommunicated but heinous sinners, magicians, witches and those under a family curse.

A manuscript discovered in the Church of St Sophia, Thessalonika, throws more interesting sidelights on the Greek Church's power of excommunication. Its main points were:

1) Whoever has been laid under any curse or received any injunction from his deceased parents that he has not fulfilled, after his death the forepart of his body remains entire.
2) Whoever has been the object of any anathema appears yellow after death, and the fingers are shrivelled.
3) Whoever appears white has been excommunicated by the divine laws.
4) Whoever appears black has been excommunicated by a bishop.

This sort of proclamation instituted the incredible habit of repeated disinterment amongst the Greeks, the Bulgarians and the other Balkan nations. The idea was to find out whether the dead had turned white or black and yellow, and on this basis ascertain whether their souls were in heaven or hell or whether they wandered the land as lustful, blood-hungry vampires.

In 1751 Voltaire in his *Dictionnaire Philosophique* wrote:

For a long time the Christians who practised the Greek ritual believed that the corpses of those Christians who practised the Latin ritual would not decompose when buried in Greece because they were excommunicated. This is precisely the contrary of what we, the Christians of the Latin ritual, think. We believe that corpses that remain intact bear the mark of eternal felicity.

Ornella Volta believes that this statement summed up the very origin of the 'indiscriminate fear of the vampire in those countries of eastern Europe where the two religions—Catholic and Orthodox—exist side by side. The body that does not decompose is therefore suspect.'

On this basis it could well be argued that the Church spread the vampire-infection by proliferate excommunications—and created an even more logical fear of the incorrupted dead. For surely, if they were incorruptible—they could also walk.

Finally, two legends illustrating some strange excommunications.

In the year 1030 St Godard, Bishop of Hildesheim in Lower Saxony, was forced to excommunicate 'certain persons for their crimes and filthy sacrileges', as Montague Summers puts it. But unfortunately for St Godard, the friends of these 'certain persons' were powerful barons and overlords who would have no truck with the power of excommunication at all. Completely defying the ban, they stoned the churchyard and buried their excommunicated friends in hallowed ground. As a result of this action Bishop Godard was forced to retaliate—by excommunicating the barons and overlords.

However, this group was not to be beaten, and their next step was to retaliate against Bishop Godard. They all turned up at the next high festival, bringing with them armed attendants. The confrontation was complete. Before Mass the excommunicated stood thronged in the pews, stonily facing the helpless Bishop Godard. But before he served Mass the Bishop turned to the congregation which completely packed the Cathedral. He then commanded all those who were under the ban of excommunication to immediately leave. The barons and overlords grinned back at him, unafraid of his command. Then, suddenly, a host of dark shadows rose from the very depths of the congregation—and passed quietly, shamefully out of the cathedral. As they passed, both barons and overlords shrank back in horror—for the shadows were the excommunicated dead. Relenting after the service, the good Bishop Godard absolved these dead and, to the horror of the living, they temporarily reappeared as they filed into their tombs. Immediately the excommunicated living hurriedly sought to be reconciled with the Church—which Bishop Godard eventually granted.

This Greek legend of excommunication occurs in the Greek *Menion* (a collection of twelve books containing the offices for the feasts within the Byzantine rite).

A disobedient Coenobite was excommunicated for disobedience by the Archimandrite. He left his monastery and arrived at the city of Alexandria, where he was captured by the Governor, and forced to worship the idols of the Temple. The Coenobite refused, and the Governor ordered his torture, and eventual execution; his head was perched out upon the city walls and his trunk was thrown into the desert.

The trunk was then taken up by the Christian community and given full funeral rights and the Coenobite was recognised as a martyr. However, on the next Sunday a complication occurred. The Deacon arrived at the part of the Mass where all excommunicants should withdraw, when out of the tomb of the martyr walked the corpse, and lingered in the narthex of the Church. When the Mass was over the corpse returned to its tomb.

Everybody then fell about in enormous confusion except for one extremely pious Basilian nun who went into a long three-day stint of prayer, intercession and fast. As a result of this an angel appeared to her, informing the nun somewhat brusquely that a major error had been made as the martyr was of course still excommunicated. Immediately a holy company left for the Coenobite's monastery and asked the Archimandrite to release the martyr from his state of excommunication. This he did, a full absolution was pronounced and the martyr found peace at last.

Some Interesting Phobias in Christian Times

The Children of Judas

Judas Iscariot was said to have red hair. He also sold Christ for thirty pieces of silver. In Rumania, Serbia and Bulgaria a specific type of vampires were known as The Children of Judas. They were red-haired, and killed their victim with one bite which drained all their blood at one go. On the flesh of the victim was then imprinted the Devil's stigmata in the shape of three scars shaped thus—XXX. These scars signified Judas' thirty pieces of silver—the price paid for the blood of Christ.

Christmas Eve

In East Prussia candles were burnt and windows were left open throughout the course of Christmas Eve. The idea was that this was the one evening when evil and the powers of darkness were silenced and the dead were friendly and bribable. Thus they were invited to sit round the hearth-side and warm themselves so that they would return the hospitality of the living by not molesting them during the course of the year—when the dead tended to be in a more vengeful mood.

The Night Wanderers

The following very strange account of the *Herlethingi* (companies of the undead) was given by Walter Map:

> In Brittany there used to be seen at night long trains of soldiers who passed by in dead silence conducting carriages of booty, and from these the Breton peasants have actually stolen away horses and cattle and kept them for their own use. In some cases no harm seems to have resulted, but in other instances this was speedily followed by sudden death. Companies of these troops of night-wanderers, who are commonly called *Herlethingi*, were very well known in England even to the present day, the reign of our King Henry II, who is now ruling over us. These armies went to and fro without let or stay, hurrying hither and thither rambling about in the most mad vagrancy, all inceding in unbroken silence, and amongst the band there appeared alive many who were known to have been long since dead. This company of *Herlethingi* was

last espied in the Marches of Hereford and Wales in the first year of King Henry II, tramping along at high noon with carts and beasts of burden, with pack saddles and provender-baskets, with birds and dogs and a mixed multitude of men and women. Those who first caught sight of this troop by their shouting and blowing of horns and trumpets aroused the whole district, and as in the manner of those border folk, who are ever on the watch, almost instantly there assembled various bands fully equipped, and because they were unable to obtain a word in reply from this strange host they incontinently prepared to make them answer to a shower of darts and javelins, and then the troop seemed to mingle with the air and forthwith vanished away out of sight. From that day this mysterious company has never been seen by man.

Aspen and Whitethorn

A vampire impaled with stakes made of either of the above rarely stood a chance. The aspen tree was said to have furnished wood for the cross whilst the whitethorn was described by Sir John Mandeville in his book *The Voyage and Travails* (1725):

> Then was our Lord yled into a gardyn, and there the Jewes scorned Hym and maden Him a crown of the branches of the Albiespyne, that is, Whitethorn, that grew in the same gardyn, and setten yt upon His heved. And therefore hath the Whitethorn many virtues. For he that beareth a branch on hym thereof, no thundre, ne no maner of tempest may dere him, ne in the house that is ynne may non evil ghost enter.

St George and the Vampire

Apart from being the patron saint of England, St George was also the patron saint of wolves, cattle and horses and is most important as a protector of the peasantry in dozens of countries. St George was fêted in the East as the 'Great Martyr' and Constantine erected one of the first Christian churches in memory of the saint. Because of this protection St George was the sworn enemy of the vampire hordes and throughout Eastern Europe St George's Eve is the most active vampire-night of all—on the part of both the 'undead' and the peasants, who barricade themselves in, never venture abroad and protect their houses with thistles, garlic and every known form of vampire deterrent. If they get through the night, on the Saint's day thistles and garlic are swopped for wreaths of flowers and roses—in honour of St George.

The peasant in *Dracula* who warned Bram Stoker's hero, Jonathan Harker, of the dangers of St George's Eve was speaking for every peasant in Eastern Europe:

> It is the eve of St George's Day. Do you know that tonight, when the clock strikes midnight, all the evil things in the world will have full sway? Do you know where you are going, and what you are going for?

It was this interaction between institutional religion and superstition that produced the hysterical vampire belief in Europe between the fourteenth and eighteenth centuries.

Part Five

The Vampire in Literature

The vampire in literature is less of a caricature than he is in most forms of entertainment yet neither poet nor prose writer has totally succeeded in capturing the spirit of dread that accompanied his visitations. Literature, in all its forms, took the vampire as a fantasy creation, and because of this the vampire has been both romanticised and popularised so that much of the real aura of fear has been watered down. The terrible atmosphere of medieval Europe has largely been left unrecorded. Yet despite the superficiality of many writers' approach to the subject, the vampire was often used as a lever for the writer or poet's own need to create fantasy—and usually malevolent fantasy at that.

Ancient Roman literature is chock-full of the most appalling accounts of the undead. The awesome Lamias were particularly prolific. They were a breed of extraordinarily bloodthirsty vampires, who seduced young men, had intercourse with them and attacked them at the peak of orgasm, drinking their blood with feverish delight. In Greek literature Phlegon relates the story of the bride Filinnius, once again a member of the illustrious undead. This story, of a young Athenian who is visited by his vampiristic dead bride, is similar to *The Life of Apollonius of Tyana* by Philostratus, whose hero Menippus narrowly escapes marrying a Lamia, who—once unmasked—admits her blood-lust quite openly, and with great bravado.

In the eighteenth century there was a good deal of debate about vampirism in various German universities—these debates being both philosophic and academic. The eastern European incidents, coupled with the rising tide of hysteria and ecclesiastical encouragement, were the subject of a mass of treatises and papers. These in turn sparked off the imaginations of a number of German writers including Heinrich August Ossenfelder, who wrote a poem entitled *Der Vampir*, Goethe, who produced the famous ballad *The Bride of Corinth*, and Bürger, who wrote the particularly chilling romantic vampire-fantasy *Lenore*, first printed in the *Gottinger Musenalmanach* during 1773.

Later, in 1796, the ballad *Lenore* was adapted and published in England and immediately became popular. In the 1790s Sir Walter Scott sought out the original of the ballad and translated it with loving care. So gripped was he that 'I well recollect that I began my task after supper and finished it about daybreak next morning.' Friends of Scott had the translation privately printed for him and several other editions, adaptations and translations followed during the final years of the century. Coleridge, possibly influenced by *Lenore*, wrote part of his famous *Christabel* in 1797 and Shelley was wrought up to a high pitch of feverish excitement by Bürger's ballad. In *Shelley and His Writings* (1858), Charles Middleton wrote of Bürger's influence:

> It is hinted, somewhat plausibly, that the *Lenora* of Bürger first awakened his poetic faculty. A tale of such beauty and terror might well have kindled his lively imagination, but his earlier pieces, written about this time, and consisting only of a few ballads, are deficient in elegance and originality, and give no

evidence whatever of the genius which soon after declared itself.

In the *The Bride of Corinth* Goethe describes how a young Athenian visited his would-be father-in-law following the premature death of his bride-to-be. He was awakened at midnight by the vampire-spectre of his dead lover who grimly intoned:

From my grave to wander I am forced,
Still to seek the Gods' long sever'd link,
Still to love the bridegroom I have lost,
And the lifeblood of his heart to drink:
When his race is run, I must hasten on,
And the young must 'neath my vengeance sink.

The young Athenian's reaction to this case-history of vampire frustration is not on record.

Walter Scott made a passing reference to vampirism in *Rokeby* with:

For like the bat of Indian brakes,
Her pinions fan the womb she makes,
And soothing thus the dreamer's pains,
She drinks the life-blood from his veins.

In 1799 Robert Southey wrote *Thalaba the Destroyer*, a beautiful example of a high-Gothic vampire ballad:

A night of darkness and of storms!
Into the chamber of the tomb
Thalaba led the Old Man,
To roof him from the rain.
A night of storms! the wind
Swept through the moonless sky,
And moan'd among the pillar'd sepulchres;
And in the pauses of its sweep
They heard the heavy rain
Beat on the monument above.
In silence on Oneiza's grave
Her father and her husband sate.
The Cryer from the minaret
Proclaim'd the midnight hour.
'Now, now!' cried Thalaba;
And o'er the chamber of the tomb
There spread a lurid gleam,

Like the reflection of a sulphur fire;
And in that hideous light
Oneiza stood before them. It was She...
Her very lineaments ... and such as death
Had changed them, livid cheeks and lips of blue;
But in her eye there dwelt
Brightness more terrible
Than all the loathsomeness of death.
'Still art thou living, wretch?'
In hollow tones she cried to Thalaba;
'And must I nightly leave my grave
To tell thee, still in vain,
God hath abandoned thee?'

'This is not she!' the Old Man exclaim'd;
'A Fiend; a manifest Fiend!'
And to the youth he held his lance;
'Strike and deliver thyself!'
'Strike HER!' cried Thalaba,
And palsied of all power,
Gazed fixedly upon the dreadful form.
'Yea, strike her!' cried a voice, whose tones
Flow'd with such a sudden healing through his soul,
As when the desert shower
From death deliver'd him;
But obedient to that well-known voice,
His eye was seeking it,
When Moath, firm of heart,
Perform'd the bidding: through the vampire corpse
He thrust his lance; it fell,
And howling with the wound,
Its fiendish tenant fled.
A sapphire light fell on them,
And garmented with glory, in their sight
Oneiza's spirit stood.

Southey did a good deal of research on vampirism in connection with *Thalaba* and in his introductory notes he cites such old friends as Arnold Paole and the vampires of Grudisch.

The poet Shelley is recorded as saying:

The Turks have an opinion that men that are buried have a sort

> of life in their graves. If any man makes affidavit before a Judge, that he heard a noise in a man's grave he is by order, dug up and chopped all to pieces. The merchants (at Constantinople), once on horseback, have, as usual for protection, a Janisary with them. Passing by the burying place of the Jews, it happened that an old Jew sat by a sepulchre. The Janisary rode up to him, and rated him for stinking the world a second time, and commanded him into his grave again.

De Sade was most enamoured with all aspects of vampirism. In *Juliette* the giant Minshi had an enormous appetite for human flesh, preserving a nice line in domestic economy by making his furniture out of the bleached bones of his victims. In the more renowned *Justine* the Comte de Gernade has a wonderfully lustful time watching the blood trickle from the veins of his victims.

On a more ethereal note there was the strange Mary Shelley/John Polidori/Lord Byron vampire syndrome. In 1816 Byron, now separated from his wife Anna Isabella, went into exile in Europe. He was to go to Switzerland, where he would link up with the Shelleys, and then go on to Italy. Conscious of the insanitary state of Europe at that time, Byron hired a doctor as both companion and medical adviser. The doctor, John Polidori, was an odd character who had already translated *The Castle of Otranto* into Italian and who was the uncle of Dante Gabriel and Christina Rossetti. He was also brilliant, moody and desperately nervous of travelling with the great Lord Byron. He had another reason for remaining extremely close to Byron: to fulfil the commission that John Murray, Byron's publisher, had given him. Polidori was to chronicle Byron's activities for five hundred guineas.

Byron and Polidori quarrelled from the very beginning. In 1816 Byron, Polidori and their travelling circus met the Shelleys—the poet himself, Mary and Mary's half-sister Claire—latterly Byron's mistress in England. Byron leased a nearby villa and settled down to a tête-à-tête with the Shelleys, from which Polidori was sharply isolated. Polidori took an instant dislike to Shelley. Claire, on the other hand, who was determined to seduce Byron again, was furious that Byron and Shelley spent so much time together—and was equally furious that when

Byron was away from Shelley, the possessive and insensitive Polidori hogged his company. So the household had its undercurrents that made the assembled company only too anxious to indulge in escapism during the evenings. Mary Shelley, in her introduction to the second edition of *Frankenstein*, wrote:

> Some volumes of ghost stories, translated from the German into French, fell into our hands. There was the 'History of the Inconstant Lover', who, when he thought to clasp the bride to whom he had pledged his vows, found himself in the arms of the pale ghost of her whom he had deserted. There was the tale of the sinful founder of his race, whose miserable doom it was to bestow the kiss of death on all the younger sons of his fated house, just when they reached the age of promise. His gigantic, shadowy form, clothed like the ghost in *Hamlet* in full armour, but with the beaver up, was seen at midnight ... 'We will each write a ghost story,' said Lord Byron; and his proposition was acceded to. There were four of us. The noble author began a tale, a fragment which he printed at the end of his poem of *Mazeppa*. Shelley, more apt to embody ideas and sentiments in the radiance of brilliant imagery, and in the music of the most melodious verse that adorns our language, than to invent the machinery of a story, commenced one founded on the experiences of his early life. Poor Polidori had some terrible idea about a skull-headed lady, who was so punished for peeping through a keyhole—what to see I forget—something very shocking and wrong, of course; but when she was reduced to a worse condition than the renowned Tom of Coventry, he did not know what to do with her, and was obliged to dispatch her to the tomb of the Capulets, the only place for which she was fitted. The illustrious poets, also, annoyed by the platitude of prose, speedily relinquished their uncongenial task.

Because of this session and also, more importantly, because of the bad vibrations between the five of them, an atmosphere of hysteria permeated the house. Shelley had hysterics when Byron recited *Christabel*, Polidori had to dose him with ether, and Mary Shelley, her mind aflame with the grotesque imagery they were creating, dreamt of the main plot of *Frankenstein* and afterwards started to write her celebrated novel. Byron himself began work on a novel based on his ghost story which Polidori read and summarised roughly as follows: A modern Greek vampire swears his travelling companion to secrecy and then undergoes a mock death. Months later, the travelling companion returns to London, only to discover his old friend the Greek vampire in English guise and indulging in some very dubious activities. But, like any honourable gentlemen, the companion is bound to his oath and therefore has to watch these demonic-vampiristic activities without being able to interfere.

Later, after many emotional scenes, Polidori was dismissed, only to turn up later in an Italian guardhouse, locked up for disorderly conduct. Byron was forced to bail Polidori, who was later ordered to leave Milan. In 1817 Polidori returned to England and took up a medical practice at Norwich. In this he failed to prosper and eventually committed suicide. A few years before his death, however, Polidori published in the April 1819 edition of Colburn's *New Monthly Magazine* a very short novella called *The Vampyre*. The preface to the story attributed the novella to Byron although in reality Polidori had written up the work from his knowledge of Byron's original idea concerning the Greek vampire and his unfortunate travelling companion.

Yet despite all the disclaimers *The Vampyre* was generally taken to be part of Byron's works and on this basis was highly successful in England and even more so in Europe. It appeared on the Parisian stage in various forms (see Part Six) and was the origin of various stage plays in England. E. F. Bleiler in his editorial notes on Polidori in *Three Gothic Novels* (Dover, 1966) says:

> In the history of the English novel Polidori's *Vampyre* has interest beyond its literary merits. It is probably the first extensive vampire story in English, and it served as the model for many later developments. It showed the direction that Romantic supernatural fiction was taking: the abandonment of the disinheritance plot that used to be almost universally present in the longer Gothic forms; the increased employment of local colour and folklore, in this case modern Greek instead of Germanic; and a much heavier use of supernaturalism, which is no longer rationalized or explained away as illusion or fraud, but is accepted within its own terms. Polidori's novel also marks a stage in the gradual shift of interest away from the earlier 'hero', who was a passive, suffer-

ing figure, to the more dynamic, action-initiating 'villain'. This change of focus is, of course, simply one aspect of Byronism.

Polidori's *Vampyre* was also the catalyst to an extraordinary work called *Varney the Vampire* or *The Feast of Blood* which was first published in 1847. It contained dozens of chapters, ran to 868 pages and its author was a prolific and action-hungry writer named Thomas Preskett Prest. He also wrote such titles as *The Death Grasp* or *A Father's Curse, Sweeney Todd, the Demon Barber of Fleet Street, The Maniac Father* or *The Victim of Seduction, The Blighted Heart* or *The Priory Ruins*, and other classic works. So successful was Prest's intricately-plotted *Varney* that in 1853 the saga was reprinted in penny parts. Here is a sample of its delights:

> The hail continues. The wind continues. The uproar of the elements seems at its height. Now she awakens—that beautiful girl on the antique bed; she opens those eyes of celestial blue, and a faint cry of alarm bursts from her lips. At least it is a cry which, amid the noise and turmoil without, sounds but faint and weak. She sits upon the bed and presses her hands upon her eyes. Heavens! what a wild torrent of wind and rain, and hail! The thunder likewise seems intent upon awakening sufficient echoes to last until the next flash of forked lightning should again produce the wild concussion of the air. She murmurs a prayer—a prayer for those she loves best; the names of those dear to her gentle heart come from her lips; she weeps and prays; she thinks then of what devastation the storm must surely produce, and to the great God of Heaven she prays for all living things. Another flash,—a wild, blue, bewildering flash of lightning streams across that bay window, for an instant bringing out every colour in it with terrible distinctness. A shriek bursts from the lips of the young girl, and then, with eyes fixed upon the window, which, in another moment, is all darkness, and with such an expression of terror upon her face as it had never before known, she trembled, and the perspiration of intense fear stood upon her brow.
>
> 'What—what was it?' she gasped; 'real, or a delusion? Oh, God, what was it? A figure tall and gaunt, endeavouring from the outside to unclasp the window. I saw it. That flash of lightning revealed it to me. It stood the whole length of the window.'
>
> There was a lull of the wind. The hail was not falling so thickly—moreover, it now fell, what there was of it, straight, and yet a

strange clattering sound came upon the glass of that long window. It could not be a delusion—she is awake, and she hears it. What can produce it? Another flash of lightning—another shriek—there could be now no delusion.

A tall figure is standing on the ledge immediately outside the window. It is its finger-nails upon the glass that produce the sound so like the hail, now that the hail has ceased. Intense fear paralysed the limbs of that beautiful girl. That one shriek is all she can utter—with hands clasped, a face of marble, a heart beating so wildly in her bosom, that each moment it seems as if it would break its confines, eyes distended and fixed upon the window, she waits, frozen with horror. The pattering and clattering of the nails continues. No word is spoken, and now she fancies she can trace the darker form of that figure against the window, and she can see the long arms moving to and fro, feeling for some mode of entrance. What strange light is that which now gradually creeps up into the air? red and terrible—brighter and brighter it grows. The lightning has set fire to a mill, and the reflection of the rapidly consuming building falls upon that long window. There can be no mistake. The figure is there, still feeling for an entrance, and clattering against the glass with its long nails, that appear as if the growth of many years had been untouched. She tries to scream again but a choking sensation comes over her, and she cannot. It is too dreadful—she tries to move—each limb seems wedged down by tons of lead—she can but in a hoarse faint whisper cry,—

'Help—help—help—help!'

And that one word she repeats like a person in a dream. The red glare of the fire continues. It throws the tall gaunt figure in hideous relief against the long window. It throws, too, upon one portrait that is in the chamber, and that portrait appears to fix its eyes upon the attempting intruder, while the flickering light from the fire makes it look fearfully lifelike. A small pane of glass is broken, and the form from without introduces a long gaunt hand, which seems utterly destitute of flesh. The fastening is removed, and one-half of the window, which opens like folding doors, is swung wide open upon its hinges.

And yet now she could not scream—she could not move. 'Help!—help!—help!' was all she could say. But, oh, that look of terror that sat upon her face, it was dreadful—a look to haunt the memory for a life-time—a look to obtrude itself upon the happiest moments, and turn them to bitterness.

The figure turns half round, and the light falls upon the face.

It is perfectly white—perfectly bloodless. The eyes look like polished tin; the lips are drawn back, and the principal feature next to those dreadful eyes is the teeth—the fearful looking teeth—projecting like those of some wild animal, hideously, glaringly white, and fang-like. It approaches the bed with a strange, gliding movement. It clashes together the long nails that literally appear to hang from the finger ends. No sound comes from its lips. Is she going mad?—that young and beautiful girl exposed to so much terror; she has drawn up all her limbs; she cannot even now say help. The power of articulation is gone, but the power of movement has returned to her; she can draw herself slowly along to the other side of the bed from that towards which the hideous appearance is coming.

European vampire fiction also proliferated and in Germany Polidori's much-disputed *Vampyre* was responsible for sparking off such fantasies as Spindler's *Der Vampyr und seine Braut*, and Bauer's *Der Baron Vampyr*. In France Gautier wrote his beautiful vampiristic prose poem *La Morte Amoureuse*, whilst back in England in 1872 Sheridan Le Fanu produced his exquisite *Camilla*—whose descriptive passages are amongst the very finest in English vampire-literature. It is the story of a female vampire guest in a castle in Styria, and includes such strange anecdotes as:

'How came the village to be deserted?' asked the General.

'It was troubled by *revenants*, sir; several were tracked to their graves, there detected by the usual tests, and extinguished in the usual way, by decapitation, by the stake, and by burning; but not until many of the villagers were killed.

'But after all these proceedings according to law,' he continued—'so many graves opened, and so many vampires deprived of their horrible animation—the village was not relieved. But a Moravian nobleman, who happened to be travelling this way, heard how matters were, and being skilled—as many people are in his country—in such affairs, he offered to deliver the village from its tormentor. He did so thus: There being a bright moon that night, he ascended, shortly after sunset, the tower of the chapel here, from whence he could distinctly see the churchyard beneath him; you can see it from that window. From this point he watched until he saw the vampire come out of his grave, and place near it the linen clothes in which he had been folded, and glide away towards the village to plague its inhabitants.

'The stranger, having seen all this, came down from the steeple, took the linen wrappings of the vampire, and carried them up to the top of the tower, which he again mounted. When the vampire returned from his prowlings and missed his clothes, he cried furiously to the Moravian, whom he saw at the summit of the tower, and who, in reply, beckoned him to ascend and take them. Whereupon the vampire, accepting his invitation, began to climb the steeple, and so soon as he had reached the battlements, the Moravian, with a stroke of his sword, clove his skull in twain, hurling him down to the churchyard, whither, descending by the winding stairs, the stranger followed and cut his head off, the next day delivered it and the body to the villagers, who duly impaled and burnt them.'

The climax is pathetically haunting:

The next day the formal proceedings took place in the Chapel of Karnstein. The grave of the Countess Mircalla was opened; and the General and my father recognized each his perfidious and beautiful guest, in the face now disclosed to view. The features, though a hundred and fifty years had passed since her funeral, were tinted with the warmth of life. Her eyes were open; no cadaverous smell exhaled from the coffin. The two medical men, one officially present, the other in the part of the promoter of the inquiry, attested the marvellous fact, that there was a faint but appreciable respiration, and a corresponding action of the heart. The limbs were perfectly flexible, the flesh elastic; and the leaden coffin floated with blood, in which to a depth of seven inches, the body lay immersed. Here, then, were all the admitted signs and proofs of vampirism. The body, therefore, in accordance with the ancient practice, was raised, and a sharp stake driven through the heart of the vampire, who uttered a piercing shriek at the moment, in all respects such as might escape from a living person in the last agony. Then the head was struck off, and a torrent of blood flowed from the severed neck. The body and head were next placed on a pile of wood, and reduced to ashes, which were thrown upon the river and borne away, and that territory has never since been plagued by the visits of a vampire.

The most terrifying of all vampire stories is Guy de Maupassant's *The Horla* whose central character is an ethereal psychic vampire which is formless yet all-powerful.

He is come; he, whom the early and unsophisticated races of the world associated with their first emotions of terror, he, whom anxious priests exorcised, whom sorcerers invoked in the darkness of the night, though unable as yet to compel his appearance; he, whom the anticipation of the temporary masters of the world invented with every conceivable form, whether monstrous or gracious, as gnome, spirit, genie, fairy, or goblin. The gross imaginings of primitive terror having passed away, men of greater perspicacity arrived at a clearer idea. Mesmer divined it, and medical research discovered and established the nature of the new power, ten years before its advent. This mysterious dominion over the human soul, which is thereby reduced to a state of bondage, is the weapon of our future Lord and Master, and the doctors of medicine have been playing with it, calling it magnetism, hypnotism, suggestion, and what not. I have seen them amusing themselves like reckless children with this horrible power. Woe unto us, woe unto mankind! for he has come, the ... the ... what is his name? ... the ... I have a feeling that he is calling out his name to me and I cannot catch it ... yes ... he is calling it ... I listen ... I cannot ... say it again ... the ... Horla ... yes ... I have heard it ... the Horla ... it is he, the Horla ... he has come.

Alas! the vulture has eaten the dove, the wolf has eaten the sheep, the lion has devoured the sharp-horned buffalo; man has slain the lion with arrow, sword and powder; but the Horla will treat man, as man has treated the horse and the ox. By the mere exercise of his willpower, he will convert man into his chattel, his slave, his food. Woe unto us!

Other notable contributions to vampire literature, with outstandingly horrible plots, are the following:

E. F. Benson's *The Room In The Tower* (malignant *revenant* complete with rotting shroud, grave-mould and creeping damp).

H. G. Wells's *The Flowering of the Strange Orchid* (vampiristic plant-life attacks botanist).

Algernon Blackwood's *The Transfer* (Human Vampire meets Psychic Vampire). Governess says of Human Vampire: 'I watched his hard, bleak face; I noticed how thin he was, and the curious oily brightness of his steady eyes. And everything he said or did announced what I may dare to call the suction of his presence.' Child says of Psychic Vampire, disguised as patch of ground in garden: 'It's bad. It's hungry. It's dying because it can't get the food it wants. But I know what would make it feel right.'

Theophile Gautier's *Clarimonde* (Monk swops his own blood for sex with beautiful female vampire).

Sir Arthur Conan Doyle's *The Parasite* (Professor battles against soul-sucking vampire in the shape of an insignificant spinster).

Reginald Hodder's *The Vampire* (Psychic vampire battles against loss of virility).

Victor Roman's *Four Wooden Stakes* (Old house, attendant crypt, blood-hungry ancestors and family going down like nine-pins).

F. Marion Crawford's *For The Blood Is Her Life* (Unrequited vampire seeks solace from former boy-friend).

Stanislaus Eric's *The True Story Of A Vampire* (Sentimental vampire has conscience over draining blood from ailing youth —conscience loses).

M. R. James's *Count Magnus* (Younger generation's explorations into ancestor's past lead to vampiristic discoveries and sudden death).

Edgar Allan Poe's *Berenice* (Premature burial and a strange relationship between cousins).

G. W. M. Reynold's *The Necromancer* (victims sacrificed to a vampire lusting after eternal youth).

'The Wife of A Medical Man's' *The Vampyre* (a teetotal tract with The Vampyre Inn as villain and drunken hero much given to hallucinatory shouting such as 'They fly—they bite—they suck my blood—I die. That hideous "Vampyre"! Its eyes pierce me thro'—they are red—they are bloodshot. Tear it from my pillow. I dare not lie down. It bites—I die! Give me brandy —brandy—more brandy.').

Notable for both its humour and its grisly drama is F. G. Loring's story *The Tomb of Sarah*. The narrator of this story's father was head of a firm of church restorers and made a special study of ancient legends. He was particularly well-versed in folklore and kept a careful record of every case he dealt with. The story, which is in the form of a diary, begins on July 17th, 1841, when he receives a commission from an old friend who is vicar at a church at Hagarstone in the West Country. He starts work and discovers that in the course of this work it is necessary to move an old tomb, on which there is an inscription reading: 'Sarah, 1630'. The inscription goes on: 'For the sake of the dead and the welfare of the living, let this sepulchre remain untouched and its occupant undisturbed until the coming of Christ.' The legend behind the tomb and its strange inscription concerns a local family named Kenyon. The last of the line, Countess Sarah, was murdered in 1630 by a madwoman who had lost both her children. Sarah had the reputation of being a witch with a familiar in the shape of a huge wolf. This familiar used to steal children for Countess Sarah, who then sucked their blood.

The church restorers moved the tomb and found it to contain a body, which was fresh, if starved-looking. Later in the evening, the village was roused by the howling of a dog and a mist rose round the church. The church restorers watched the church and saw a large dog leaving and returning. Later it was discovered that the local sheepfold had been raided and on reviewing the corpse it was evident that the Countess Sarah was looking much better, with lips firm and red, eyes staring and with dark froth at the lips. Immediate prevention was then necessary and a piece of mortar was taken from the tomb in order to prevent vampiristic attack. The church restorer and the vicar decided to investigate and make an attempt to lay the vampire. It was not long before Countess Sarah was seen rising from the tomb in human form, whilst her would-be exorcists drew a circle on the floor, in which they stood. Dog roses and garlic were also laid around the tomb and various preventive implements such as sharp knives and pointed stakes were placed within the circle. The exorcisors then awaited the return of the Countess Sarah. Appreciating the sprung trap, the wily Countess made an attempt to seduce the vicar who nearly succumbed to her charms! The church restorer then ordered her back to her tomb and as the sun rose the Countess did in fact shrink back over the circle of flowers and return to her tomb. The burial service was then read over her and a stake was driven through her heart. The Countess writhed, shrieked and then lay still. Later the body was found to have turned to dust.

In 1897 Bram Stoker published his classic tale of vampirism which immediately achieved enormous popular appeal. Descriptively the story, set in the traditional Transylvanian setting, is remarkably evocative, particularly at the beginning as Jonathan

Harker, the ill-fated solicitor's clerk, journeys towards the castle of his client, Count Dracula. Harker was particularly unheedful of the following warning:

> Just before I was leaving, the old lady came up to my room and said in a very hysterical way: —
>
> 'Must you go? Oh! young Herr, must you go?' She was in such an excited state that she seemed to have lost her grip of what German she knew, and mixed it all up with some other language which I did not know at all ... She was in such evident distress that I tried to comfort her, but without effect. Finally she went down on her knees and implored me not to go; at least to wait a day or two before starting. It was all very ridiculous, but I did not feel comfortable. However, there was business to be done, and I could allow nothing to interfere with it. I therefore tried to raise her up, and said, as gravely as I could, that I thanked her, but my duty was imperative, and that I must go. She then rose and dried her eyes, and taking a crucifix from her neck offered it to me. I did not know what to do, for, as an English Churchman, I have been taught to regard such things as in some measure idolatrous, and yet it seemed so ungracious to refuse an old lady meaning so well and in such a state of mind. She saw, I suppose, the doubt in my face, for she put the rosary round my neck, and said, 'For your mother's sake,' and went out of the room. I am writing up this part of the diary whilst I am waiting for the coach, which is, of course, late; and the crucifix is still round my neck. Whether it is the old lady's fear, I do not know, but I am not feeling nearly as easy in my mind as usual. If this book should ever reach Mina before I do, let it bring my good-bye. Here comes the coach!

When Harker finally arrives at his destination he sees 'a vast ruined castle, from whose tall black windows came no ray of light, and whose broken battlements showed a jagged line against the moonlit sky'. The first few chapters of Stoker's *Dracula* are the most effective and it is upon these that dozens of films and plays have been based. Stoker followed up his original work with a collection of stories entitled *Dracula's Guest* and another vampiristic novel called *The Lady of the Shroud* (1912).

Perhaps the man who was closest to the subject of the undead was Edgar Allan Poe, whose mother complex heavily influenced the majority of his work on the macabre. Many of his stories concerned a dead woman appearing in the shape of a living woman. Shattered by the death of his own mother, Poe tended to see the 'marital bed as a bier' (as Ornella Volta puts it) and chose as companions only women who themselves looked consumptive and as near as they could be to death. This extraordinary relationship seemed to be the only one he could achieve—for as his women grew sicker he loved them even more dearly. Death was the final consummation of his love and his choice of the frail ensured that Poe's loved ones frequently did end in the grave. The visitation of Berenice, the subject of Poe's famous short story, is indicative of his obsession with the satisfaction of death.

> The forehead was high, and very pale, and singularly placid; and the once jetty hair fell partially over it, and overshadowed the hollow temples with innumerable ringlets, now of a vivid yellow, and jarring discordantly, in their fantastic character, with the reigning melancholy of the countenance. The eyes were lifeless, and lustreless, and seemingly pupilless, and I shrank involuntarily from their glassy stare to the contemplation of the thin and shrunken lips. They parted; and in a smile of peculiar meaning, the *teeth* of the changed Berenice disclosed themselves to my view. Would to God that I had never beheld them, or that, having done so, I had died!

In the nineteen-twenties American vampire literature suddenly took precedence over its counterparts in England and the rest of Europe, where the popularity of both Gothic and 'horror' novels had begun to wane. Fantasy magazines became showcases for imaginations; *Weird Tales* in particular specialised in the most grotesque tales of vampirism. H. P. Lovecraft wrote *The Tomb* (1926) and *The Shunned House* (1937) whilst Greye La Spina wrote *Fettered* (1926), and Clark Ashton Smith wrote *The End of the Story* (1930) which involved a student hero falling prey to a Lamia. In the nineteen-thirties *Weird Tales* carried a succession of vampire serials and stories, including *Lord of the Lamia* (1935), *The Vampire Master* (1933), *Horror From the Hills* (1931) and *Revelations in Black* (1935) amongst many other works of demonry.

Finally, we come to the comic-book vampire who owes more to the cinema vampire creation than the legendary one. No self-respecting vampire would be happy with his comic-book image.

Sandwiched as he is between the comic-book werewolf and the comic-book zombie, the comic-book vampire is a travesty of real terror. Yet despite this the strip-cartoon vampire has a very special personality of his or her own. In *Curse of the Vampires* (*Chilling Tales of Horror*, October 1969) a female of the species admits all to her mortal lover, who reacts by saying:

> 'But there's still ONE CHANCE, Lisa. My studies have convinced me that vampirism ISN'T supernatural, but physical! There's a dangerous operation to remove a faulty gland at the base of the brain.'

Lisa replies:

> 'I'll gladly risk my life, Joe. FOR OUR LOVE.'

Unfortunately the operation is only temporarily successful, as the story reveals:

> 'Yes, Lisa—why so STRANGE? Can it be that the FULL MOON strikes with fatal fascination? That the operation has given only temporary relief, rather than cure? That you're—CHANGING?'

Poor old Lisa—and poor old Joe.

In *Vampire Slayer* (*Eerie*, No. 18) a vampire-hunter falls in love with a female vampire whose twin sister is a ghoul. The hunter, fooled into thinking his vampire lover was mortal because she cast a reflection in the mirror, gets his crunch-line in final-frame dialogue. Says Corinne (the vampire):

> 'I'm afraid I haven't played quite fair with you, dear. That wasn't me last night. You see, even on board ship I neglected to mention I had a TWIN SISTER! Luckily Colette has no reflection problem. You see, SHE'S A GHOUL!'

And Colette adds gleefully: 'Remember your promise, Corinne. For helping you out last night, I get what's left when you're finished!'

This leaves the vampire-hunter merely exclaiming: 'GYAHHHHHHHHH.'

Eerie, No. 24, introduces in comic-strip form a first chapter to *Dracula* that 'was excised because of the length of the book'. In it Jonathan Harker has a preliminary adventure before he meets Dracula, which involves him in some strange activities on St

George's Eve, concluded by an attack by a wolf and his rescue by soldiers. Undeterred by these exhausting episodes, Harker strides out of the last frame into his better-known encounters with Count Dracula. During the course of this first adventure Harker has the following dialogue with his coachman:

Whilst we were talking, we heard a sort of sound between a yelp and a bark. It was far away; but the horses got very restless, and it took Johann all his time to quiet them.

HARKER: It sounds like a wolf ... but yet there are no wolves here now.

Remarking that the snow-storm would soon come, Johann climbed to his box as though the time had come for proceeding on our journey. I did not at once get into the carriage.

HARKER: Tell me about the place where the road leads.

JOHANN: It is unholy. The village. No one lives there hundreds of years. Men died there and were buried; and sounds were heard under the clay, and when the graves were opened, men and women were found rosy with life, and their mouths red with blood. And so, in haste to save their lives (aye, and their souls!) those who were left fled away to other places, where the living lived, and the dead were dead and not ... not something else. Get in! WALPURGIS NACHT!

All my English blood rose at this. I took from the seat my oak walking stick and closed the door, pointing to Munich.

HARKER: You are afraid, Johann. Go home; I shall return alone; the walk will do me good. WALPURGIS NACHT does not concern Englishmen.

In *Pursuit of the Vampire* (*Eerie*, No. 24) the local Burgomaster turns out to be the vampire, whilst the hero turns out to be a werewolf. The final frames produce this telling dialogue:

'You Burgomaster! You cast no reflection in the water!'

'You are too observant, my friend! You should have been satisfied with those two girls I allowed you to kill! Now, for your meddling, you are going to die.'

'The greed of the vampire! The bloodlust! Night after night, another victim—I can't let you destroy this village. I need it for myself. Every full moon!'

Dell comics produced a superman Dracula, out to cleanse the nasty reputation of his ancestors by fighting evil-doers. His pledge reads as follows:

'I pledge by the strange powers which have become mine to fight against the injustice, corruption, evil and greed which fills this earth in the hopes that somehow my example will be an example to all men!'

Back now to less worthy vampire motives in *The Coffin of Dracula* (*Creepy*, No. 9) in which a pastiche of the good Count perishes, staked and drowned in a coffin hurtling down to the ocean floor.

'The ocean boils and foams, drawing the wreckage into its dark depths—swallowing the large black box, incasement of blacker secrets, dragging down THE COFFIN OF DRACULA.'

The narrator adds:

'Tsk! Tsk! Looks like the Count's SPIRITS have been DAMPENED—or will this be a case of what goes DOWN must come UP?'

The female vampire has always been associated with sensuality rather than friendliness, but the comic-book figure *Vampirella* is downright fresh. Here is how she introduces herself:

HI, THERE! WELCOME TO THE COOLEST GIRL-MEETS-GHOUL MAG ON THE MARKET! My name's VAMPIRELLA. I'm the NEWEST thing in comic magazines! And if you take me home with you, YOU can call me ... VAMP! (That's if I don't call you first!) I've put out the call to all the creepiest eeriest artists in the country (and you know what country: TRANSYLVANIA!) ... and it'll be a BLOODY pity if anyone in the whole wide world doesn't get the word about this way-out mag of fantastic females! My AMAZING ADVENTURES explode here exclusively every issue and in addition you get half a dozen other sock-it-to-you SHOCKERS for gals and guys who're wise to the best in BEWITCHING COMICS! What more do you want—BLOOD? YOU got it! Get VAMPIRELLA magazine!!

CHECK YOUR HEARTBEAT before reading this magazine and if it hasn't risen 100 beats per minute by the time you lay the issue down (if you CAN lay it down!) you need a transplant and we will give you one free. Just tear off the TOP OF YOUR HEAD and mail it to me, VAMPIRELLA, care of the GHOST OFFICE. If you're my kinda bird or BOYFRIEND, you'll lose your mind over me anyway, so ... LOOK! READ! GASP! SHIVER! over this FIRST COLLECTOR'S EDITION!!

In a jokey collector's edition of *Werewolves and Vampires* the camp horror is well illustrated by this excerpt:

> A Vampire is one of three things (and we use the word 'THING' advisedly): a silent movie Femme Fatale, an undead human who rises from his grave at night to suck the blood of the living, or a blood-sucking bat. Of course an old-time movie Vamp could also be an old bat and, since they were silent, no one would know the difference. The element that tends to confuse us is the fact that the true, undead Vampire can also become a bat by day and a living corpse by night. We must realize that anyone, dead or undead, who goes on a bat can get stiff.
>
> The real Vampire was the sucker named in the folklore of the Slavs. Consequently most Vampires are big Slavs. They would rise from their coffins in the blackest hours of the night to seek and suck the blood from the necks of their victims, thus drawing nourishment from the life-blood of the sleeper. The truth is that the old-time movie Vamps also liked to neck but, being in no way artistic, they didn't draw blood. Many of them couldn't even walk a straight line.
>
> Victims of a Vampire's grisly feeding habits pine and die and they in turn become Vampires, for while they pine they become part of the Vampire's family tree and later branch out on their own looking for more saps to drain. From this it is easy to see how anyone, from willowy blondes to oak-line labourers can become victims of the ghoulish Vampire and carry on his horrendous heritage.

Attendant to the comic-book is a host of vampire gimmickry, most of which is amazingly and disturbingly realistic. Here is a selection:

> DRACULA'S DRAGSTER.
> IMAGINE DRACULA on the drag strip! You can put him there in the way out, ghastly ghostly DRACULA DRAGSTER ... a horror on wheels. Flames shoot from the exhaust ... a bat perches on the radiator ... eerie decorations adorn the front bumper. Sculptured Dracula steers the Dragster with one hand ... holds a magic potion in the other while his red cape flies behind him. It looks as though Dracula is driving a coffin. And why not? That's what it is! You'll enjoy the ride with Dracula, and you can for only 98c, plus 27c for postage and handling.

MONSTER FOOT!

PUT YOUR BEST FOOT FORWARD wearing a grotesque MONSTER FOOT! Create a riot shuffling along, monster-style. Giant size; made of long-lasting latex rubber; riotously painted. Goes on over shoe. Full price only $1.50 each foot; $3.00 for complete pair.

MONSTER HAND!

SANTA NEVER SAW CLAWS like these! Fierce-looking monster hands you wear over your hands, like grotesque gloves. Tucked inside a coat or shirtsleeve, the hands look horribly natural. Have fun and start right in with your own Monster Hands. $1.50 for 1 hand; $3.00 for the pair.

DRACULA'S OWN 'RUBBER BAT'

IF IT'S TRUE that people fear bats, you'll have the time of your life when they walk in on this one. DRACULA'S OWN RUBBER BAT, so real it may even scare you. Suction cup lets you put him on wall, closets, fences, beds, etc. Then have fun driving folks crazy with fear.

The comic-book vampire is a travesty of the medieval vampire; the latter was a product of mass hysteria, the comic-book vampire is a synthetic product used simply for mass titillation.

Part Six

The Vampire as Entertainer

The Vampire in The Theatre

The vampire has been reduced to a figure of fun in the theatre. It was only the early cinema that was to revive him fully and to restore the ridiculed vampire to his former state of demonic power.

Polidori's central character Lord Ruthven, from his disputed work *The Vampyre*, appeared on stage in Paris at the Théâtre de la Porte-Saint Martin on June 13th, 1820. The melodrama was written by Charles Nodier with music by Alexandre Piccini. The play was an enormous success and was equally successful when it was published in book form. The melodrama had uniformly bad notices from the critics yet these condemnations completely failed to undermine the play's popularity. A revival was put on in 1823 with the same actors and the same huge success. In 1851 Dumas, in collaboration with Maquet, wrote a drama called *Le Vampire*, which was produced at the Ambigu-Comique on December 20th, 1851. Dumas described it as a *Drama Fantastique En Cinq Actes, en Dix Tableaux* and it had a vast array of characters. The play, based once again on Polidori's story, features the incorrigible vampire Lord Ruthven. As a result of Nodier's and Dumas's work Paris was suddenly besieged by vampire plays, mainly of a very inferior quality. One critic remarked: 'There is not a theatre in Paris without its vampire! At the Porte-Saint-Martin we have *Le Vampire*; at the Vaudeville *Le Vampire* again; and at the Variétés *Les Trois Vampires* or *Le Clair de la Lune*.' Predictably enough *Le Vampire* also features Lord Ruthven and is set in Hungary. Written by Scribe and Mélesville, the piece was described as a *comédie-vaudeville* in one act. Montague Summers, writing in *The Vampire: His Kith and Kin*, has this to say of the play:

> This elegant little piece opens with nuptials of Hermance de Mansfred at the castle of the Baron de Lourdorff, to whom she is betrothed. It appears that she has trifled with the affections of Adolphe de Valbern, now supposed dead. Her sister, Nancy, acknowledges that she loved Adolphe, but kept silence owing to his courtship of Hermance. Adolphe's uncle, the Count de Valberg, who knows nothing of the two ladies, fearing his nephew is unworthily entangled has had him held in military detention at Temesvar, whence however he has disappeared. The intrigue of the seventeen scenes, although clearly unravelled in the play, is a little complicated, and it must suffice to relate by an accident Adolphe appears at the castle. Upon being asked his name he answers: 'Lord Ruthven. An Englishman,' whereupon he is immediately taken to be a Vampire and the servants are thrown into a state of panic. Eventually he is reconciled to his uncle who recognizes him as the brave young hero by whom his life was saved on a recent battlefield; Nancy's fidelity is rewarded with the hand of the man she loves, and who now realizes that Hermance's heart was never his; so that the curtain falls upon a double wedding.

Les Trois Vampires was a farce (which did *not* feature Lord Ruthven) and others followed, including an extraordinary piece by Désaugiers entitled *Cadet Bureux, Vampire*; another farce called *Encore un Vampire* (1820) and yet another, in the same year, called *Le Vampire*, a melodrama in three acts.

The sombre Ruthven appeared on the English stage in 1820 at the English Opera House. Written by James Robinson Planché, this musical play was an adaptation of Nodier's original. However the adaptation was amazingly free, as can be seen from Planché's remarks at the time:

> *The Vampire*, or *The Bride of the Isles*, was produced at the Lyceum, or English Opera House, as it was then called, 9th August, 1820. Mr. Samuel James Arnold, the proprietor and manager, had placed in my hands, for adaptation, a French melodrama, entitled 'Le Vampire', the scene of which was laid, with the usual recklessness of French dramatists, in Scotland, where the superstition never existed. I vainly endeavoured to induce Mr. Arnold to let me change it to some place in the East of Europe. He had set his heart on Scotch music and dresses—the latter, by the way, were in stock—laughed at my scruples, assured me that the public would neither know nor care—and in those days they certainly did not—and therefore there was nothing left for me but to do my best with it. The result was most satisfactory to the management. The situations were novel and effective; the music lively and popular; the cast strong, comprising T. P. Cooke, who made a great hit in the principal character, Harley, Bartley, Pearman, Mrs. Chatterley and Miss Love. The trap, now so well known as 'the Vampire trap' was invented for this piece, and the final disappearance of the Vampire caused quite a sensation. The melodrama had a long run, was often revived, and is to this day a stock piece in the country.

Poor Lord Ruthven, his vampire dignity totally shattered by the wearing of the kilt, was described in the stage directions, together with the other leading character, Lady Margaret:

> *Ruthven*, Silver breast plate, studded with steel buttons; plaid kilt; philibeg; flesh arms and leggings; sandals; Scotch hat and feathers; sword and dagger. *Lady Margaret*, white satin dress, trimmed with plaid and silver; plaid silk sash; Scotch hat and feather.

The Vampire Trap, a very sophisticated and much acclaimed apparatus, was described as follows:

> A vampire trap consists of two or more flaps, usually india-rubber, through which the sprite can disappear almost instantly, where he falls into a blanket fixed to the under surface of the stage. As with the star trap, this trap is secured against accidents by placing another piece or *slide*, fitting close beneath when not required, and removed when the prompter's bell gives the signal to make ready.

Further transitions took place in 1828 when *Der Vampyr*, an opera, opened in Leipzig. Based on the French melodrama and its English version, the scene was thankfully changed from Scotland to Hungary where Ruthven, despite the fact that he now had to sing everything, was restored to something of his former glory. In his memoirs Planché wrote:

> In the summer of 1829 I had the opportunity of treating the subject of 'The Vampire' in accordance with my own ideas of propriety. The French melodrama had been converted into an opera for the German stage, and the music composed by Marschner.
>
> Mr. Hawes, who had obtained a score of it, having induced Mr. Arnold to produce it at the Lyceum, I was engaged to write the libretto, and consequently laid the scene of action in Hungary, where the superstition exists to this day, substituted for a Scotch chieftain a Wallachian Boyard, and in many other respects improved upon my earlier version. The opera was extremely well sung, and the costumes novel as well as correct, thanks to the kindness of Dr. Walsh, the traveller, who gave me some valuable information respecting the national dresses of the Magyars and the Wallachians.

In 1861 a ballad, *Il Vampiro*, was produced in Milan and a fabulous piece named *Guten Abend Herr Fischer! oder, Der Vampyr* was later successful in Germany.

1852 saw yet another vampire play, this time by Dion Boucicault, which was called simply, *The Vampire*. It opened at the Princess's Theatre on June 19th and received this notice from Henry Morley in his *Journal of a London Playgoer*:

> If there be any truth in the old adage, that 'when things are at

the worst they must mend', the bettering of Spectral Melodrama is not distant; for it has reached the extreme point of inanity in the new piece which was produced on Monday at the Princess's Theatre, under the attractive title of *The Vampire*.

Its plot is chiefly copied from a piece which some years ago turned the Lyceum into a Chamber of Horrors; but it has been spun out into three parts, facetiously described as 'Three Dramas'!: the little period of a century has been interposed between each part; and, in order that the outrage on the possible shall be complete, the third part is projected forward into the year that will be 1860! By this ingenious arrangement, the resuscitation of the original *Vampire* has been enabled to supply the lovers of the revolting at the Princess's with three acts of murder—that is, two consummated, and one attempted; but, as the delicate process of vampirical killing is exactly after the same pattern in each case, the horror is quite worn out before the career of the creature terminates. Nothing but tedious trash remains.

To 'an honest ghost' one has no objection; but an animated corpse which goes about in Christian attire, and although never known to eat, or drink, or shake hands, is allowed to sit at good men's feasts; which renews its odious life every hundred years by sucking a young lady's blood, after fascinating her by motions which resemble mesmerism burlesqued; and which, notwithstanding its well-purchased longevity, is capable of being killed during its term in order that it may be revived by moonbeams—such a ghost as this passes all bounds of toleration.

The monster of absurdity was personated by its reviver Mr. Boucicault, with due paleness of visage, stealthiness of pace, and solemnity of tone; the scenery, especially a moonlit ridge amidst the heights of Snowdon, was beautiful, and the costumes were prettily diversified; but the dreary repetition of fantastical horror almost exhausted even the patience which a benefit enjoins. Unfortunately, the mischief of such a piece, produced at a respectable theatre, does not end with the weariness of the spectators, who come to shudder and remain to yawn; for it is not only 'beside the purpose of playing', but directly contravenes it; and though it may be too dull to pervert the tastes of those who witness its vapid extravagances, it has power to bring discredit on the most genial of arts.

A vinegary notice, but once again this did not prevent the play's success. In fact the play was revived in both London and New York under the title of *The Phantom*.

One other production, after this first impetus of stage vampiry, is particularly worthy of note. A burlesque version of the vampire theme, founded upon 'a German legend, Lord Byron's story and a Boucicaultian drama' was given in 1872 at the Royal Strand Theatre which was advertised as 'Production of a Bit of Moonshine in Three Rays entitled "The Vampire" written by R. Reece.' One critic wrote of Edmund Terry's performance in the central rôle: 'Mr. Terry's make-up as the Vampire was something extraordinary, and he worked with unflagging energy to add "go" to the novelty.' *The Illustrated London News* described Terry as 'the Hibernian plagiarist with the broadest of brogues and the most ghostly of faces.'

The Vampire in The Cinema

If the stage made a pastiche of the vampire, then the cinema, except for a few very interesting exceptions, certainly did likewise. Mostly the fiend was tamed, and the awesome credibility of the vampire cult was nullified. The story of the screen vampire is mainly one of missed opportunities except for some interesting early work and a number of gruesome and imaginative Hammer films which established Christopher Lee as a cult figure in his commanding rôle as Dracula.

The count was first committed to film in 1921 when a German film-maker, Henrik Galeen, adapted Stoker's novel for the screen. The location was Bremen, the film was titled *Nosferatu* and the script was remote from Stoker's original plot. This was largely because Galeen and his director F. W. Murnau wanted to avoid copyright. The film, which was of course silent, provoked a chilly enough atmosphere but was basically both unsubtle and unsuccessful. It was only the ending that really struck the right note of brooding Nordic horror.

In 1931 Tod Browning (who made the overpoweringly horrible film *Freaks*) made *Dracula* which starred the Hungarian actor Bela Lugosi who so identified himself with the rôle that to millions of cinema audiences he *was* Count Dracula. So intense was Lugosi's obsession with the part that when he eventually died in a nursing home, he, too, was totally convinced that he was Dracula. Made by the studios already renowned for the early Frankensteins, Browning's *Dracula* was beautifully directed and beautifully photographed by the German camera-man Karl Freund. It carefully follows Stoker's original, evocatively reproducing Dracula's forbidding castle with its empty, echoing chambers, its unmentionable horrors behind locked doors and the attendant howling, ravaging wolves. Transylvania was bathed in a sinister twilight whilst its superstitious villagers cried wild and terrible warnings to the solicitor's clerk, Jonathan Harker. Such was Lugosi's popularity, with his alien Hungarian accent and his magnificently forbidding stature, that he received a flood of mail—as much as any big romantic star. In 1933 he told the press that ninety-seven per cent of his correspondence came from women. Lugosi with his remotely intoned 'I am—Dracula' was a particularly haunting personality and the only actor in the Dracula rôle who has ever been able to convey the sheer force of evil. Alexander Walker the film critic writes of Browning's *Dracula*:

> The 'vampire' theme probably owes its origins to the primitive belief in the regenerative power of human viscera, of the sacrificial victim whose blood refreshes the tribe. *Dracula* established that the supernatural had box-office appeal provided it was sufficiently fleshy and bloody, though the film had redeeming touches of jocular Gothic wit—as when the Count at dinner spots a tempting pinprick of blood on a guest's hand and refuses other refreshment murmuring 'I never drink ... wine'.

In 1935, when Hollywood was churning out a proliferation of mediocre horror films, Browning remade *London After Midnight* as *The Mark of The Vampire* with Bela Lugosi as the vampire and Lionel Barrymore as the detective. Despite brilliant photography Browning's second vampire film was not nearly so successful, largely because of its unrealistic visual gimmickry.

Sheridan Le Fanu's story *Camilla* was adapted by the Danish director Carl Dreyer at roughly the same time as Browning's *Dracula*. Called *Vampyr* or *The Strange Adventures of David Gray*, the film was streets ahead of Browning's *Dracula* or Murnau's *Nosferatu*—in fact it was one of the few really brilliant horror films ever made. The story, which has strong lesbian overtones, concerns two beautiful young girls. One is victim and the other is vampire. The film, a talkie, opened with this prologue:

> There exist certain beings whose very lives seem bound by invisible chains to the supernatural. They crave solitude. To be alone and dream ... their imagination is so developed that their vision reacts beyond that of most men. David Gray's personality was thus mysterious.

Working on a very small budget, Dreyer's company rented a château and used nearby locations. There was no studio work. In his fascinating book *Horror Movies* (Secker & Warburg, 1967) Carlos Clarens relates how Dreyer described his film to his crew, before they started shooting:

> Imagine that we are sitting in an ordinary room. Suddenly we are told that there is a corpse behind the door. In an instant the room we are sitting in is completely altered; everything in it has taken on another look; the light, the atmosphere have changed, though they are physically the same. This is because *we* have changed and the objects *are* as we conceive them. That is the effect I want to get into my film.

Dreyer did exactly this—and filmed *Vampyr* as a total fantasy. In an attempt to get imprecise, eerie images Dreyer took the unprecedented step of shooting the entire film through gauze that had been placed three feet in front of the lens. Clarens says that this gave the following effect:

> The characters seemed to be bathed in an eerie light as if they were at the bottom of the ocean or in perpetual dusk. To match this quality, Dreyer avoided brusque movements, pared the action to a few gestures and the dialogue to a few phrases, only half heard. The camera followed the somnambulistic hero, David Gray, in and out of his 'strange adventure' in long tracking shots that somehow never pierced the white mist of the dream.

The basic story-line of Dreyer's original and imaginative film is particularly credible:

> David Gray arrives at the village where a bed has been kept for him at the inn. Later that night a strange old man enters his

room and whispers: 'She must not die, do you understand? She must not die.' He leaves a small box in David's care to be opened in the event of his death.

Leaving the inn, David sees the wandering shadow of a one-legged gamekeeper and follows it into a deserted building, where the shadow curls up near its owner. The walls of the house are covered with shadows. David has stumbled upon the witches' sabbath! The music stops and the shadows fade when an old lady enters and orders an end to it. The old woman is then visited by a doctor who, David discovers, lives next door to the haunted house. The one-legged gamekeeper is building a coffin. David sees the doctor hand the old woman a bottle of poison.

David follows the shadow of the one-legged man to a nearby chateau. As the chatelain comes to the door, David recognizes him as the old man of his dreams; he is revealed as the mysterious old man who visited David earlier in the evening. A shot rings out and the chatelain drops to the ground wounded. He dies shortly after in the arms of his younger daughter, Gisèle. Leone, the older daughter, is dying of a strange sickness. David opens the box, which contains a book called Strange Tales of The Vampires.

Later that night, Leone rises from her bed and is found in the castle grounds; the old woman is seen by her side. The girl's condition is critical and the doctor is called. He asks David for his blood for a transfusion. David agrees; later, weak from the loss of blood, he has a vision of his own coffin. He feels himself locked in it and taken to the graveyard. The old woman peeks through the coffin's transom. She is the vampire and the doctor her accomplice.

David wakes up in the graveyard. He has wandered. With the help of an old servant from the chateau, he locates the grave of the old woman (as mentioned in the book). He finds the body fresh and ruddy. They then drive an iron pole through her heart. The body turns to dust and Leone is freed from her curse.

The doctor and the gamekeeper are pursued by the ghosts of their victims. The gamekeeper is hurled down a flight of stairs and killed. The doctor is locked into the cage of a flour mill and suffocates. David and Gisèle meanwhile walk at last into the light.

Vampyr was premièred in Berlin and immediately disappointed the critics—because they thought that any kind of horror film, however superior, was beneath the attention of a director as great as Dreyer. The film was released during the heyday of

Hollywood horror and retitled *Castle of Doom*. It was considered unconventional and therefore uncommercial. *Dr Terror's House of Horrors*, a compilation film made in the early forties, had some of Dreyer's *Vampyr* footage in it.

In 1935 Marguerite Chapman became the victim of *Dracula's Daughter*, a blood-lusting female vampire played by Gloria Holden who lured other females to their death by means of a hypnotic ring and an oriental manservant. Just before the war compilation films such as *House of Dracula* appeared in which a loose background framework contained a series of seemingly totally unrelated characters such as mad scientists with their deformed assistants, mummies, wolf men, Frankensteins, zombies and of course the good Count himself. Lugosi, Strange, Chaney and Karloff were often involved, whilst Lon Chaney Junior made a considerable impact in the leading rôle of *Son of Dracula*, which was released in 1942. Lugosi, now making some very poor quality vampire films, cropped up in *Return of The Vampire* where, for once, he was not playing Dracula, but appeared as a vampire named Armand Tesla who lurked in the bomb-damaged buildings of wartime London. Drake Douglas, in his book *Horrors* (1967), describes two particularly striking sequences in the film:

> Two Cockney grave-diggers return to the cemetery after an air raid to re-inter the dead. They find one corpse with a spike driven through its heart. When they remove the spike, the 'corpse' groans; it is Tesla, who had been staked twenty years before. Tesla's chief adversary sits playing the family organ, while Lugosi (in evening clothes, of course) threatens her. With a sweeping gesture, she removes the music book from the rack and reveals a lighted cross; Lugosi disappears in a clap of thunder. Finally, Tesla—who has slain his werewolf assassin—is dragged into the sunlight and the flesh runs from his skull like melting wax, a delightfully gruesome end.

Between 1943 and 1960 very few horror films were made, until Hammer Studios took over Universal's rôle, remaking many of the old horror film classics.

Bela Lugosi died in 1957 and in 1958 a new screen vampire appeared—Christopher Lee as Count Dracula, with Peter Cushing as Dr Van Helsing. *Dracula* was Hammer's first vampire film, and was in Cinemascope and Technicolor. This gave full scope to blood-dripping lips, blood-red eyes and blood-red wounds. The film ends with a fight between Van Helsing and Count Dracula—a fight that culminates in Dracula being imprisoned by the power of the crucifix. He falls into a patch of sunlight and crumbles away to dust—only to be resuscitated in many later films.

Brides of Dracula, with David Peel taking over the Dracula rôle, had a more unusual story-line. Yvonne Monlaur plays a young girl who is spending the night at the mysterious castle of the decrepit but sinister Baroness (Martita Hunt). There, the young girl discovers the alarming fact that the Baroness keeps her attractive-looking son (David Peel) shackled to his bedroom wall by means of a silver chain. Anxious to release him the girl pinches the Baroness's keys—and unshackles a bloodthirsty vampire. Incidental detail is poor, however, for the true vampire connoisseur—Peel is seen to emerge in daylight at least once. Don Sharp's *Kiss of The Vampire*, also with Peel as Dracula, was only marginally successful, but when Lee returned in *Dracula Prince of Darkness* it was obvious that only Christopher Lee could in any way approach the vampiristic *panache* of Lugosi. But unreality stepped in again when Lee stepped out into the sun—daylight is fatal to the true vampire. *Dracula Has Risen From The Grave* (1968) was highly imaginative and much the most successful Hammer vampire movie so far. Vampire-bites become festering wounds rather than pinpricks decorated by Max Factor and the film opens with a girl's half-naked bleeding corpse suspended head down within the casing of a church bell. The sexual connotations of vampiredom are emphasised here whilst a macabre fairy-tale-like quality hovers in the air.

Christopher Lee is a very different Dracula from Lugosi. Lee is tall, menacing, almost bat-like. But his resonant and very English accent make the Count a considerably less sinister figure than the Lugosi version. Lee believes that the films are fantasies and on this basis violence is then permissible. He sees the Count as partly sexual, partly pathetic and finds it a challenge to make him as convincing as possible. During the filming of *Dracula Has*

Risen From The Grave, Hammer received the Queen's Award for Industry—so it can safely be said that the good Count was not only a catalyst to Britain's economy but also one of her prestigious exports.

Finally a word on some foreign vampire movies. Mexico has particularly specialised in vampiristic films and the most noted director here is Mendez who was responsible for *El Vampiro* (*The Vampire*, 1957) and *El Ataud du Vampiro* (*The Vampire's Coffin*, 1958). These collectors' pieces are shot à la Browning, and Clarens says of them:

> Grafting to the arid locale the unlikely meteorological readings of a dewy English fen and to the landscape eternally gloomy mansions and haciendas, these films draw every ounce of effect from sets shrouded in artificial fog (which besides rendering them photogenic also conveniently hides their limitations) and borrow from Browning the Castle ... there is one last outpost in Mexico of the old-fashioned, pre-psychological monster-rallying horror show in which science has not come to science fiction but is more the practice of black magicians and spirits of the night.

Perhaps the only real classic Vampire work in the last thirty years was the Italian picture *The Mask of The Demon*, known in America as *Black Sunday* and in England as *Revenge of The Vampire*, and released in 1968 after a number of years' battle with the censor. The film is based on a story by Nikolai Gogol which was concerned with the Slavic conception that Satan walks the earth once every hundred years—and that auspicious day is Black Sunday. The story is set in traditional vampire country—Moldavia. A vampire trial is under way. There are priests, flickering fires, leafless trees and thick fog. A woman, tied to a cross, is having a golden mask of Satan hammered into her face. Its interior is lined with sharp iron spikes. This is the traditional Moldavian punishment for vampirism and witchcraft. The story takes place two centuries later—on Black Sunday. A doctor and his assistant, en route to a medical convention, arrive at a ruined chapel. They explore—and find a strange sarcophagus. In the stone, at the head of the corpse, is a glass panel through which can be seen the mask of Satan—placed over the head of the corpse. At the breast of the coffin is a wooden cross. As the two stare at the coffin in horror a huge bat swoops down upon them—a bat that the doctor manages to kill. In the struggle the glass of the sarcophagus is broken and the blood of the slain mammal drips on to the mask.

Meanwhile, back in his castle, the ruling prince sits fearfully before the fire. He knows it is Black Sunday—and is uneasy, for his daughter Katya strongly resembles the long-dead vampire woman. The prince has reason to be worried for in the coffin the vampire woman is being revived by the blood of the bat. She then calls to her followers and a satanist, plus mask, rises from his grave in an adjacent cemetery. This male vampire then enters the castle via a secret passageway and confronts the prince, who collapses. A doctor is called but is intercepted, becomes a vampire and attends the prince. Next morning the original doctor's assistant arrives to find the prince dead with a vampire's mark at his neck. Meanwhile the older doctor tells him on no account to interfere. Of course the assistant does just this by discovering the secret passage and confronting the recently revived vampire woman. Meanwhile his senior practitioner seeks help from the village priest. They arrive at the tomb to find Katya and the vampire woman together—but unfortunately they both claim to be Katya. Finally the young doctor makes up his mind and advances on the woman he imagines to be Katya. As he raises the stake high above his head he sees that she wears a crucifix—and of course he knows that no vampire could possibly wear such a symbol. He then tears the cloak from the supposed Katya—revealing the pitted and grave-rotted hag beneath. She is then burnt at the stake.

Black Sunday serves to underline all the missed opportunities of countless other films concerned with vampires. It is in black and white and contains little sunshine or daylight—if the film had been shot in colour then the whole effect would have been ruined. Visual, unspoken horror is the keynote combined with a beautiful sense of atmospherics.

The Vampire on Television

In the United States during the late 'sixties and early 'seventies *Dark Shadows*, the ABC-TV Gothic suspense series, achieved spectacular success with its collection of resident ghouls, vampires, warlocks, witches and monsters. Here is how the company describes their satanic soap opera:

> *Dark Shadows*, the Gothic suspense series which made its debut on the ABC-TV daytime schedule in June, 1966, moves into its third season in the Fall of 1968 with new terrors and mysteries waiting in the wings.
>
> The unique weekday contemporary drama—starring stage and screen luminary Joan Bennett as Elizabeth Collins Stoddard, mistress of Collins house, and Jonathan Frid as the 175-year-old family vampire, Barnabas Collins—is styled in the tradition of the Gothic novel.
>
> It is a suspense story centering around the tale of a young girl who has become the governess to a 10-year-old boy in a house filled with strangeness and intrigue.
>
> The setting is the tiny fishing village of Collinsport, Maine—and the great brooding mansion that looms above it on Widow's Hill. It is in this house that the series is played as the young governess Victoria Winters (Alexandra Moltke) is surrounded by ominous terrors and drawn into the dark mysteries of the Collins family, founders of the fishing fleet that still sails from the village's sheltered harbour.

Jonathan Frid, the actor who plays the 175-year-old vampire Barnabas Collins, has dozens of fan clubs, most of whose members are women. One woman, from Carmichael in California, wrote: 'There is no escape from the burning light you create! In simple words you could bite ME anytime for I would not be able to resist your fatal charms.'

The show is watched by an audience of six million (mainly housewives and schoolchildren) on Monday to Friday afternoons.

Part Seven

The Vampire Today

Vampires still proliferate in the twentieth century. Sometimes they kill just for the sight of spilt blood—sometimes, although these occasions are rare, they drink it. Most of these modern vampires are psychotic and have abandoned the traditions of their forebears. It is much more likely for your twentieth-century vampire to be a pallid-faced little man with a greasy tie and carpet slippers living in the suburbs than a Gothic monster. Peter Kürten, for instance, a German vampire who has already been discussed in Part Two, lacked the personality of his vampiristic ancestors, committing his squalid crimes in an untraditional and particularly ugly manner. No self-respecting vampire would have drowned his playmates at an early age (as Kürten did when he was a child) or committed sadistic acts against sheep (as Kürten did when he was thirteen). There is however an obvious link between Kürten and the traditional vampire. The link is sexual. The discharge of semen is often regarded with great concern by a pubescent boy masturbating for the first time. He is immediately aware that this discharge emanates from his own body and that it is both warm and sticky—like blood which is also warm and sticky. There is thus an immediate association between blood and semen, and the same guilt or elation can be brought about by the shedding of either. There is probably a sexual motive for most crimes of violence, particularly really brutal assault or murder. This is one of the basics of Freudian teaching, and is exemplified by that well-known post-war vampire John George Haigh, who was tried at Sussex Assizes in July 1949.

Haigh was born in 1910. His parents were members of the Plymouth Brethren—an extremely puritanical religious sect, who forbade all worldly pleasures. Alcohol and gambling were obvious sins to be guarded against, but the home also considered radio, films and newspapers as sources of corruption. Haigh was not even allowed to have any friends in the house—presumably because they might bring in some corruptive influence. The Haigh parents' God was a wrathful God and the only salvation from His vengeance and the wickedness of the world was the 'blood of the heavenly lamb'. Haigh's mother also believed in the portents of dreams and influenced her son to believe in them too. At an early age young John began to dream the same dream—a dream that was to return to him, at ever decreasing intervals, throughout his life. In his words (from his confession) Haigh says of his awesome fantasy world:

> I saw a forest of crucifixes which gradually turned into trees. At first I seemed to see dew or rain running from the branches. But when I came nearer I knew it was blood. All of a sudden the whole forest began to twist about and the trees streamed with blood. Blood ran from the trunks. Blood ran from the branches, all red and shiny. I felt weak and seemed to faint. I saw a man going round the trees gathering blood. When the cup he was holding in his hand was full he came up to me and said 'drink'. But I was paralysed. The dream vanished. But I still felt faint and stretched out with all my strength towards the cup.

I woke up in a semi-comatose state. I always kept on seeing those hands holding out a cup to me that I couldn't quite reach, and that terrible thirst, unknown to any other modern man, never left me.

For three or four days I always had the same dream and each time I woke up, my horrible desire always became stronger. You will now understand what happened to young Swan when he found himself alone with me that autumn evening. I knocked him out with the leg of a table, or a piece of tubing: I don't remember exactly now. Then, I slit his throat open with a penknife. I tried to drink his blood but it wasn't easy. I didn't know yet which was the best way to go about it. I held him over the kitchen sink and tried somehow to gather the red liquid. In the end, I managed to drink directly from the wound, with a sense of deep satisfaction.

A deeply religious man, Haigh could never understand why Christ had been allowed to suffer death so slowly upon the cross. As a result he killed his own victims efficiently and speedily, causing them the minimum amount of suffering. At sixteen he became a Church of England choirboy and later became an assistant organist. He also took the Bible literally and the passages 'Drink water out of thine own cistern and running waters out of thine own well' (Proverbs, v, 15) and 'He that believeth in me, as the scripture hath said, out of his belly shall flow rivers of living water' (John, vii, 38) caused Haigh to drink liberally of his own urine. He drank this liquid every day, up until the time of his trial.

Haigh murdered nine people and drank the blood of all his victims—a fact that caused an incredible sensation at Sussex Assizes. Bernhardt J. Hurwood, in his book *Terror by Night* (1963) explains Haigh's reaction to the trial:

The only time he became ruffled was when his crimes were referred to as murder. He was completely unconcerned with right or wrong, laws, or his victims. The killings were of a ritual nature to him, he said they were his destiny. He insisted that he followed no plan since the slayings were the result of divine revelation and he vaguely suggested that they might have something to do with eternal life. When the judge asked him if he were not concerned about his fate he remained at ease and compared himself to Christ before Pilate on trial.

Dr Henry Yellowlees, a psychiatrist brought in by the defence, extracted from Haigh a summary of his dreams—dreams that were catalysts to his murders. Of the moment of killing Haigh said: 'Then I went out and fetched a drinking glass and made an incision in the side of her neck, and collected a glass of blood which I drank.' This took place directly after the murder of his final victim—the unfortunate Mrs Durand Deacon. Other killings were described in the following ways: 'I tapped her on the head with a cosh and tapped her for blood', or 'I hit him on the head with a cosh, withdrew a glass of blood as before and drank it.'

Necrophilia and indeed cannibalism are still the components of the vampire's contemporary image. In October 1958 two psychiatrists, Franklin S. Klaf and William Brown, presented in the *Psychiatric Quarterly* a paper entitled 'Necrophilia, Brief Review And Case Report'. Introducing their subject, Messrs Klaf and Brown pointed out that:

> Among early psychiatric writers on the subject, Krafft-Ebing called the perversion a horrible manifestation of sadism, but Moll objected because no actual pain is caused. He called it a variety of ALGOLAGNIA (abnormal and distorted activity of sexual impulse toward persons of opposite sex with a desire for experiencing or causing pain). These authors agreed in considering the cause to be some congenital defect. Wulffen divided necrophilia into three types: LUST MURDER in which murder precedes the sexual act with the corpse; NECROSTUPRUM in which the corpse is stolen; NECROPHAGY in which the corpse is mutilated and parts of it eaten.

They also give a couple of ghoulish case histories. The first concerned:

> A 24-year-old epileptic, a quiet, detached, stolid person with no abnormal ideation, (who) used to have fantasies of naked women. He wanted sex relations with a corpse but was fearful of contagion. He would enter cemetery chapels seeking female corpses. Finding one, he would put it on the ground and then masturbate but would have no sexual contact with the body. On one occasion, he did insert his finger in the vagina of a corpse. His morbid sexual acts were not related to his seizures.

The second involved:

> A 50-year-old man who was arrested when found kissing the lips and touching the breasts of a female corpse; his necrophilic activity began six years after the death of his mother; he cut out death notices, preferring the obituaries of middle-aged or elderly women; he had no heterosexual experiences and limited his contacts with cadavers to kissing and fondling, after which he would masturbate in a men's room or at home. He had strong desires to be a morgue attendant because 'It would satisfy me; if I couldn't see corpses, I might lose control.'

Earlier, in 1932, a psychiatrist named Brill published, once again in the *Psychiatric Quarterly*, a paper entitled 'The Sense of Smell in the Neuroses and Psychoses'. Under this seemingly innocent banner Brill related an amazing case of necrophilia involving a man who had been blind from childhood, who, in childhood, had played with dead animals and who, in adult life, could only derive sexual pleasure from fantasising about intercourse with dead women. Fortunately he never went the whole hog.

> His description of what a dead woman would offer him reads like a gourmet's idea of a Lucullan feast. He dilated upon all delicacies of decayed flesh, how to cure it to bring out the odour, etc.; but as the smell of a human body would attract too much attention he finally decided to be satisfied with a dead horse.

Vampirism still exists on a primitive level although European belief, except in particularly remote places, has virtually died out. It was reported in 1912 that a Hungarian farmer had gone to a cemetery, disinterred a corpse, stuffed stones and garlic in its mouth and staked it. This old method, handed down from father to son, had not been reported for many decades.

Yet, in an equally primitive area during the nineteen-sixties an actual example of the live vampire type was recorded. His name was Florencia Roque Fernandez, he was aged twenty-five, his occupation was stone-masonry and he lived in Monteros, a town in north-central Argentine. 'I don't know what made me do it,' was the statement Fernandez made to the police when arrested for nocturnally biting at the throats of at least fifteen women.

Many activities of the Mau-Mau were decidedly vampiristic.

Vampirism occurred in the oath-taking ceremonies which were designed to bind the members of the organisation together as rigidly as possible. Ione Leigh, writing in 1954, said that there were eight different forms of oath-taking, each with its attendant ritual.

> The first oath, which is the mildest, is taken in a darkened room where an arch of sugar-cane or banana-leaves has been erected. In an atmosphere of gloom, the candidate divests himself of all European articles such as watches, shoes and clothing. Rings of Igoka grass are then placed over his head and wrists, and standing naked before the arch he takes the oath. Seven *sodum* apples are included in the ritual to bring misfortune to him if he breaks the oath; the eyes of a slaughtered sheep, pierced with *mugai* thorns, also denote the fate of those who break their vows.
>
> A 'banana-bell', which has been hollowed out and filled with a mixture of blood and earth, is rotated seven times around his head, after which a stick of wild hibiscus is dipped into the blood and put to his lips. He licks the blood, and bites the chest of the slaughtered sheep seven times. Blood is then drawn from his arm and mixed with the sheep's blood, which all initiates must drink. This forms the 'blood-brotherhood'. Live cats and dogs and certain parts of human bodies are sometimes nailed to Mau Mau altars.

As the ritual oath-taking progresses the ceremony becomes infinitely more barbaric and vampiristic. Ione Leigh continues the macabre description:

> For the fourth oath, which is usually taken before an African becomes a Captain in the Mau Mau army, a dead body has to be provided. At the ceremony the fingers of the dead man are bent seven times, and his eyes pricked seven times. A Major takes the fifth oath. He is required to bite the brain of a dead African seven times. For a Brigadier, the brain of a *white* man has to be provided. The candidate proceeds to eat seven pieces of it. A General, who takes the seventh oath, is required to eat, besides the brain, the wrist-bones of a white man, broken up and mixed with his excrement and blood.
>
> For the last oath, a man and a child must first be killed. The heart of the child is cut from its body, and pricked seven times with a nail; the brains and blood of the dead man are then mixed with the blood of the oath-takers, and all members are required to drink the draught.

Appalling as these ceremonies are it is interesting to note how many of the rites are still associated with ancestor worship, with belief in the drinking of the blood of one's enemies and the transfer of strength that drinking blood implies.

Other contemporary instances of vampirism are too broad and too numerous to dwell upon. Such figures as Aleister Crowley, the so-called practising magician, spring to mind. On being introduced to a friend of Isadora Duncan's Crowley asked if the friend would like to be the recipient of the 'Serpent's kiss'. He immediately took her hand, raised her wrist to his mouth and bit deeply at it. To the consternation of all sitting on the terraces of the restaurant in Montparnasse Crowley then proceeded to drink greedily of the quick-flowing blood. Crowley also indulged himself in certain sacrificial rites including a black mass in which Raoul Loveday was involved. Loveday was forced to help kill a cat, to have a magic sign traced on his forehead in the cat's blood and eventually to drink a warm and glutinous cup of the liquid.

However, Crowley was, by the standards of others, a mere dabbler in the ritual of blood. More professional contemporary exponents included the blood-drinking Russian Baron Roman von Sternberg-Ungem who believed himself to be the reincarnation of Genghis Khan and who was ultimately caught, tried and executed by the Bolsheviks in 1920; the demon La Bête who in the Paris of the 'twenties copied such past masters of blood-ridden orgies as Gilles de Rais and the Marquis de Sade, and who eventually turned up as a mass murderer at Ravensbruck; the blood-lusting voodooist Papa Doc, François Duvalier, infamous ex-President of Haiti; the dehumanised killer of Auschwitz, Commandant Rudolph Hoess; and Charles Manson and his family of bloodthirsty monsters.

Perhaps the best clinical observation of a living vampire comes from Ornella Volta's book *The Vampire*. The account, published in Paris in 1935, is from a paper entitled *Anomalies et Perversions Sexuelles*. It was submitted by a Doctor Craven and discussed a very straightforward example of female vampirism in a thirty-year-old Portuguese woman:

The thoughts and fantasies of the subject all moved around the idea of blood, which she expressed by means of bloodthirsty metaphors and symbols. Blood for her is the symbol of love, hate, anger, and passion. She wants to know in what way human blood is different from animals' blood and has set herself this problem: what aspect would blood have if it were to lose its colour? What would be the appearance of a body deprived of its vital liquid? Would it be pale and cold? Would it diminish in size? When it rains, she imagines that it is raining blood and the mere idea of blood dripping from a disintegrating cloud in a completely clear sky sends her into ecstasy. She likes to suck and swallow blood, but does not dare to do so, for fear of making its owner suffer. She drinks red wine only because it has the colour of blood, and, for the same reason, likes blood oranges.

She has the habit of amusing herself with mental images of foetuses and corpses of mammals. She thinks she hates her little seven-year-old boy because he does not resemble her husband. The hate the child inspires in her has led her to entertain homicidal desires from time to time. She would then like to kill him, not with a knife, but by breaking his neck with her own two hands. Moreover, she has experienced the same homicidal impulses towards her husband. She would like to do away with him, strangling him and keeping his corpse in her bedroom.

She would also like to dispose of her father's body and, if she could touch her mother's skull with her hand, she would be infinitely happy. She also makes plans regarding the eventual use of the corpses of her husband and two children. She would like to eat their flesh, without swallowing it and raw, of course, so as not to lose the flavour of the blood.

Instead of a true and proper sexual union, she greatly prefers to suck the blood of her partner from a little hole made in the cavity of his ear. During the orgasm she seems to die and she then remains immobile like a corpse.

Epilogue

At the height of vampire belief, in the eighteenth century, the French philosopher Jean Jacques Rousseau wrote:

> If ever there was in the world a warranted and proven history, it is that of vampires: nothing is lacking, official reports, testimonials of persons of standing, of surgeons, of clergymen, of judges; the judicial evidence is all-embracing.

Man has never accepted that death is the end and that dust is merely dust. For centuries he has believed that the slain lay vengeful in their graves, waiting for the life-force of blood that would allow them to rise from their tombs and return once more to seek succour from the living. This fear of the vengeful dead transcended all rational explanation and contributed to the vast weight of material that Rousseau termed 'a warranted and proven history'. This book has analysed the background of that 'warranted and proven history' and examined the true import of that life-force of both the mythical and the living vampire—blood. When Gilles de Rais was asked by his judges for some kind of explanation for his appalling wave of bloodshed he replied:

> that he had done them and perpetrated them following his own imagination and his thought, without acting on anyone's advice and according to his own bent, purely for his own pleasure and carnal delectation and not for any other purpose or end.

It could be argued that de Rais was a fourteenth-century psychotic who was of no universal significance, but his attitude has been echoed throughout the centuries. Martin Gershen in his book *Destroy or Die* (Arlington House, 1971) explains a G.I.'s attitude to the My Lai massacre in Vietnam thus:

> It was like the first time you masturbate.... You feel guilty because you think you shouldn't do it, yet somewhere you heard it was perfectly natural and anyhow it's irresistible, so what the hell.

Our ancestors could not elude the fear of the vengeful dead and vampires ranged the world—nowadays their influence is dead. Some people may find this regrettable. 'It is not that I feared to look upon things horrible,' said Edgar Allan Poe in his story *The Pit And The Pendulum*, 'but that I grew aghast lest there should be nothing to see.'

Is this to be the fate of man? That even in his retributive imagination 'there should be nothing to see'? Better, then, the return of the vampire.

Bibliography

Abbot, G. F.: *Macedonian Folk-Lore* (Cambridge, 1903)

Allatius, Leo: *De Graecorum Hodie Quorundum Opinionatibus* (Cologne, 1645)

Andree, Robert: *Ethnographische Parallelen und Vergleiche* (Stuttgart, 1878)

Bendann, E.: *Death Customs, An Analytical Study of Burial Rites* (Kegan Paul, Trench, Trubner & Co., 1930)

Billson, C. J.: *County Folklore: Leicestershire and Rutland* (London, 1895)

Briggs, K. M.: *The Anatomy of Puck* (Routledge & Kegan Paul, 1959)

Burton, Sir Richard: *Vikran and the Vampire* or *Tales of Hindu Devilry*. Edited by Isabel Burton (Tilston & Edwards, 1832)

Butler, Ivan: *The Horror Film* (Zwemmer, 1967)

Byron, Lord: *Fragment of a Novel* from *Three Gothic Novels* (Dover Publications, New York, 1966) and *The Giaour* (John Murray, 1813)

Calmet, Augustin Dom, O.S.B.: *Traité sur les Apparitions des Esprits, et sur les Vampires, ou les Revenants de Hongrie, de Moravie*, etc. (First edition, Paris, 1746)

Clarens, Carlos: *Horror Movies* (Secker & Warburg, 1967)

Clébert, Jean-Paul: *The Gipsies*. Translated by Charles Duff (Vista, 1963)
Cooper, Gordon: *I searched the World for Death* (John Long Ltd, 1940)
Corvo, Baron: *Chronicles of the House of Borgia* (London, 1901)
Crooke, William: *Introduction to the Popular Religion and Folklore of Northern India* (Allahabad, 1894)
Dorson, Richard M.: *The British Folklorists, A History* (Routledge & Kegan Paul, 1968)
Dorson, Richard M.: *Peasant Customs and Savage Myths* (Selections from *The British Folklorists*, Vol. 1) (Routledge & Kegan Paul, 1968)
Douglas, Drake: *Horrors* (John Baker Ltd, 1967)
Doyle, Sir Arthur Conan: *The Parasite* (1891)
Elg, Stefan: *Beyond Belief* (Tower Books, 1967)
Encyclopaedia of Religion and Ethics, Vols 8 and 12 (T. & T. Clark, 1908)
Ennemoser, Joseph: *History of Magic*. Translated by William Howitt. 2 volumes (Henry G. Bohn London, 1854)
Frazer, Sir James: *The Golden Bough* (Macmillan, 1925)
Gautier, Théophile: *La Morte Amoureuse* (originally appeared in Chronique de Paris, 1836) and *The Beautiful Vampire* (London, 1927)
Giles, Raymond: *Night of the Vampire* (New English Library, 1969)
Grant, Kenneth and Symonds, John, eds: *The Confessions of Aleister Crowley* (Jonathan Cape Ltd, 1969)
Groome, Francis Hindes: *Gipsy Folk Tales* (Hurst and Blackett Ltd, 1899)
Haestier, Richard: *Dead Men Tell Tales* (John Long Ltd)
Hamel, Frank: *Human Animals* (Rider, 1915)
Hartmann, Dr Franz: *Premature Burial* (London, 1896)
Henderson, W.: *Folklore of the Northern Counties of England and the Borders* (Folklore Society, 1879)
Hodder, Reginald: *The Vampire* (London, 1913)
Hogg, Garry: *Cannibalism and Human Sacrifice* (Robert Hale Ltd, 1958)

Hurwood, Bernhardt J.: *Monsters and Nightmares* (Belmont Books, 1967)
Hurwood, Bernhardt J.: *Monsters Galore* (Gold Medal Books, 1965)
Hurwood, Bernhardt J.: *Terror by Night* (Lander Books, 1963)
Huxley, Aldous: *The Devils of Loudoun* (Chatto & Windus, 1952)
Hyde, Douglas: *Beside the Fire* (London, 1890)
James, M. R.: *Ghost Stories of Antiquary* (Arnold, 1905)
Jones, Russ: *Dracula* (Ballantine Books, 1966)
Keats, John: *Lamia* (London, 1820)
King, Francis: *Ritual Magic in England 1887 to the Present Day* (Neville Spearman, 1970)
Lawson, John Cuthbert: *Modern Greek Folklore and Ancient Greek Religion* (Cambridge University Press, 1910)
Le Fanu, Sheridan: *Camilla: In a Glass Darkly* (Bentley London, 1872)
Levi, Eliphas: *The History of Magic*. Translated by A. E. Waite (Rider, 1913)
MacKenzie, D.: *Scottish Folklore and Folk Life* (London, 1935)
Mandeville, Sir John: *The Voyage and Travails* (1725)
Map, Walter: *De Nugis Curialium*, edited by M. R. James (*Aneddota Oxoniensia*: Medieval and Modern Series Part XIV) (Oxford, 1914)
Maple, Eric: *The Dark World of Witches* (Pan, 1965)
May, Hubert: *On the Truths Contained in Popular Superstition, with an account of Mesmerism* (William Blackwood, 1854)
Otescu, I: *Beliefs of the Roumanian Peasant Concerning the Sky and the Stars*
Nodier, Charles: *Le Vampire* (Paris, 1820)
Planché, James Robinson: *The Vampire* or *The Pride of the Isles* (London, 1820)
Polidori, John: *The Vampyre* from *Three Gothic Novels* (Dover Publications, 1966)
Prest, Thomas Preskett: *Varney the Vampire*, or *The Feast of Blood* (1847)

Puckle, Bertram: *Funeral Customs, their Origin and Development* (Werner Laurie, 1926)
Ralston, W. R. S., M.A.: *Russian Folk Tales* (Smith, Elder & Co., 1873)
Ricaut, Paul: *The Present State of the Greek and Armenian Churches* (London, 1679)
Riva, Valeria and Volta, Ornella: *The Vampire, An Anthology*, English adaptation by Margaret Crosland (Neville Spearman, 1963)
Rohr, M. Philip: *Dissertatio de Masticatione Mortuorum* (Leipzig, 1679)
Roman, Victor: *Not at Night* (London, 1925)
Ross, Marilyn: *Barnabas Collins* (Paperback Library, 1968)
Rudorff, Raymond: *Monsters* (Neville Spearman, 1968)
Sade, Marquis de: *Justine* (Olympia Press)
St Clair, S. G. B. and Brophy, Charles A.: *Twelve years Study of the Eastern Question in Bulgaria* (London, 1877)
Sharper-Knowlson, T.: *The Origins of Popular Superstitions* (Werner Laurie, 1851)
Shelley, Mary: *Frankenstein* (London, 1818)
Sisistrari, Ludovico Maria: *Demoniality*. Translated from the Latin by Montague Summers (The Fortune Press, 1927)
Skeat, W. W.: *Malay Magic* (Macmillan, 1900)
Southey, Robert: *Thalaba the Destroyer* (London, 1801)
Spence, Lewis: *An Encyclopaedia of Occultism* (Routledge & Kegan Paul, 1920)
Spence, Lewis: *Myths and Legends of Babylonia and Syria* (Harrap, 1916)
Spindler: *Der Vampyr und sein Braut* (Hanover, 1826)
Sprenger and Kramer: *Malleus Maleficarum*. Translation by Montague Summers, published by the Pushkin Press London, 1948 (Cologne, 1484)
Steiger, Brad: *Ghosts, Ghouls and Other Peculiar People* (Merit Books, 1965)
Stoker, Bram: *Dracula* (London, 1897)
Stoker, Bram: *The Vampire* (Constable, 1897)
Stone, Mrs.: *God's Acre. Historical Notices relating to Churchyards* (John W. Parker, 1858)

Summers, Montague: *The Vampire: His Kith and Kin* (Kegan Paul, Trench, Trubner & Co. Ltd, 1928)
Summers, Montague: *The Vampire in Europe* (University Books, 1929)
Sure Henham, Sir Frank A.: *Malay Sketches* (London, 1895)
Thompson, R. Campbell: *The Devils and Evil Spirits of Babylonia* (London, 1903)
Volta, Ornella, and Riva, Valeria: *The Vampire, An Anthology.* English adaptation by Margaret Crosland (Neville Spearman, 1963)
Volta, Ornella: *The Vampire* (Tandem Books, 1965) (Original edition by Editions Jean-Jacques Pauvert)
Willoughby-Meade, G.: *Chinese Ghouls and Goblins* (Constable, 1928)
Wright, Dudley: *Vampires and Vampirism* (1914)
Yardley, Edward: *The Supernatural in Romantic Fiction* (Longmans Green, 1880)
Zopfius, John Henrich: *Dissertatio de Vampiris Seruiensibus* (Halle, 1733)

Index

Note:

n refers to footnote on page cited

not every species of vampire is listed in index; see under country of origin

books and plays are listed under their authors, films under their titles